YESTERDAY AGAIN

YESTERDAY AGAIN

by BARRY LYGA

SCHOLASTIC PRESS · NEW YORK

Library of Congress Cataloging-in-Publication Data

Lyga, Barry.
    Yesterday again / by Barry Lyga. — 1st ed.
        p. cm. — (Archvillain ; 3)
    Summary: Twelve-year-old Kyle Camden is annoyed because his superpower identity, the Azure Avenger (often called the Blue Freak), has been labeled as a villain by the town of Bouring — but when he builds a time machine, so that he can go back and prove that the hero Mighty Mike is an alien, he finds out that all of his assumptions are wrong.
    ISBN 978-0-545-19654-3
    1. Superheroes — Juvenile fiction. 2. Extraterrestrial beings — Juvenile fiction. 3. Time travel — Juvenile fiction. [1. Superheroes — Fiction. 2. Extraterrestrial beings — Fiction. 3. Time travel — Fiction. 4. Science fiction.] I. Title.
    PZ7.L97967Yes 2013
    813.6 — dc23

2012014423

10 9 8 7 6 5 4 3 2 1   13 14 15 16 17

Printed in the U.S.A.   23
First edition, January 2013

The text type was set in Sabon.
Book design by Christopher Stengel

Also by Barry Lyga

ARCHVILLAIN

THE MAD MASK

For Jody, who saw it through

Previously in
ARCHVILLAIN

Kyle Camden has superpowers!

(This is not as cool as you'd think.)

Kyle got his powers one night when a strange alien plasma storm hit the town of Bouring. The result? Kyle's intelligence (which was already pretty high to begin with) got boosted off the charts, and he discovered powers of flight, invulnerability, and superstrength. Not bad, eh?

But the same plasma storm that gave Kyle his powers also brought Mighty Mike to Earth.

Mighty Mike claims to be a good guy. He rescues kittens from trees and helps little old ladies cross the street and (oh, yeah) saves Kyle's best friend — Mairi — when she gets snatched up by a monster made out of dirt. (Kyle prefers to call it an "Animated Soil Entity," or ASE.) But there's something off about Mike, and only Kyle notices it. It's not just that Mike seems to have amnesia and a little bit of brain damage, and it's not just that he's become the most popular kid in Bouring (a role once filled by Kyle himself).

It's that he hasn't bothered to mention that he's an alien.

Only Kyle knows, and he can't tell — if he revealed that he'd seen Mighty Mike the night of the plasma storm, people would figure out that Kyle is the other superpowered kid in town, the mask-wearing, prank-playing Azure Avenger. (Unfortunately, the newspaper calls him the "Blue Freak" instead . . . but what do newspapers know anyway?) Kyle realizes that Mike must have a reason for keeping his alien origins a secret . . . and that reason is probably pretty evil. How could it not be?

As the Azure Avenger/Blue Freak, Kyle has tried any number of ways to force Mighty Mike to reveal his alien heritage, but they always seem to backfire. Like the time he tried to, er, vaporize Mike's pants with a high-powered laser. Pretty much every time Kyle tries to do something right, it gets misinterpreted as evil.

Recently, Kyle met the Mad Mask, a criminal genius who tricked Kyle into helping him build Ultitron, a ten-story-tall robot designed to destroy all that is beautiful in the world. As part of his evil master plan, the Mad Mask also kidnapped Mairi and tried to destroy the town of Bouring's landmark lighthouse. All of this after double-crossing Kyle. So, yeah, Kyle realized that maybe teaming up with a lunatic wasn't such a great idea after all.

Still, Kyle saved the day, rescuing Mairi and wrecking the Mad Mask's plans — but he did it underground, in the Mad Mask's sewer lair (gross!), while Mighty Mike was aboveground, making it look like he beat Ultitron single-handedly. So everyone still loves Mighty Mike, while the cops and the whole U.S. military want to get their hands on the poor Blue Freak. . . .

CHAPTER
ONE

There was a huge pothole in the middle of the road outside Mairi MacTaggert's house. Her mother said it had been caused by an errant Sidewinder missile fired by an Army helicopter three weeks ago when a giant robot tried to destroy the town of Bouring, but her father claimed it was from the Blue Freak, the local supervillain.

Mairi wasn't sure who was right, but she didn't really care. She just couldn't stop staring at the pothole every time she left the house. Whether the pothole had been caused by the good guys or the bad guys didn't matter to her. What mattered was that it was less than thirty feet from her front door. Thirty feet wasn't really that far. The Whatever that made the pothole could just as easily have come crashing through the roof of her house and . . .

Well, it couldn't have done anything to *Mairi*. Because at the time the Army was blowing up the robot and the Blue Freak, Mairi was busy being a kidnap victim, unconscious and tied up somewhere in the grotesque sewer system running beneath Bouring, held captive by a lunatic called the Mad Mask.

But her *parents* had been home.

Her parents had been thirty feet away from —

Mairi stared at the pothole and tried not to think about it, but it wasn't easy.

It was, after all, a really, really big pothole.

The school bus slowed a little more carefully than usual. The day before — the first day of school since the Siege of the Blue Freak — the bus had come careening down the road at its usual breakneck pace (Mairi's best friend, Kyle, once joked that their bus driver was a retired Indy 500 driver) and had made a sickeningly hollow *THWOMP* sound when it hit the pothole. Today, the driver was being a bit more careful.

With a last backward glance at the pothole — Thirty feet! Just thirty feet! — Mairi boarded the bus.

Toward the back was, as always, Kyle, slumped low in his seat, as though trying to hide.

Mairi sat down next to him.

"Hi, Kyle," she said.

Kyle cleared his throat and flicked his eyes in her direction, not lingering. "Hi," he said, then turned to stare out the window as the bus gently pulled away. *Uh-thump*, the wheels murmured as the bus went over and through the pothole.

Mairi stared at Kyle, mentally urging him to speak, even just to turn and look at her. He had been like this since the Siege. Barely speaking to Mairi. The previous day, in school, he had hardly spoken at all, even when he had a chance to correct a teacher.

That just wasn't like Kyle. Not at all.

He had become sullen and withdrawn and quiet. He no longer played the pranks that had made him famous among kids and infamous among adults. (No one could ever prove that Kyle was the prankster, but everyone still knew it.) All he did now was listen to his iPod — custom painted with blue flames — and mutter to himself.

Mairi wanted her best friend. She needed him back. She had stuff to talk to him about. Important stuff. About being kidnapped. About her time underground with the Mad Mask. Three weeks later and she was still having strange dreams — her doctor said it was natural, that being kidnapped by the Mad Mask was very traumatic.

Mairi needed someone to talk to. Someone who would listen. But her parents were dealing with the ramifications of the attack on Bouring. Heck, *everyone* was dealing with that. Leaving Mairi on her own. With nothing but those dreams. Those dreams. That mask . . .

Strangely, though, in her dreams, it wasn't the Mad Mask she was afraid of, even though he was the one who kidnapped her, who threatened her, who knocked her unconscious with some sort of poison gas.

In her dreams, she was *worried* about the Mad Mask, but her real fear was reserved for the Blue Freak.

She saw him in her dreams and she saw him take his mask off, but then . . .

Nothing. Nothing there. Under the mask, she saw only a blank.

No face.

And yet . . . And yet, she felt like she knew him anyway. As though even faceless he was familiar to her. But she just couldn't place . . .

She sighed and looked over at Kyle, who was still doing his best emo impression, gazing moodily out the window, earbuds firmly fixed in his ears.

Her parents had no suggestions as to how to get through to Kyle. She even talked to Mighty Mike, Bouring's resident superpowered kid and the one who'd saved the town from Ultitron and the Blue Freak. But even though Mike was capable of miraculous physical feats, he had no advice or insight into Kyle's problems.

Mairi didn't know what to do. She wanted her friend back.

For some reason, just then, she thought again of her dream. She didn't know why, but it was like she relived her dream in that moment. The plain nothing under the Blue Freak's mask.

She found herself pulling away from Kyle, without being sure why. Kyle was her friend. Even though he was being an idiot right now. He was still . . .

Wasn't he?

CHAPTER
TWO

"... reconfiguring the IPv6 tech specs to redirect folding processes," Erasmus was saying, "which means that we can —"

"Knock it off," Kyle mumbled under his breath, making certain that no one else could hear him. No one except for Erasmus, the artificial intelligence built into his iPod. Erasmus was developing some kind of scheme to divert something like a third of the Internet's computing power to Kyle's own computer so that — in one swift burst of computing — Kyle could launch a brute-force hack attack on the military computers holding Mighty Mike's sealed medical tests. But Kyle had lost his taste for super-stuff. For crazy science. For being a "villain."

The reason why sat right next to him on the bus, and Kyle couldn't even look at her without feeling a now-too-familiar pang in his heart:

Guilt.

When Mairi had been kidnapped by the Mad Mask, Kyle had sworn to rescue her. Unlike the time she'd been threatened by the ASE (Animated Soil Entity), this time he wouldn't put the well-being of the town above Mairi's. This time, he let Mighty Mike and the Army distract Ultitron while he — Kyle — headed into the sewers to hit the problem at its source: the Mad Mask. And in defeating the Mad Mask, he also rescued Mairi. Double score.

But something went wrong. One of the Mad Mask's MadDroids ripped off Kyle's mask and Mairi saw that her best friend and the "evil," "villainous" "national security risk" — the Blue Freak — were one and the same.

Kyle had no choice. He couldn't put Mairi in the position of knowing that Kyle was the Blue Freak. She would have been questioned by the government and would have to lie about his true identity. She would have to live with a horrible secret.

So he erased her memory, using the brain-wave manipulator he'd built.

The brain-wave manipulator was gone now, crushed into useless scrap metal when the enormity of what he'd done had hit Kyle. He had erased Mairi's memory! He played with his best friend's *brain*.

Sure, he'd done the same to his parents, but somehow that didn't seem serious. They were adults and they had plenty of boring adult stuff in their lives, so who cared if they forgot a few convenient facts?

But Mairi was his best friend.

Kyle couldn't look at her. Couldn't talk to her. Didn't even want to think about her, though that was impossible, of course. And meanwhile — when all he wanted to do was to wallow in his guilt and self-pity — Erasmus kept chattering away.

Like now. Even though Kyle had told him to shut up, Erasmus just kept prattling on, now indignant.

"Who are you to tell me to stop talking?" Erasmus demanded. "At least I'm still using my brain for something other than pointless, moody emotionalism. Unlike someone I could mention, using no names, but his initials are *Kyle Camden*."

Erasmus was smart — he was beyond smart, actually, having been patterned on Kyle's own brain waves and personality — but he didn't possess much in the way of sympathy. Kyle sighed and removed his earbuds. Erasmus could blather on as much as he wanted, but there was no way he could force Kyle to listen.

After school, Kyle once again curled up in his seat on the bus and ignored the world on the way home. When Mairi tried to say good-bye to him, he just shrugged and mumbled something to her as she got up and made her way down the bus aisle. All he wanted was to be home, inside, away from the world.

As he walked to his front door, a neighbor gasped and pointed to the sky. Without thinking, Kyle looked up . . .

. . . and saw Mighty Mike. Just for a lingering moment, his green-and-gold costume sparkling against a cottony white cloud.

Kyle ground his teeth. He knew things about Mighty Mike that no one else knew, things no one else could be bothered to find out. Mike claimed to have amnesia. He claimed just to be a kid with superpowers, a kid living with his foster parents on the other side of Bouring. But Kyle had been there that night. The night of the plasma storm that gave him his own powers. And he'd seen Mighty Mike, awash in the plasma, emerging from it. . . .

An alien.

A liar.

And yet as angry as the mere sight of Mighty Mike made Kyle, he just couldn't get worked up enough to do anything about it. Not now. Not since . . .

He squeezed his eyes shut tight, but all he could see was the dreamy, dazed look on Mairi's face as the brain-wave manipulator selectively rearranged her neurons. . . .

He growled and kicked at one of the heavy, concrete planters his mother had placed along the front of the house. It instantly shattered into a million pieces. Oops! Kyle looked around furtively. Whew. No one had been watching. He quickly scooped up the pieces.

And the plants.

And the dirt.

He didn't know what to do with it, so he just zipped around to the backyard and dumped it all in the woods. But when he came back around to the front, he saw that the planters were uneven now — Mom had put four on each side of the door and now it was lopsided. So Kyle grabbed up another one and buried it in the woods. There. Now everything was even.

Biggest intellect on the planet. Superstrength and superspeed and all that. And what was he?

He was a landscaper!

Sheesh.

Things couldn't get any worse, could they?

Inside, he tossed his books and his backpack on the floor and went down to the basement. His parents never used the basement, so Kyle had turned it into a lab/workshop for himself.

He hadn't gone down there since the night Ultitron and the Mad Mask were defeated.

"Oh, finally returning to the basement," Erasmus said as soon as Kyle slipped his earbuds back in. "Good. There's work to be done. Mighty Mike won't destroy himself, you know."

"Not now, Erasmus. Please."

Erasmus simulated a sort of *harrumph!* sound, but fell silent. Kyle didn't want to listen to the AI — he had put the earbuds in to listen to music. He fired up a playlist and roamed the basement.

In one corner: the remains of his biochemical forge, which had once churned away to create a bacterium that would remove Mighty Mike's powers. Now it was a heap of junk, disassembled at the order of the Mad Mask, to be used as parts for Ultitron.

And over here: the workbench where Kyle had worked tirelessly and feverishly to assemble Ultitron's "motivational engine."

And piled on a chair: the shredded remains of Kyle's Azure Avenger costume, ripped by MadDroids and then perforated by Army ordnance when Kyle tried to save the town of Bouring and got shot at for his efforts and his bravery.

And on a shelf against one wall, next to a leaden jug of radioactive dirt from Mighty Mike's "landing site," the Mad Mask's mask, a heavy piece of ebony wood with two eyeholes and a single inlaid tear made out of ivory.

Everywhere Kyle looked, he was reminded of the Mad Mask. And Ultitron. And the lair in the sewers.

And the look on Mairi's face . . .

It was almost Thanksgiving. Kyle had nothing to be thankful for.

*　　*　　*

By the time his parents got home from work, Kyle had already done his homework (a superbrain made homework a snap) and now lay on his bed, the bedroom door closed. This was what he did every day and had done every day since Ultitron's defeat: come home, do homework, chill out until dinner, shovel dinner in, then retreat to his bedroom for privacy until bedtime.

Today, something changed. There was a knock at his door. Lefty — the fat white rabbit who lived in a cage in Kyle's room — jumped in surprise.

"Come in," Kyle said reluctantly.

His father poked his head in the room. "How — how you doing, kiddo?"

Kyle winced at the stutter. His father stuttered on the words "how" and "why" — a side effect of the brain-wave manipulator. Another reminder of what Kyle had done.

"I'm fine," Kyle lied, shrugging.

"You sure?" Dad came into the room and leaned against the wall, trying to look casual. But Kyle could tell there was something on his mind.

"I'm fine, Dad. Really." Kyle said it with all the earnestness he could project. He really didn't want to talk to anyone.

"I have to be honest . . ."

Why? Is someone holding a gun to your head?

"Mom and I are sort of worried about you."

"I'm fine," Kyle said for the third time, annoyance beginning to creep in. He hated repeating himself. He especially hated repeating *lies*; why couldn't people just believe him the first time? Then he wouldn't have to lie so often.

"You haven't been talking much. At all, really," Dad said, speaking as though Kyle hadn't just served up a perfectly believable lie to end the conversation. "What about your new friend? Theodore? He hasn't been around for a long time."

Kyle froze. "Theodore" was the name he'd given his parents for the Mad Mask, since the Mad Mask was hanging around the house a lot while they worked on Ultitron. Just hearing the name made Kyle depressed.

"You're quiet," Dad went on. "You're sullen. And you just spend all of your time alone in your room. You haven't even seen Mairi in weeks."

Dad stopped talking and gazed at Kyle. Kyle realized that he was supposed to say something at this point.

But he had nothing to say. So he just shrugged.

"Look, did you guys have a fight or —?"

"No, Dad."

"Did you disagree about something? Did you —?"

"Dad, really — everything's fine. Just leave me alone. I'll come down for dinner when it's ready." Kyle flipped over onto his belly so that he didn't have to look at his father anymore.

"You're not . . . you're not coming to the time capsule burial with us?" Dad sounded shocked. Kyle didn't care, and he showed it by not answering.

"We're worried about you," Dad pressed. "Is there something else going on? Sometimes when, uh, when boys and girls get to be your age, um . . . things can get . . . complicated, you know?" Dad started stuttering; it had nothing to do with the brain-wave manipulator. "We just — your mom and I, I mean — we just want you to know that we're here for you and if you're having, you know, if you're having, well, um, *new* feelings about Mairi or *complicated* feelings, well, Mom and I, we're here for you. . . ."

"Please stop it," Kyle groaned into his pillow. "Just. Stop. It."

"You probably think you're alone in this. You probably think you have to handle it on your own. But Mom and I can help. We can teach you —"

And that was it. Kyle couldn't take any more. Teach? His parents, with their merely mortal brains, were going to teach *him*? Teach him what? How to waste six hours a night on the couch watching stupid TV shows?

"Stop it," he told his father again.

"We've been there before. We know what you're going through and —"

Kyle rolled over and sat up so quickly that he was

a blur. "Stop it!" he yelled at his father. "Just stop it! There's nothing you can teach me!"

Lefty scampered into a corner of his cage and cowered there, shocked.

Dad swallowed, his Adam's apple bobbing. He stared at Kyle for a long moment. Kyle returned the stare and didn't back down.

"It's almost time for the time capsule burial —"

"Go without me."

Dad mumbled something about money for pizza being on the kitchen counter and backed out of the room, shutting the door as he left.

Good.

from the top secret journal of
Kyle Camden (deciphered):

What is good?

What is evil?

Philosophers and priests and logicians and scientists and even regular people have been wondering this almost forever. And don't believe what they tell you in school or on TV: No one has figured it out yet. No one.

The classic example, of course, is hurting someone. Hurting someone is supposed to be bad and wrong and evil. But what about self-defense? What about soldiers in war?

Even in the case of something as cut-and-dried, as black-and-white, there are exceptions.

I did something good. No one can ever convince me otherwise. Mairi was in danger and I did everything in my power to rescue her. I saved her from the Mad Mask and also saved the entire town of Bouring while I was at it. The Mad Mask could have hurt or killed Mairi, if not for me. Heck, she would have ended up Numero Uno on the government's speed dial for dealing with the "Blue Freak" if not for me! And if losing a little, tiny piece of her memory is the price of not being maimed or murdered or locked up in a government dungeon some-where, then I think that's an okay trade-off.

Right?

I did something good! I saved my best friend's life! I saved a lot of lives! I'm the good guy! I did the right thing!

So why does it feel like I did something evil?

Why do I feel bad and guilty?

CHAPTER
THREE

A knock at her window made Mairi jump in surprise. She spun around, and of course it was Mighty Mike, hovering at the window, grinning in at her.

"I never get used to that!" she exclaimed as she opened the window to let him in.

"It is pretty enterprising," he admitted.

Mairi thought for a moment. Mike had some odd combination of amnesia and brain damage, which made translating his mangled English a challenge at times.

"I think you meant that it's pretty *surprising*," she guessed.

Mike nodded slowly. "That sounds more likely, doesn't it?" He sighed and his shoulders slumped, and suddenly — even though he wore a gaudy costume and a cape — he looked nothing like a superhero and everything like a depressed boy.

"Don't worry," she told him. "Your memory will come back. I'm sure of it. And your speaking is getting better. It really is." She patted him on the shoulder to reassure him.

Mike shrugged. "I hope so. I get frustrated sometimes. When I say something and I can tell I said it wrongly, but no one will correct me. They just intend like they understand me."

"I know. People are afraid of offending you. Oh, and it's 'wrong,' not 'wrongly.' And probably '*pre*tend.'"

"Okay. Thank you, Mairi. You're my only real friend." He gave her a sad smile and Mairi couldn't help herself — she threw her arms around him and hugged him. It was like hugging something chiseled out of diamond, so dense and hard was Mike's body, but she hugged him anyway. After a moment, Mike hesitantly returned the hug, careful not to crush her with his Mighty Strength.

"You're great," she told him. "Be patient. Everything will work out."

After the hug lingered for a moment, Mike broke it and said, "Are you ready to go?"

"Yep!"

With a grin, Mike swooped Mairi into his arms. She shrieked with delight as he hurtled out the window and then they were airborne, soaring over the town.

Mike had offered to fly Mairi to the annual burial of the Bouring Time Capsule. Every year for the past thirty years, the town of Bouring buried a time capsule just before Thanksgiving. There was a large parcel of land not far from the school that had been donated years ago for the purpose. It was divided into fifty sections, one per year. At the end of fifty years, the first time capsule would be dug up and opened; the fifty-first would then be buried there.

So far, no time capsules had been opened yet, but the entire town turned out for the annual burial. The whole thing was like a carnival — businesses had booths, restaurants set up grills and cooked, the mayor spoke. . . . It was a big deal and lots of fun.

Usually, Mairi and her family went with Kyle and his family. But this year Kyle was . . .

Mairi decided not to think about Kyle. Instead, she tightened her arms around Mighty Mike's neck and enjoyed the feel of the air blowing against her.

It only took a couple of minutes to get to the burial site. Mike could have gotten there even faster, but when he carried Mairi he had to fly a little slower — she could be hurt by the great speeds otherwise.

There was a crowd gathered down there, milling about in the crisp late-November evening. Mike had flown Mairi a bunch of times now, but every time seemed amazing and brand-new. Especially a time like this, when she could see almost the entire town of Bouring down below her: her teachers, her parents, Kyle's parents. . . .

Kyle was nowhere to be seen.

Of course. Mairi was surprised to find that she wasn't even surprised. Kyle had changed so much lately that she hadn't really expected him to be here at all.

The crowd began cheering as they spied Mighty Mike, and then Mairi's stomach did that weird little dip it always did when Mike descended.

"Easy," he murmured in her ear. Mike knew she hated landings.

In an instant, it was over, and she joined her parents in the crowd. Mike waved to the cheering townspeople and made his way to a spot in the field cordoned off with red, white, and blue ribbons. This was the spot designated for this year's time capsule burial. The mayor and Sheriff Maxwell Monroe waited there, smiling and waving. Along with them was an older man Mairi didn't recognize, who stood next to a large platform. The time capsule itself rested on that platform.

It was roughly three feet high and two feet around, shaped like a bullet, with a small door set into it. It gleamed silver in the sun. Engraved along its nose-cone were the words: *TOWN OF BOURING — MEMORIES AND LIVES*, followed by the year. Anyone could put something into the time capsule each year in the two weeks leading up to its burial, and Mairi always did. This year, she had put in a photo album containing one picture for every day of the last year. The previous year, she and Kyle had goofed off and put in pictures of their pets — his rabbit, Lefty, and her cat, Sashimi.

Kyle.

She pushed the thought away. No point getting depressed. Not when this was supposed to be fun.

The mayor spoke into a microphone, asking everyone to settle down and be quiet. When the crowd fell silent, she said, "I want to thank you all for coming out today. It looks like the weather is cooperating — I think this is the warmest it's been since July!"

Everyone laughed. The fall had been bitterly cold; today was the first day in a long time Mairi had been able to go out without a heavy coat.

"I am so pleased," the mayor went on, "to have with us today Mr. Walter Lundergaard, founder and CEO of Lundergaard Research, and the man who so generously donated the land for the time capsules many years ago. Mr. Lundergaard?"

So *this* was the man who ran Lundergaard Research. The facility was located near Bouring and had always been a mystery to most of the town, considering that it did so much top-secret work for the government. Mairi thought maybe she'd seen a picture of Lundergaard once or twice, but he'd never come to a town event like this before.

He stepped up to the microphone and cleared his throat annoyingly right into it.

"It's a real honor and a pleasure to be here today," Lundergaard said, his voice slightly cracked, but still bright. "The town of Bouring and my own research campus have both suffered in recent weeks." He paused while everyone thought of the devastation wrought by Ultitron.

"It's in times like this," Lundergaard went on, "that it is imperative we pull together — as a community — to honor our past and look to our future."

The crowd went wild with applause. Mr. Lundergaard executed a small but polite bow, then stepped away from the microphone, yielding to the mayor.

"Every year," the mayor said, "we gather here to bury the town time capsule in this plot. Well, *almost* every year."

Everyone looked in the same direction: toward the plot reserved for the year 1987. It was part of the town legend. How the time capsule had simply disappeared overnight from its secure resting place the night before it was scheduled to be buried. No one knew what had happened to it, and so the 1987 plot was the only empty one from the past.

"This year," the mayor continued, "our usual team of diggers who dig the hole the night before and then fill it in afterward won't be necessary. Because this year, we are proud to have the capsule buried by our town's mightiest resident: Mighty Mike!"

The crowd went wild as Mike took the microphone. Mairi clapped until her hands burned.

"Thank you. Thank you," he said. "I am ironed to —" He broke off for a moment, gazing at Mairi, who was shaking her head and mouthing *honored* to him.

"I'm sorry," he said, grinning sheepishly. "I meant to say that I am *horrored* to be here and to be asked to participate in the time capsule burial. Thank you for making me a part of your town."

Oh, well. She tried.

Mike handed the microphone to the sheriff, who cautioned everyone to stand back and watch out for "flying dirt."

And then Mighty Mike turned like a top, spinning so fast that he was just a green/gold blur, rapidly descending into the ground. Despite Sheriff Monroe's warning, the dirt that geysered up from the ground formed a tight column that arced away from the crowd and settled into a neat heap. For a moment, Mairi had a flashback to the dirt monster that had nearly killed her a few weeks ago, but she pushed past it and clapped and cheered along with everyone else.

It took Mike less than a minute to excavate a hole ten feet deep and five feet across. He popped up from the hole, covered in dirt, then spun once more in the air to shake off the dirt. The crowd applauded even more loudly.

"Wait!" he said, holding up a hand. "Wait!"

The crowd kept cheering. They couldn't tell what Mairi could tell — that Mike was concerned about something. What was wrong?

"There's something down here already!" Mike called.

The crowd's raucous applause mutated into confused babbling. Something *down* there already? What was he talking about?

Mike dived back into the hole and hauled out something bullet-shaped. About three feet high and two feet around. As dirt fell away from it, it gleamed silver in the sun.

It was a time capsule.

The crowd gasped in shock. At the front of the crowd, Mairi could see what most people couldn't. Engraved along its nose-cone were the words:

TOWN OF BOURING — MEMORIES AND LIVES — 1987.

CHAPTER
FOUR

The entire town of Bouring, Kyle knew, would be at the burial of the time capsule. Usually Kyle enjoyed these events — he always tried to put something genuinely interesting and useful into the time capsule, though he also tended to put in practical jokes. He couldn't help himself — he was a prankster by nature and the idea of pranking people fifty years in the future pleased him. One year, he had put in an envelope marked "URGENT AND IMPORTANT," then stuck a sheet of specially treated flash paper inside it. As soon as someone opened the envelope, the paper inside would vanish in a burst of smoke and light. Heh.

But this year, he just couldn't be bothered.

Erasmus was low on power, so Kyle scrounged around for his charging cable but couldn't find it. Mom must have taken it again. She did that sometimes, when she left her own charger at work. So Kyle just plugged Erasmus into his computer with a USB cable and let him charge that way.

His parents were at the burial ceremony, so Kyle was alone except for Lefty and Erasmus. Lefty cocked his head this way and that, following Kyle as he paced the bedroom.

"I wish I could be *in* that time capsule, Lefty. Believe me. I wish I could just tuck myself inside it and go to sleep and wake up fifty years from now when they dig it up. Because then I wouldn't have to deal with any of this nonsense. Mighty Mike and the Mad Mask and everyone in the world thinking I'm the Blue Freak and all of that. It would be so much easier to skip everything. Almost like having a . . ."

He trailed off and stopped right in front of Lefty's cage, staring down at the white rabbit. He stared for so long that he lost track of time and probably would have stood frozen like that for hours if Lefty hadn't gotten impatient and started rattling the cage door for attention.

Kyle snapped out of it and fed Lefty a piece of dried papaya, then snatched up Erasmus and raced down to the basement. As soon as he slipped the earbuds in, he started barking to Erasmus: "Six feet of copper cabling! Three steel panels, measuring eighteen inches by thirty-one inches each! The guts of a PlayStation 2!"

"Wait!" Erasmus cried out. "Wait! What are you doing?"

"Inventory!" Kyle shouted. He spun around in the

center of the basement. Yeah, he had a lot of junk. Leftover parts. Stuff that was useless.

Useless until it was *used*.

And there, tucked away in a corner, under an old garden tarp, were the remains of his father's old motorbike, which hadn't worked since Kyle was born. Kyle had started tinkering with it when he'd first gotten his superpowers, then had gotten distracted by the Mad Mask and by other plans.

But his original plan for the bike . . .

"Inventory? Why?"

"I need you to index everything we have. All of it. And cross-reference it to the blueprints I uploaded for the motorbike. Do it. Now."

"The motor . . ." Erasmus didn't breathe, so he didn't really know how to gasp, but he did a decent digital impression. "But that means —"

"That's right, Erasmus!" Kyle chortled. "We're building a time machine!"

Moving at superspeed and with Erasmus's help, Kyle soon had an accounting of all of the gadgets, gizmos, widgets, and leftover technological junk at his disposal.

"It still won't work," Erasmus said. "We're missing the material to make a power conduit — that copper wiring won't be able to handle the massive amounts of electromagnetic energy from a time machine. And you can't collect the stellar zero-point energy without some kind of super-reflective surface. And the —"

"I know!" Kyle barked. "I know!" He resisted the urge to punch the wall in frustration — even though the concrete was almost a foot thick, he would still end up buried to his elbow, if not his shoulder.

He settled for grabbing a solid steel crowbar and twisting it into a pretzel shape instead. It had seemed so easy. . . . He'd understood the basic theoretical physics for time travel for weeks now. He just lacked a way to put his knowledge into practice. But he still needed some very expensive components. And with his Blue Freak costume shredded, he couldn't just . . .

"Kyle," Erasmus said with a gentleness that surprised Kyle, "what are you thinking? Talk to me."

"I'm thinking that I need to ask for money for Christmas this year," Kyle said. He fumed. Christmas was a month away! Why couldn't his family be *Jewish*? Hanukkah was right at the beginning of December this year, only a week away!

"That's not what you're thinking," Erasmus said. "Your heart rate is elevated. Your breathing pattern has deviated from normal by one percent. You're upset."

"Of course I'm upset! I want a time machine and I can't have one!"

"Right. But *why* do you want a time machine?"

Kyle sighed with exasperation. "We've been over this before. If I can travel back in time, I can record Mighty Mike's arrival on Earth. Then I can show it to the world and prove he's an alien and that will force him to tell the world why he's really here."

"I don't believe you."

Kyle marched over to his shelf unit and plucked a video camera from the bottom shelf. "What about this? I fixed up the old camcorder last week. Why else would I do that?"

"Kyle, you based me on your own brain patterns and logical development. I think almost exactly the way you do. I know what you're really up to."

"Oh, really, short circuit? Then why don't you tell me, if you're so smart?"

"Absolutely," Erasmus said with infuriating and self-assured calm. "You want to travel back in time to the Mad Mask's attack and change things so that you never needed to erase Mairi's memory. That will, in your estimation, expiate your sin and release you from your guilt."

"Shows what *you* know. That's totally *not* what I plan to do," Kyle lied.

"Kyle, I can tell when you're lying."

"I'm sure you believe that."

"Your plan would not work in any event. The past is fixed. You can't change it. Everything that has happened . . . has happened. It can't be altered."

"Oh, yeah?" Kyle sneered. "Figured that out based on all the time travel you've done?"

"It's simple logic. If you could change the past so that you never erased Mairi's memory, then you would never have had a reason to go into the past in the first place. Your success would erase the reason for your trip."

"Time paradox nonsense," Kyle said. "Time isn't set in cement. If I change the past — *when* I change the past — the rest of the universe will be altered, but my memories will still be the same because I'll be . . . I'll *have been* out of sync with the universe when the change happens. Happened. Will have happened." Verb tenses had clearly not been designed to take into account time travel. Kyle figured he would have to get around to reinventing verb conjugation one of these days. *Someone* had to do it.

"Paradox isn't *nonsense*, Kyle. In fact, most theoretical physicists agree that even if you *could* travel through time, you could only go forward —"

"Everyone is traveling forward in time. One second at a time. That's no big trick."

"— and furthermore that even if you *could* go into the past, you would only be able to travel back as far as the moment the time machine was actually switched on —"

"Most theoretical physicists have IQs under two-fifty. Why should I listen to them? They can't even properly visualize thirteen-dimensional space. They haven't harnessed dark energy."

"Neither have you."

"I could, if I had the proper equipment." Kyle sighed and put the camcorder on the top shelf, next to the jar of dirt and . . . and . . .

"Whoa," Kyle whispered.

"What? What is it? Based on your inflection and intonation, I assume you've had some sort of epiphany."

Kyle stared at the Mad Mask's mask, those conjoined, off-center half circles of black wood, that gleaming ivory tear.

This wasn't the only such mask in the world. There was another.

"Ultitron . . ." Kyle said softly.

The Mad Mask's ten-story-tall killer robot, Ultitron, had an identical mask for its face, so that the world would know that the Mad Mask was behind it. (Not that it helped — the idiots who ran the world still thought that Kyle had put together the robot.)

And right now, Ultitron's deactivated robotic "corpse" was still junked exactly where Mighty Mike had left it: on the site of the abandoned coal mine on the outskirts of Bouring. The Army had been guarding it for the past few weeks while a team of scientists picked their way over and under and through it, trying to figure out what made Ultitron tick. They never would, of course, because Ultitron had been powered purely by the Mad Mask's psychic ability to control machinery and electronics.

But in the meantime . . .

"Ultitron?" Erasmus asked. "What *about* Ultitron? It's . . . Oh." Because Kyle and Erasmus thought almost exactly alike, it took Erasmus only a moment to realize what Kyle had realized.

Ultitron was junk, true, but it was *high-tech* junk. There was a wealth of components and parts to be scavenged there. Pieces of technology and raw materials just there for the taking.

Kyle's Azure Avenger costume was in shreds, but he still had the Mad Mask's mask. He was wearing a plain red T-shirt and blue jeans. Nothing identifiable or unique.

He slipped the ebony mask on. "Come on, Erasmus. We've got work to do."

"Work? What kind of work?"

"We're going Dumpster-diving."

CHAPTER
FIVE

At the time capsule burial plot, the crowd surged forward, desperately curious to see what appeared to be the legendary Lost Time Capsule of 1987. Mairi was almost crushed in the ensuing rush forward, but she managed to worm through spots in the throng and make her way to the front of the mob. From here, she had an excellent vantage point on the stage. She fished in her pocket for her tiny video camera. This was something worth recording!

"Please remain calm!" Sheriff Monroe said into the microphone. His words said "Please," but his tone said "I'm about ten seconds away from drawing my gun." A few deputies on the scene tried to keep the crowd from rushing the capsule. Mighty Mike stood near the capsule, puzzled.

"Seriously, folks," the sheriff said in that tone of voice he usually reserved for when Kyle did something prank-y and annoying.

Mairi zoomed in on the capsule with her camera and stared at the screen. The capsule looked legit, but how could she be sure? It's not like she had a book titled *Images of Time Capsules from the 1980s*. But the design of the time capsules used in Bouring hadn't really changed much in the past few years, so why would they be different even that long ago? Time capsules were pretty simple things — you stuck stuff in them and buried them underground.

She tried to remember what her mother had told her once about the missing time capsule. Her parents had been the same age back in 1987 that Mairi was now, and the story of the missing time capsule had buzzed the air of Bouring like curiosity-seeking bees for weeks, eventually passing into the territory of town lore and mystery: The night before a time capsule burial, the capsule was always left safely in storage at the sheriff's office. That year — 1987 — the sheriff at the time (Sheriff Monroe's father, Milton Monroe) had locked it up in his office as usual. The next morning, it was gone. No sign of forced entry. Nothing.

A search ensued, but the time capsule was never recovered. And so the hole dug in the spot for 1987 had been filled in without a time capsule, and beginning the following year, it became standard protocol for a deputy to sit with the time capsule all night.

So . . . someone had stolen the capsule in 1987 and then . . . buried it in the wrong spot?

But why? And how? How could someone have buried it ten feet down before someone else noticed a hole being dug? And how —

The mayor's voice snapped Mairi out of her thoughts of the past and brought her back to the present. The deputies and Mighty Mike had managed to keep the crowd from rushing forward any more, though the noise of chatter and excitement kept building.

"Folks!" the mayor boomed from the microphone. "Folks, please! I understand how excited you all are! I think we're . . . It's pretty amazing. We came here to bury this year's time capsule and instead we've found one we thought lost forever."

If someone had stolen it, Mairi wondered, why? What was the point of stealing it and hiding it? If Kyle had been alive way back in 1987, she would assume it was one of his weird pranks. But what was the point of a prank no one understood? Why steal a time capsule? They weren't *good* for anything. Unless . . .

"I know that the people of 1987 intended for this to be opened awhile from now," the mayor went on, "but this is a special circumstance, as I think you'll all agree."

Unless there was something inside the time capsule, something that the thief didn't want anyone to see. Could that be it?

"So I think that — as long as no one objects — we're going to go ahead and open this time capsule right now."

The crowd roared its approval.

Mairi said nothing. She was still thinking. Was there something in there that the thief wanted hidden? But then why not just take it *out* of the capsule? The thing was welded shut, but if you were going to the trouble of stealing it, would it be that much more effort to open it?

So then in that case, maybe . . . maybe . . .

"They put something . . ." she whispered. "The thief didn't want to take something *out*. He wanted to *put* something *in*!"

"Mighty Mike, we don't seem to have a cutter here," the mayor said, chuckling, "so could you do the honors?"

What could someone put into a time capsule that they had stolen? It had to be something horrible, right? Which meant that . . .

On the screen of Mairi's video camera, Mike tilted his head.

"Do *what* to the honors?" he asked.

"Don't do it," Mairi tried to shout, but only a whisper came out. Something bad was about to happen. She could feel it in her throat, her tongue, her lips — all had gone dry and thick and useless.

The mayor laughed expansively. "Could you just open the time capsule?" she asked.

"Don't!" Mairi shouted, her voice finally returning. "Don't!"

But no one heard her over the crowd noise, and Mighty Mike grasped the top of the time capsule in his child-sized but incredibly strong hands. With a single wrenching twist, he ripped off the nose-cone. Mairi had a perfect, up-close view of it on her screen.

The crowd bellowed as though with a single, thrilled voice.

And then something exploded and the world went white for an instant. Mairi could see nothing, could hear nothing. . . .

And then she saw a blur. A green-and-gold blur, like the colors of Mighty Mike's costume —

It *was* Mighty Mike. Flying toward her, reaching out, screaming —

"MAIRI!!!"

CHAPTER
SIX

Kyle soared over the town of Bouring, bearing due west toward the old coal mine. A billion years ago — back when Kyle's parents had been kids — Bouring had been a coal town. But the mine had been shut down a long time ago; it was now nothing more than an open sore on the face of the local ecology, cordoned off by ten-foot-high fencing topped with razor wire. There were lots of impressive-looking signs that said things like NO TRES-PASSING and DANGER! but Kyle didn't care much for the signs. He had actually come out to the coal mine the first night he'd discovered his superpowers, testing his strength and speed in the relative privacy of the mine, where no one would care what happened when he unleashed his full strength.

Now the signs were augmented with new ones. Government warnings. Military warnings. Violators will be shot on sight, etc.

Yeah, they could shoot at Kyle all they wanted. Bullets just bounced off.

He hovered over the coal mine, high enough up that none of the guards down below could see him. Ultitron lay there like a broken toy. A broken ten-story-tall toy. Its arms — ripped off by Mighty Mike — lay over to one side, as though Ultitron had dropped them somewhere and couldn't remember where.

It was getting close to dusk, and from here it appeared as though most of the scientists and lab rats and government geeks assigned to pick through Ultitron had knocked off for the day. There was only a small crew near the left arm. Other than that, there were about a dozen armed guards in a standard formation around the fence.

No one was looking up.

Morons.

Kyle drifted down slowly, not wanting to catch anyone's eye.

"Kyle," Erasmus said suddenly.

"Not now."

"But I'm picking up something on the police band. There's —"

"I said not now." And then Kyle did something he rarely did: He switched off Erasmus. He didn't need distractions right now.

Ultitron loomed larger and larger in his view as he descended. He expected a shout of alarm at any moment, but it never came, and soon enough he was concealed behind the massive bulk of the robot.

His memory was better than most computers' these days, so it was no big deal to recall the "shopping list" of components he'd come up with back at home. Fortunately, he was also able to remember most of the schematics to Ultitron, so he would be able to get to the right places inside the gigantic structure and not waste a lot of time fiddling around, looking for —

"Hey! Hey, you!"

Kyle sighed. Oh, man — he *really* didn't want to have to mess with the military.

Again.

"You're *kidding* me!" Kyle raged, shooting straight up into the sky.

"What's happening?" Erasmus asked. Kyle had switched him back on as soon as the guard called out to him.

"Block their signals!" Kyle shouted. "All military frequencies! Now!"

"But what about —"

"Just do it!" Kyle screamed, visions of entire platoons and brigades bearing down on him and firing up at him scrolling through his mind. "Block all military and police frequencies in the entire *town*!"

"I already *did* it," Erasmus said rather snottily. "I did it as soon as you asked me to. Well, *ordered* me to is more like it. I react in microseconds, remember? But we need to talk about the police band that I —"

"Make sure that's blocked, too. I don't want them switching to a local frequency." Kyle spun in midair and swooped down. Below him, the guards were converging around the (un)lucky one who'd spotted Kyle. Suddenly, a flurry of bullets came at him, a reverse rain of lead.

Kyle dodged the bullets. They couldn't hurt him, but he didn't want to crack the mask he wore. Or get holes in his clothes. His mom wasn't a genius, but even she would probably wonder why he had bullet holes in his favorite jeans when she did the laundry.

"Condition red! Red!" a soldier screamed just as Kyle flicked him twenty feet with a tap from his right hand. The soldier groaned and tried to get up, then collapsed, unconscious.

More armed guards rushed at Kyle, still firing, even though they had to know it was pointless. More shouts of "Condition red!" into the shoulder-mics they all wore. But no help was coming, thanks to Erasmus's jamming frequency.

Kyle counted them quickly. Good. All of the soldiers were here, focused on him. None of them were running away to get help in person. They figured they would get through on the radio. By the time they realized their mistake . . .

"The police band is down now, as you ordered," Erasmus said, insisting on interrupting Kyle's fight. "But you need to know: Something's gone wrong at the time capsule burial."

"This is the sound of me not caring," Kyle said. "We have more important things to worry about." He side-stepped a bullet, then another, then another, making his way to the soldier who was firing at him. At this speed, the bullets were like fat little slugs just hanging in the air, barely moving. Kyle actually flicked one away with the tip of his index finger. Kyle had to give the soldier his props: There was a kid moving toward him at superspeed, and the guy just stood his ground and fired. Pretty brave.

Kyle thunked two fingers against the soldier's helmet. *BONGGGG!* The guy passed out. He would have a heck of a headache when he woke up, but would be otherwise unhurt.

But that was just one soldier, and there were more than a dozen here, all of them converging on Kyle, now coordinating tighter and tighter bursts of gunfire. If he took these guys out one at a time, he'd be here forever. And Kyle had more important things to do than to play Dodgebullet with the U.S. Army.

So he lifted one foot and stomped the ground.

The ground rumbled and shook like a miniature earthquake, radiating out from Kyle's superpowered stomp all the way to the soldiers, who suddenly started dancing like they'd been zapped with electricity. The gunfire stopped.

Kyle spun around like a top and a burst of wind peeled away from him, knocking down everyone in its path. Before the stunned soldiers could regain their feet or their weapons, Kyle was on them at superspeed, knocking each one out cold with a carefully placed, superstrong finger-flick.

"Now for the scientists . . ." he muttered, flying over the hulk of Ultitron and in the direction of the left arm, where the science guys clustered in a terrified huddle, as if jamming themselves closer together would provide some kind of safety.

Kyle hovered over them for a moment. He had figured he would just knock them out like he'd knocked out the soldiers, but all of a sudden that seemed . . . wrong. The soldiers had been shooting at him — getting physical with them was appropriate and fair. Heck, they were soldiers; they got *paid* to have people get physical with them.

But these guys . . . These poor guys who thought they knew science (*no one* knew science like Kyle knew science) were just cowering there like mice backed into a corner by a lion.

"Oh, great. One more thing to deal with. Like I don't have enough on my plate. You guys are gonna give me a headache," Kyle complained. He thought for a moment, then darted down at superspeed, snatching up a length of strong cable that had been pulled from Ultitron and spooled loosely on the ground. He tied it tightly around the scientists so that they couldn't escape.

"If you behave and don't yell your heads off, I'll untie you before I go," he promised, then made for his original goal: the wreckage of Ultitron and the wealth of free electronic gizmos and gadgets within.

CHAPTER
SEVEN

Mairi barely had time to shout in surprise as Mighty Mike snatched her up in his arms and sped away with her. The next thing she knew, she was standing on a small bluff overlooking the time capsule burial plots. Her hair stirred in the telltale wind that always meant Mighty Mike had just flown away.

What had happened? Mike had opened the time capsule and then there'd been that light and then —

Suddenly, there were more people next to her on the bluff. More wind. Mike was flying people here, then darting back to the crowd to grab more people. Because . . .

Because . . .

Mairi finally *looked* at the time capsule burial area.

"Oh, no," she whispered.

The flash of white light had gone away, but in its aftermath was chaos. It took a moment for Mairi to realize exactly what was going on down there, but once she realized, it made her shiver as though this fine weather had gone incredibly, massively bad.

Some people were standing still. So still that Mairi thought — against her will, but she thought it anyway — that they might actually be dead. Other people were writhing on the ground as though in pain. Others were . . . They were . . .

She couldn't quite believe her eyes, but other people were moving at incredible speed, running here and there, as if panicked by something . . .

And they were hitting one another . . .

Mike swooped and dodged in and around the crowd, grabbing people, separating the fighters. But it was a losing battle. There were too many of them, moving too fast, and the ones who were paralyzed, the ones in pain . . . they were sitting ducks for the fast movers.

Some of the police seemed unaffected and they were wrestling with the *other* police, who had gone crazy like the other townspeople. Mighty Mike moved swiftly, disarming the ones who'd been affected. Sheriff Monroe was shouting orders into the microphone, and as Mairi watched, the mayor took a swing at him, almost smacking him in the back of the head as her mouth hung open, slack.

What was *happening*?

And her parents. Where were —

Just then a fist came out of nowhere. It would have connected with frightening strength if Mairi hadn't dodged at the last minute.

It was Mr. Rogers. The school gym teacher. His teeth were gritted, his lips pulled back in a horrible grin so taut that it must have been painful. But his *eyes* . . . his eyes were somehow blank and full of hate at the same time.

And he moved so fast . . . swinging at her again now.

Mairi backed up and nearly bumped into Miss Schwartz, her science teacher. For an instant, she relaxed, relieved. Miss Schwartz was her favorite teacher and Mairi was one of Miss Schwartz's favorite students, practically a teacher's pet. But then Mairi saw the look of madness in Miss Schwartz's eyes and she knew that no one would be playing favorites. Not today. Not now.

Mairi ducked as Miss Schwartz swung at her, then rolled to one side, sprang up to her feet, and sprinted off, running down the side of the hill that led away from the burial area.

Mairi ran as fast and as far as she could. At first, she checked over her shoulder to see if she was being followed, but then she tripped and almost went facedown on the sidewalk. She decided that getting far away was more important than checking to see if someone was chasing her.

Besides . . . no one was following. It slowly dawned on her that she was running away from nothing. And had no idea where she was running *to*.

She slowed as she neared the northernmost tip of Major Street, suddenly aware of the burning in her lungs and the sore pain lancing through her legs. She leaned against a mailbox and tried to catch her breath.

What was happening? Why had people gone crazy all of a sudden? Why had —

No. Wait. It wasn't that "people" had gone crazy. It's that *some* people had gone crazy. Maybe the people closest to the time capsule . . .

No. No, that wasn't it. Because Sheriff Monroe had been right next to it and he seemed all right. And the mayor, standing next to the sheriff, had gone crazy.

And other people had just stopped moving completely.

Mairi thought again of her parents. What had happened to them? In the chaos and confusion, she hadn't been able to find them before running. She felt ashamed all of a sudden. What if her parents hadn't been affected by the, by the *whatever-it-was*? What if they were scared and under attack like Mairi had been? She had run away. Abandoned them . . .

She spun around, clenching her fists, determined to return to the scene and find them, but before she could take a single step in that direction, she felt a familiar breeze press against her and then Mighty Mike soared into view, hauling Sheriff Monroe with him. The sheriff's hat was missing, his shirt was torn, and a trickle of blood ran from one corner of his mouth, but he didn't seem badly hurt. Just angry.

"Mairi! Don't travel!"

"Don't go back there," the sheriff clarified as he got his feet under him. He gazed at her grimly. "It's not pretty."

"My parents —"

"— are all right. Well, as all right as anyone. I saw them both. They're unconscious and no one is bothering them."

"But —"

"Look, it's under control. For now."

"I made a wind tunnel and sucked all the air away," Mike said. "Everyone went to sleep."

"That . . . that's a great idea," Mairi said, impressed.

"It was the sheriff's idea," Mike said modestly. "I only utensiled it."

Implemented? Sure, maybe. Mairi shook her head, furious with herself for trying to correct Mike's vocabulary at a time like this.

"That won't last forever," she said. "They'll wake up and start hurting one another again. What do we do?"

" 'We' aren't doing anything, young lady," Monroe said, hitching up his gun belt. His handcuffs jangled. "I'm finding a safe place for you to hide out until this is over. Then I'm calling in the National Guard, and Mike and I will get started isolating the dangerous ones from the rest."

"I want to help."

Monroe shook his head. "No way. No civilians. Especially no kids." He sniffed. "Although it's pretty darn suspicious that your little friend isn't around when this happened."

Kyle? Did Sheriff Monroe really think that *Kyle* was responsible for this? For a moment, Mairi's loyalty to her friend swelled to the surface and overwhelmed her fear. Kyle played pranks, yes, but this was far beyond anything he could do. How would he have access to the 1987 time capsule, for one thing? It had vanished long before Kyle was even born!

But then she thought of her dreams. Of the Mad Mask. The mystery face behind the mask.

And Kyle's behavior lately. So quiet. Sullen. Not himself at all. Was he up to something? Had Kyle finally crossed the line and done something dangerous?

Monroe was staring at her as if he expected her to argue with him and defend Kyle. But Mairi just said, "I don't know where he is."

The sheriff nodded. "Let's find a safe place for Mairi here, Mike. And then let's get to work."

Mighty Mike swept Mairi into his arms.

"Wait," Mairi said. "Wait. Before you take me away,

tell me, please: What's going on? What's happening to everyone?"

And Sheriff Monroe said the scariest thing Mairi had ever heard from an adult:

"I don't know."

CHAPTER
EIGHT

Kyle knew that the soldiers would eventually wake up, so the first thing he did was tie all of them up at superspeed. But even that was only a temporary solution. He was pretty sure that if one of them didn't check in at some sort of base on a regular schedule, the Army would send more soldiers. So he had to move quickly.

Fortunately, moving quickly was something he was really, really good at these days.

He sped around Ultitron's deactivated body, ripping open hatches, tearing through wiring and cabling, smashing his way into the innards of the thing. Unlike the Army and the government scientists, Kyle knew that Ultitron wasn't actually a robot — it was just a mass of electronics and components jumbled together at random — so he didn't feel bad about breaking Widget A in order to get to Widget B.

Erasmus walked him through the process, consulting the schematics for Ultitron that still resided on his hard drive. Kyle gathered everything on his "shopping list" and soon had a respectable pile of stuff he would have to haul back home. He pried a sheet of metal from Ultitron's left leg, and twisted and mangled it until it formed a rough sort of bucket. Then he dumped his newfound treasures into it and lifted it over his head. It weighed close to a ton, he estimated.

"Kyle, now that you're done with this, you really should —"

"Not. Now." Kyle heaved out a breath and focused. He'd never tried flying with such a burden before. He would have to move very fast, lest someone see him near the Camden house with the "bucket." And he would have to do it without dropping anything.

He sucked in another breath, then exhaled as he launched himself skyward. For a second, he tilted to the right, unbalanced by his burden, but he quickly righted himself and sped home.

Luckily, no one saw him. Of course — the time capsule burial. Everyone would be there, on the other side of town. He couldn't have planned his heist for a better time!

He realized, with a small shock, that he'd completely forgotten to release the scientists as he'd promised. Oops. He would have to go back later. No biggie.

"There's a serious problem," Erasmus said. "Something happened at the burial ceremony. Details are sketchy, but it seems that the town is out of control."

"I'll fix it," Kyle said, landing in his backyard.

"You don't even know what 'it' is!"

"Trust me. I'll take care of it. Now just let me get this stuff inside and get to work."

Once inside, Kyle took off his stolen mask and got to work. He had Erasmus play something fast, with a strong beat, and then he worked at his top speed, blurring the air in the basement as he zipped from workbench to shelf to the time machine and back again.

He'd never been able to work so quickly before; he usually had to watch his noise level because his parents were always right upstairs and, while they weren't all that bright, the incredible racket of superspeed gadgetry in the basement would surely have caught their attention. (Even then, they would wait for a commercial before budging from the TV — they always forgot they could pause with the DVR, further proof of their idiocy.)

But now he could cut loose. And he did.

Soon, he was sweating, the beads of sweat wicking away from him as he dashed from spot to spot. Flecks of his perspiration, hurled from his brow and sent splattering by his great speed, dotted the basement walls.

"It was when they opened the time capsule, it seems," Erasmus said. "Reports are incomplete. And someone keeps babbling gibberish into the police band, so it's tough to figure out exactly what —"

59

"Get off the police band," Kyle ordered, "and calculate the tolerances needed to recapture a neutrino flow in this capacitor I'm building. I don't want it to explode when I turn on the time machine."

He stripped wires and crimped them together, then soldered them into place. He scrounged around for an old DVD player, unscrewed its shell, and pried it apart to access the goodies within. He needed the small laser and lens assembly that read the DVD during playback. It wasn't terribly powerful, but it was accurate enough for his purposes to act as a controlling mechanism.

Kyle had been designing and redesigning and re-redesigning his chronovessel (it sounded much more impressive than *time machine* even though it meant the same thing) for weeks and weeks now. He had mentally gone over each aspect of it, carefully and cautiously examining it from all angles in the vast intellectual reaches of his enhanced brain. At the same time, he'd fed his ideas and schematics and plans into Erasmus so that the AI could give them the once-over and offer any suggestions, too.

In short, Kyle had already built his time machine. Now it was just a matter of assembling the parts.

The DVD laser. Wiring and cables from Ultitron. A chunk of solar panel. He opened up the motorbike's gas tank — which was now useless; chronovessels didn't operate on gas — and reinforced it with steel, then began adding the computer components that would control the time travel technology. He had grabbed a fistful of processors from Ultitron and now was wiring them to run in parallel, creating in effect a supercomputer in the shell of the motorbike. In order to travel through time, the chronovessel had to calculate millions of variables all at once and make changes to its systems in less than microseconds. Kyle's brain was fast enough and powerful enough to do the math, but even at superspeed, it would be impossible to keep up by typing into a computer. This is why he needed his new, special supercomputer — it was connected directly to the heart of the time travel circuitry and could make the changes instantaneously.

"This is going to work," Kyle whispered. Sweat gathered on his forehead and he wiped it away, still huddled over the glowing soldering iron as he pieced together another component. "It's really going to work."

"Of course it's going to work," Erasmus said in a huff. "We designed it."

Erasmus didn't understand. He couldn't understand. He was an artificial intelligence, not a person. Yes, he was based on Kyle's personality and brain waves, but he couldn't really feel the world, couldn't experience it any other way than through Kyle's voice in the microphone or through the information that streamed through his police band and his Wi-Fi connection. With each passing day, Erasmus became less and less like Kyle, and more and more like, well, Erasmus.

"I designed it," Kyle retorted. "You double-checked it."

"I found the flaw in the zero-point energy collector," Erasmus reminded him, "and figured out new efficiencies in the trans-light —"

"Enough!" Kyle said. "I get it. I get it. You were very helpful. Are you happy now?"

There was a period of quiet, electronic sulking, during which Kyle finished assembling the guidance controls for the chronovessel. As he was busy installing them into the motorbike, Erasmus piped up again, his voice noticeably subdued.

"Kyle, the police band has gone dead."

"Of course it has. I had you block it."

"No, you don't understand. I'm blocking it, but people should still be *trying* to use it. It's just that none of their signals would go through because of me. But no one is trying to use it. At all."

"Well, good. It won't distract us anymore."

Another moment of silence. And then:

"Kyle, the police band *never* goes dead."

Kyle paused. "What are you saying?"

"You don't live in the virtual world like I do. The police band is *always* active. There's always something going on, even if it's just two deputies complaining about the sheriff or someone calling in for a doughnut run. There's always something."

"And now there's nothing."

"Nothing at all. Silence. Dead silence."

Kyle bolted an old Xbox controller onto the handlebars of the motorbike.

"Did you hear me? Dead silence. No one is —"

"I heard you," Kyle said, adjusting the position of the controller. "I'll fix it."

"How?"

"I'll fix all of it," Kyle said. He stood and stretched. "The chronovessel is finished. I'll fix everything by going back in time."

CHAPTER
NINE

Mighty Mike flew off; Mairi watched him go, his green-and-gold costume melting into the darkening sky as he went. In an eye blink, he was gone, leaving her there on Major Street as the sun dipped into the western horizon.

"It'll be all right," Sheriff Monroe promised her in his most convincing adult voice. "Let me get you somewhere safe while he tries to get to the bottom of this."

The sheriff's voice was usually calming, but right now Mairi wasn't buying it. Just moments ago, the sheriff had called out on his shoulder-mic for the dispatcher back at the sheriff's office to alert the National Guard, but no one had answered. He'd then tried his deputies in the field, but again no one had answered.

Nothing could get through. It was like Sheriff Monroe was shouting for help from the bottom of a well and no one could hear.

Mairi wasn't a cop, but she figured when a sheriff called for help and no one answered, that was pretty bad news.

"Come on," Monroe said, taking her hand. "We're going to the office. It's the safest place in town. There's a good sturdy door with a lock and there's the arm —" He shook his head, stopped talking, and started walking.

A good door with a sturdy lock? What did he mean? Mairi had gone on a field trip to the sheriff's office in elementary school, so she knew the place. (In fact, now that she thought about it, that was the day Kyle's feud with Sheriff Monroe began — Kyle had somehow managed to glue the sheriff's gun into its holster.) The only door with a sturdy lock she could think of was —

"Are you putting me in *jail*?" she asked.

"Hush," the sheriff said, his mouth set in a grim line. "Not planning on it, but if worse comes to worst, it might be the safest place."

Mairi's mind raced. Jail. That was crazy. And what else had he been talking about? The arm? The arm? What kind of *arm* —

Oh. Wait. Not an arm. An *armory*.

"Are you going to shoot them?" she demanded. She thought of her parents. Of Kyle's parents. Of her friends and teachers. Everyone she knew was in Bouring, and any one of them could be roaming the streets, looking to hurt someone, the way Mr. Rogers and Miss Schwartz had tried to hurt her. And the sheriff was thinking about the weapons stored at his office?

"You can't kill them!" she pleaded. "They don't

know what they're doing! It's not their fault! Let Mighty Mike figure out a way to —"

Sheriff Monroe stopped walking and spun around to glare at Mairi, his eyes wide and angry, his jaw set. He jerked her arm once, as if to make sure he had her attention, but Mairi could focus on nothing *but* him.

"Listen, Mairi: I don't know what's going on here. No one knows what's going on here. My job is to protect people, and right now you're the only person I see who needs protecting, so I'm going to do whatever I can for you. And, yeah, if I can help those other poor folks, I'm gonna do that, too. But if it comes down to you or them, or *me* or them, well, I have to be prepared to do what has to be done. Do you understand?"

Mairi opened her mouth to answer, but the sheriff's eyes went even wider and he said something that sounded like, "Uch!" and he collapsed right in front of her, his nerveless, strengthless fingers releasing her hand as he crumpled to the street in a heap.

Behind him, grinning and making a strange mewling sound, stood Melissa Masterton, Bouring Middle School's guidance counselor. Or, as Kyle referred to her: the Great Nemesis. Ms. Masterton's eyes were crazy as she glared at Mairi.

Worse yet: Her mouth was smeared red, her teeth stained scarlet. . . .

Mairi couldn't move; her heart skipped a beat, then skipped another one, she was so shocked. Had Ms. Masterton actually been *biting* —

And then — with relief — Mairi realized that it wasn't blood. It was just Ms. Masterton's usual garish red lipstick, smeared all over her face and teeth. Whew!

Ms. Masterton stared as though looking straight through Mairi, who was still rooted to the spot, too terrified even to run. For a moment that seemed to last an infinity, Mairi watched and waited for Ms. Masterton to attack her, her mind spinning, wondering how long the guidance counselor would make her wait before lunging. . . .

Finally, Mairi's muscles unlocked; she shook herself out of her shock-induced paralysis and ran. Ms. Masterton jerked and advanced on Mairi. Mairi fled back along Major Street. Ms. Masterton loped along after her, swinging her arms and making a terrifying, high-pitched keening sound, a desperate sort of noise that made Mairi think of the howl of starving babies, turned up to eleven. She ran as fast as she could — Ms. Masterton had longer legs, but Mairi was younger, smaller, faster.

And more desperate.

She ran down Major Street, her breath setting fire to her lungs, her legs protesting, her feet pounding the pavement. What was happening to the town? Why hadn't it affected her? Or the sheriff? What about her parents? What about —

Oh, no!

Her thoughts flew away like frightened sparrows as she spied a throng of people advancing up Major Street, headed right toward her. There was no mistaking their loose-limbed, chaotic gaits — these were more strange zombies, now formed into a posse. They shoved and pushed one another out of the way, but did not seem to actually hurt one another, instead moving with terrifying intensity toward her.

Mairi skidded to a halt and checked over her shoulder. Ms. Masterton bounded down Major Street. Mairi did not want to imagine what would happen if Ms. Masterton caught her.

She forced herself to remain calm, not to panic. She needed a place to hide. Somewhere where she would be safe until Mighty Mike could rescue her.

But what if Mighty Mike has become one of them by now?

The thought was too horrible, the question too heart-breaking — Mairi forced it right out of her head, ejecting it like a weak and fragile baby tooth.

Instead, she gathered her wits about her and looked right, then left. A furniture store — BOURING FURNITURE — FOR YOUR EXCITING LIFESTYLE! — on one side, a bank on the other. The furniture store was more inviting, probably because it had a big window in front. A nice, big breakable window.

Mairi darted to that side of the street and found a chunk of pavement that still hadn't been picked up since Ultitron's attack. The streets of Bouring were littered with the stuff, even weeks later. She hurled the pavement at the window.

And it bounced off.

Oh, come on!

The crowd of zombies (Were they actually zombies? She didn't know, but it was easier to think of them that way.) had spotted her now and rushed toward her. Ms. Masterton howled and picked up her pace. Maybe, Mairi thought, they would collide in the middle of the street and finish each other off.

Yeah, right. Because that's how her luck was turning out today.

She picked up the chunk of pavement again, this time holding it over her head with both hands, and threw it as hard as she could at the window. The glass shivered and a long crack appeared, spiderwebbing out in all directions to form a haphazard pattern of fissures.

Even though her arms were tired, Mairi once again picked up the pavement chunk. She was too tired to throw it again, so this time she rammed it straight at the heart of the map of fissures in the glass. The glass obligingly shattered — at last! — and Mairi cried out in triumph, then gasped in pain. Her arm had caught on a jagged shard of glass, ripping her coat sleeve from the wrist to the elbow . . . and gashing her arm. Blood seeped out and stained the window.

She bit her lip hard against the pain and forced herself not to look at the blood again. The zombies were closer, almost on top of her, and Ms. Masterton was only steps away. And the opening in the window was too small to crawl through.

In desperation, Mairi tossed the piece of pavement as far across Major Street as she could, shouting, "Go fetch!" Despite herself, she laughed at the stupidity of it.

But it worked. The zombies seemed suddenly captivated by the movement of the pavement. They all — including Ms. Masterton — altered their course and made for the spot where the chunk had landed.

Mairi didn't question her good fortune; she stripped off her coat and used it to protect her hands as she broke off larger pieces of window glass, then carefully slipped into Bouring Furniture.

The lights were off, but there was enough light coming from the streetlamps outside that she could make out the showroom. A check over her shoulder revealed that the zombies had already become bored with the chunk of pavement and were looking around. She stood completely still for a moment, then realized that she was standing right in the window — a sitting duck. She had to find a hiding place. Now.

As soon as she moved, the zombies — Ms. Masterton had joined the crowd — made a group sound that seemed to be a cousin to "Aha!" and converged on Bouring Furniture.

Mairi ducked behind a sofa and looked around. To her surprise, she spied a flight of stairs behind the counter and cash register. Of course. It was a two-story building, after all.

She darted from cover, running to the stairs. Behind her, she heard the window crack and groan as the zombies pounded a larger opening.

Up the stairs, she hit a landing, made a half turn, and ran up a second flight. She was in some sort of office-type area, dusty and messy, with some big chairs covered in plastic against a wall. It looked like it was used for spare storage, too.

An idea occurred to her. She got behind one of the big chairs and pushed with all her might. Her bloody, gashed arm shrieked in pain, but she forced herself to ignore it. A slashed-up arm was way better than whatever fate those zombies had in store for her.

Finally, she got the big chair moving, shoving it along the floor until it hit the edge of the top stair . . .

. . . and toppled down the stairs onto the landing, just in time to crash into Miss Hall, her history teacher. She made no sound, just fell backward and collided with the wall.

Adrenaline pumping with both triumph and terror, Mairi shoved the other big chair down the stairs, too. It joined its twin. Zombies came up onto the landing and had to maneuver around both of them.

It wasn't enough.

She ran to the desk; the wheeled desk chair went easily, knocking down a couple of zombies, entangling a couple more.

Now the desk.

It turned out to be easy, too, thank goodness. Someone had put those plastic furniture movers under each of its feet, and the whole thing glided across the floor with little effort. Which was just as well — Mairi's right hand had gone slick with her own blood and she was having trouble keeping a grip on the desk.

But she managed to struggle it across the room and push it down the stairs. It bounced and crashed down the steps, tilting at a crazy angle, jamming in the stairway.

Her little blockade would only hold for so long, but at least she had a minute to catch her breath. She looked around the office/storage area. There was a filing cabinet and two bookcases, but they looked too heavy to move. Still, she would have to figure out a way — the zombies would work around the desk and chairs eventually. But those bookcases would really jam them up. . . .

Just then, she spied something through the office's lone window: a ladder.

She raced to the window. It was dirty and dusty, but she could make out a wrought-iron balcony and ladder. A fire escape!

With the sounds of zombies pressing against the furniture filling her ears, she heaved open the window and hauled herself through.

The street below was filling with zombies, still pouring into the store. She couldn't go down . . . but as long as she didn't hit the lever to release the ladder, they couldn't come up, either. So that was good.

There was a second ladder, though, bolted to the wall, that went up to the roof. Mairi always hated it in movies and TV shows when people ran away to the roof. What could you do on the roof? What was so great and safe about the roof?

Well, right about now, what was so great and safe about the roof was that there were no zombies there. If she could get up there and figure out a way to block the ladder . . . or even take it down . . .

She'd be safe until Mighty Mike could come.

If he came.

What if this . . . *plague* affected him, too? As best Mairi could tell, there wasn't anything in the world that could really, truly hurt Mighty Mike. The dirt monster and Ultitron had stymied him and stunned him, but he'd recovered quickly. This, though, this was like a disease. Or radiation. Or something else. Something invisible.

Whatever was affecting the people of Bouring, it was something that Mike couldn't punch or fly around. And maybe that meant it could hurt him.

The thought of a zombie Mighty Mike . . .

Just then, a sound from behind snapped her attention back to the present. The zombies were shoving at the furniture blocking the stairs.

Mairi scrambled up the ladder to the roof. It was colder up here and she shoved her hands into her pockets, then scanned for something — anything — that could help her: a ladder to another part of the building, a door, something she could use to signal for help.

Nothing. The roof was just flat, with a two-foot brick parapet running around it. The hulk of an air-conditioning unit squatted in one corner, but she didn't think that would be much help. She was alone. She was trapped.

From below, she could hear the zombies in the stairwell.

Mairi looked up: Mighty Mike was flying overhead!

"Help!" she shouted, waving her arms. "Help!"

And then she realized that the flying figure didn't have a cape. Or a costume. It looked like someone in jeans and a T-shirt, carrying . . . Was that a *motorbike*?

If it wasn't Mighty Mike, then the only other person who could fly was . . .

Mairi swallowed hard. The sounds of furniture moving and breaking from below increased. What did she have to lose? Maybe the Blue Freak would have pity on her. It was better than being attacked by zombies.

"Help!" she screamed again, jumping and waving her arms as if her life depended on it. And maybe it did.

"HELP!!!"

CHAPTER
TEN

Kyle zipped over the town, his earbuds firmly in place. Erasmus was feeding him a never-ending stream of information; he couldn't hear anything but the AI's voice in his ears, and he had the wind blowing at him. He was flying high enough that no one could make out his face, so he'd left the Mad Mask's mask back at home. Besides, that thing was dark and smelly and it made his voice all weird and echo-y. How on earth had the Mad Mask been able to wear it all that time?

"Okay, all the calibrations make sense," Kyle told Erasmus. They had adjusted the chronovessel's settings back home. Once they arrived at the proper location, they would make the final tweaks, and then that would be that.

"You have to make sure that the antimatter production disks don't generate too many positrons or —"

"I know," Kyle said. "I know." He was messing with serious forces of nature in the chronovessel. Dark energy. Antimatter. Zero-point energy. Concentrated neutrino plasma. All of it running through his dad's old motor-bike. Yeesh.

He looked down as he flew overhead and saw a crowd of people clustered in Major Street, milling about. "That's weird," he mumbled, almost to himself, but of course Erasmus heard everything. "They seem to cluster around things that move. Whenever the wind makes one of the traffic signals move, they lunge at it."

"Well, maybe they have movement-based vision, like frogs?"

Kyle paused for a moment, hovering over the town. "I don't think so. Something else seems to be at work here."

"Could it —"

"Can you read back a transcript of the police band? Start with the first sign of something wrong and go until it went dead."

"I can do better than that."

Kyle expected a dry recitation in Erasmus's slightly robotic voice, but instead the AI played back a recording in perfect digital sound. At first there was just mild panic:

"Received word 2213 at time capsule burial. Sheriff on scene."

"Reporting in, uh, Deputy Travers. On scene at the — What the heck is —"

But then things got more and more panicked. . . .

"They're moving too fast! I can't even —"

"— did they come from? Who the —"

At one point: the sound of flesh on flesh. Knuckles against jaw. Someone being hit. Hard.

And then someone else.

A babble of voices. Panic, mounting. And then something Kyle had never heard before, something he never imagined: the sound of an adult, a grown-up, screaming in absolute terror.

Kyle swallowed, hard. Eventually, the recording went to dead static. Erasmus let the static play for long seconds before terminating the sound.

"This is bad," Kyle said.

"You should do something."

Kyle hesitated, then shook his head. "No. Not now. I can fix everything in the past. Whatever happened, it happened when they dug up the time capsule. I can intercept it in the past."

"It doesn't work that way!" Erasmus protested. "We've talked about this! You can observe the past, but you can't change it."

"I disagree." Kyle flew away, to the football field behind Bouring Middle School. That was where the plasma storm had touched down, where he had gained his superpowers, where Mighty Mike had landed on Earth. This was where they would be able to rewatch recent history . . . and record it.

"Time is like a river," Kyle said as he landed near the spot where the plasma storm had intersected the ground. It was easy to locate — the dirt was still disturbed from where the ASE had risen up and nearly killed Mairi. "You can dam up a river, redirect it, and it's still a river."

"Time is *not* like a river," Erasmus said. "Time is a function of particle physics and superstrings. If you try to change anything, at best you'll create a parallel timeline. This is our universe."

He displayed a line on his screen:

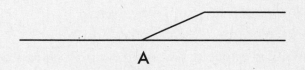

"If you make a change in the past — let's say at Point A — you'll cause the universe to split at that point."

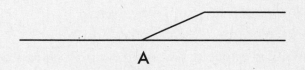

"And then you'll end up with *two* universes, one with the change you made and one without it."

"Fine. Then I'll live in the one where I made the change."

"It doesn't work that way! There's *already* a Kyle in that universe, only *he* never traveled in time because he didn't need to. Because you made it so that he had no reason to."

Kyle set the motorbike on the ground and did a last-minute check of its systems. "You worry too much, Erasmus. This is all going to work out," he promised.

"Going back to record Mighty Mike's arrival is one thing. That's just observing something. No impact other than some photons and neutrinos out of place. But trying to stop the time capsule disaster, too — that's too much. You'll go from observing the timestream to interfering with it and who knows *what* —"

"Look, we're going to come back to the present *one second* after we left. So if it turns out I can't fix things in the past, we'll be back in no time at all and I can save the town then. Okay?"

Erasmus seemed to think that over. "All right. But you should know that I think you forgot to lock the basement door when we left the house."

Kyle rolled his eyes. Erasmus always had to drive the knife in just a little bit. "You're right. I did. Mea culpa. You are so much smarter than me, Erasmus." Kyle served it up with a thick, heaping helping of sarcasm.

Erasmus ignored the sarcasm. "You should set up the chronovessel over in the cornfield."

That was true. The motorbike no longer actually moved or ran — it was just a shell for the time travel machinery — which is why Kyle had flown here to the spot he wanted to record. But if he time traveled right here, he would pop into the past in front of his past self and Mighty Mike. Not a good idea.

So he hauled his equipment into the cornfield near the football field. The corn was harvested or dead now, but there were still enough stalks to provide some cover.

And besides, they weren't going back to that night. Not right away.

Kyle hadn't told Erasmus, but he had set the chrono-vessel to make a little side trip first.

First, they would go back just a few weeks. Right before the Mad Mask kidnapped Mairi. Kyle would go to prevent that, then continue on to the night of the plasma storm. He would rescue Mairi, change his own past, and show Erasmus who knew more about time travel physics.

Then he would record Mighty Mike's arrival on Earth and show it to the world, proving that Mighty Mike was an alien and a threat.

It wasn't just a win-win scenario. It was win-win-win-win-win!

It took a few more minutes to finish calibrating the chro-novessel. The last job was to mount the video camera on the front of the motorbike. It was old and still used digi-tal tapes a little smaller than a deck of cards. Kyle soldered it into place, made sure the battery was charged and there was a tape in it.

He was ready.

"We're going to travel through time," he said, his voice filled with awe. "I can't believe it."

"That's been the plan all along," Eramus said sarcastically. "You've been working on the chronovessel since you built *me*."

"I know. It took some time."

"No pun intended?"

"Right. It just seems . . . *real* now. We're really going to do it."

"Give me access to the systems," Erasmus said. "I'll monitor the trip."

Kyle straddled the motorbike; he felt like an action-movie hero. He pretended the bike could still rev and vroom.

Set between the handlebars, just below the camcorder, was a smallish screen — Kyle had taken it from his old Nintendo 3DS. Now it displayed the chronovessel's onboard computer. He activated the Wi-Fi chip he'd installed in the chronovessel, and now Erasmus was tied into the systems.

"All systems are go," Erasmus announced. "Hey, wait a second! You have the destination set for —"

Before Erasmus could say anything else, Kyle thumbed the activation button.

A pattern of shapes and colors exploded before Kyle's eyes, then exploded again. And again. And again. Just when his eyes and his brain caught up to the dizzying, disorienting bursts — like fireworks that erupted into more fireworks and from there into even more fireworks — it would start all over again, a rapid-fire series of lights and glowing, sparkling pinwheels that seemed unending. He thought he would be trapped like this forever, unable to see anything but the constant and ever-shifting array of resplendent chromatics.

elyK dehctaw eht dlrow dlof dna dlofnu dnuora mih. ytilaeR emaceb imagiro. siH dnim detsiwt dna dekrej dna dellup ekil tlas-retaw yffat.

gnihtoN saw laer.

gnihtyrevE saw laer.

sihT si tahw doG sees, elyK thguoht. *sihT si tahw ti skool ekil.*

dnA neht —

And then —

Sparks flew into Kyle's eyes. Smoke erupted from the front of the chronovessel, near the neutrino collector. Kyle shouted for Erasmus, but his words didn't come out. There was no time for them; he was moving faster than sound, faster than words. Faster than light itself.

Sound suddenly collided with him again as the universe hiccuped and spat him out. The smoke exploded up and out in a mighty, gushing cloud, blinding him, choking him. He waved furiously, trying to blow it away, but only succeeded in unbalancing himself and falling off the chronovessel.

After a single, silent moment, the world rushed back in as the smoke cleared. Kyle lay on the ground, coughing.

Had it even worked? Had he traveled through time?

"You idiot!" Erasmus raged. "You lying, cheating . . . *scoundrel*!"

Kyle's whole body hurt for the first time in a long time. He felt like he'd just had the flu for a week . . . and then got beaten up by six big guys with crowbars and bad attitudes.

"Lay off, Erasmus," he managed to say, catching his breath on the ground. His mind was spinning and churning. Something was wrong with his thoughts.

"You lied to me! You didn't want me to triple-check the systems because you programmed a different destination time period! We were supposed to go all the way back to Mighty Mike's arrival, but you programmed it for just a few weeks. You wanted to rescue Mairi from the Mad Mask!"

Kyle shook his head. "Of course I did. I *told* you I did. But we have a bigger problem."

"There *is* no bigger problem."

Kyle tried to count from one to a googol using only prime numbers.

He couldn't.

"Erasmus . . . something's wrong with my head."

"I'll say! You're not thinking clearly and you haven't been thinking clearly since —"

"No, seriously. There's something wrong. I can think all right, but a lot of my superintelligence — the memorized Wikipedia, stuff like that, higher order stuff — it's all scrambled." Kyle swallowed hard, tamping down his panic. "My brain is messed up. It must be a side effect of the chronovessel. I'm still smart, but I can't make the same connections I used to make."

If he was expecting sympathy from Erasmus, the next moment dashed that hope:

"Well, I hope you're happy with yourself," Erasmus ranted. "I'm not picking up anything at all from the chronovessel's systems. They're completely burned out. All because you told me to prep it for one trip and then set it up for another. None of the systems were properly calibrated. You act like traveling through time is like riding your bike down to the corner store —"

Kyle pushed himself up on his elbows, noticing something, something that cut through his concern over his malfunctioning brain. "Hey, Erasmus."

"Don't 'Hey, Erasmus' me, you, you, you *rapscallion*! All that work! Ruined! You don't *deserve* to travel through time. You're irresponsible, reckless —"

"Hey, Erasmus, I think it worked."

"— inconsiderate, rude, and . . . What did you say?"

Kyle looked around. He couldn't be 100 percent sure, but he thought that the cornstalks around him looked different. More densely planted.

"The corn . . ." he said, and stood up. He was a little wobbly, but he stayed upright.

To his left, the chronovessel was a smoking ruin, its frame charred and blackened like Mom's last attempt to grill steak. But he barely noticed. There was noticeably more corn than there had been mere moments ago; tall stalks of it reached for the sky.

"It worked . . ." Kyle whispered.

"Are you —"

"It worked!" he howled at the top of his lungs, thrusting his fists in the air. "It worked! I did it! I did it! I traveled through time!" He danced a little jig right there in the cornfield.

"Kyle," Erasmus said. Kyle ignored him and fist-pumped repeatedly, alternating fists. He'd done it! The single most complicated problem in physics and he had *solved* it! He had done what everyone said was *impossible*! This was totally worth scrambling his brains a little bit.

"Kyle," Erasmus said again, this time with a note of panic in his voice.

"Don't start lecturing me," Kyle said threateningly. "I will crack you open and take out your battery. I'm celebrating! You should be psyched, too — you helped."

"Kyle, I'm *blind*."

Kyle chuckled. "No kidding, genius. You don't have eyes."

"That's not what I — I mean there's nothing out there."

"Out where?"

"Out *there*! All I'm picking up is your voice on my microphone. I'm scanning on Wi-Fi, on Bluetooth. On 3G and 4G cellular bands. But there's nothing."

Kyle stood perfectly still. It was so *quiet*, he realized.

"What does this mean?" he asked.

"The police band. The cell phone satellites. The local Wi-Fi hotspots. The *Internet*. None of them are there. It's all *gone*."

CHAPTER
ELEVEN

Mairi kept screaming "Help!" for a good two or three minutes after the Blue Freak (who hadn't looked all that blue from her vantage point on the roof) had vanished in the distance, headed in the direction of Bouring Middle School. She could only imagine what nefarious outrage he planned to perpetrate. Maybe another dirt monster or giant robot. Or maybe big, sparkling vampire lice. Or . . .

Or maybe turning people into zombies?

Mairi shivered and turned around. She could hear scrabbling and scratching on the fire escape. The zombies would be up on the roof soon. A quick scan of the roof told her what she'd already been sure of: There was nothing up here to use as a weapon. Nothing to throw down on them as they came up the ladder.

Running here to hide hadn't been such a great idea after all. She had been right to think movie people were idiots for going up the stairs.

She ran to the ladder, not to go down, but rather to see if she could somehow dislodge it from the roof and the wall. It would strand her up here, but at least she would be safe.

The ladder was bolted to the roof with two big steel bolts. All she needed was a wrench.

Which, of course, she didn't have.

Just then, a head of hair poked up over the parapet, almost right in her face. Mairi shrieked and recoiled as the Great Nemesis — the nickname seemed very appropriate all of a sudden — popped up from the ladder, still grinning that horrible red grin.

Mairi turned to run; her ankle twisted under her and a bright flare of pain flashed there for half a second, blotting out the rest of the world. She blinked through it and lurched away from the Great Nemesis, keenly aware that it didn't matter how fast or slow she ran — there was nowhere to go.

Running/limping as fast as she could, she made it to the other end of the roof before she collapsed, her ankle protesting. Behind her, she could hear feet crunching the gravel and tar paper laid out on the rooftop.

Fine. Fine, then.

If this was the end, she wouldn't go out like a wimp. She would be brave and strong.

She rolled onto her back, leaning against the parapet. A horde of zombies, led by the Great Nemesis, bore down on her.

Mairi wished she could have seen Sashimi one last

time. Thinking of her cat brought tears to her eyes, and she didn't bother to move to wipe them away. She hoped Sashimi was okay. She hoped someone would find the cat and take care of her.

Her parents, of course. Wherever they were. She hoped they knew she loved them, even when she didn't act like it.

She wished she could have seen Mighty Mike. Thanked him for being her friend. Told him that she forgave him for having to leave her with the sheriff.

And Kyle. She wished she could have seen him again. Despite everything.

As the zombies approached, she squeezed her eyes shut. So tight that patterns of light swirled there.

Any moment now.

Any

moment

now.

CHAPTER
TWELVE

"Settle down," Kyle said as soothingly as he could. He turned Erasmus over in his hands, looking for signs of damage — a dent or a ding that could indicate the AI had been jostled during time travel. "Don't panic. You probably got banged up a little and some wires came loose internally —"

"Nothing's loose!" Erasmus said. "I've run a complete diagnostic. Everything is functioning. There's just nothing *out there*."

"Don't be ridiculous. We only went back a few weeks. The Internet and the satellites were all there back then. I bet your diagnostic software is all messed up. I'll sneak into the house and fix you up, okay?"

"But —"

"Don't worry about it. It's all good. I promise." He slipped Erasmus into his pocket and pushed through the corn to the football field.

But there was no football field. Just more corn.

He must have gotten turned around somehow. After the smoke and being thrown from the chronovessel. He went in another direction.

More corn.

What the heck . . . ? He had set up the chronovessel about ten feet from the edge of the cornfield. He shouldn't have to walk more than that far in any direction and he'd eventually be back out in the open. But every which way he walked, he saw only corn. He was starting to hate corn. Stupid corn.

"This is ridiculous," he muttered. He flew up a few feet, just enough that he could see over the corn and get his bearings.

"Uh-oh," he said.

"Uh-oh?" Erasmus asked. "*What*-oh?"

"I, uh . . . I don't think we're in Bouring anymore."

There was no football field. There was no Bouring Middle School. Just acres and acres of corn in every direction.

"Oh, boy," Kyle said and told Erasmus.

"Where *are* we? *When* are we?"

"Wait!" Kyle shouted, relieved. "We *are* in Bouring! I see the lighthouse!"

The Bouring Lighthouse. Mairi's mom's pride and joy. The most useless tourist attraction in the world. Bouring was totally landlocked, but for some reason there was a lighthouse just outside town. Had been forever. No one knew why. No one knew much about it at all, actually. But there it was, standing against the horizon. Whew!

"But if we're in Bouring, then why can't I connect to anything?" Erasmus asked. Kyle realized that Erasmus felt the same way Kyle would feel if suddenly he'd been struck blind and unable to feel, smell, or taste.

"I'm going to figure this all out," he told Erasmus. "Don't you worry."

He settled back down to the ground and sat next to the burned-out husk of the chronovessel. Was some sort of static feedback emanating from the motorbike and its installed systems, blocking Erasmus's various radios? No, no — that didn't make sense. . . . If only his brain would work right. . . . He hoped this side effect was temporary.

Kyle stared up at the sky. Cassiopeia . . . The Big Dipper . . . A clear night. The stars like glittering diamonds on a field of deepest black. What was wrong up there that Erasmus couldn't connect to any of the cell phone satellites? Had the chronovessel done something to technology? The thought thrilled Kyle with fear. Had he accidentally wiped out technology? Like an electromagnetic pulse? Erasmus still worked, but Erasmus had been within the chronovoltaic field generated by the zero-point energy conversion unit.

He checked over the chronovessel. None of the

onboard systems would even boot up. The only thing working, he noted with a strange sort of satisfaction, was the video camera, which still switched on. Kyle positioned himself in front of the camera.

"This is Kyle Camden, humankind's first successful chrononaut, reporting from an undefined time in the past." A thought occurred to him. "Or, possibly, the future. Some sort of malfunction in the chronovessel has sent me to —"

"Are you actually recording yourself for posterity?" Erasmus yelled. "We've got a crisis here and you're making home movies!"

"Sorry." He clicked off the video camera. "It just helps me think sometimes. I'm wondering if we're in the future. Maybe someone bulldozed the school and planted corn here. Or maybe the chronovessel didn't actually send us through time at all. Maybe it channeled the chronometric energies and caused accelerated time revving in the immediate area, making the corn grow all over the place."

"I *told* you we shouldn't have done this," Erasmus sulked. "I knew no good would come of time travel."

"You said no such thing. You just didn't want me to try to change the past."

"Because that way lies folly! Breaking the fundamental rules and laws of the universe can only lead to —"

"Oh, pipe down about the fundamental rules and laws of the universe! I could go back in time and toss George Washington into orbit and change history and the universe wouldn't even notice. The laws of physics wouldn't even blink."

"Are you crazy?"

"I'm not going to *do* that. I'm just making a point. You have no sense of scope or size because you're all locked up in that little iPod. You don't understand how enormous the universe is."

"Current estimates place the size of the universe at —"

"That's not what I'm talking about. The universe is so vast, so enormous. . . . Do you really think the universe will notice such a small perturbation as the changing of someone's history in Bouring? The universe is like a skein of interwoven threads, a tapestry. But the tapestry is so gigantic that you can never see the whole thing at once. And no one would notice if a single red thread suddenly turned blue."

"Well, if you're lost in time, your parents will eventually notice. And that won't be good."

"True. Let's figure this out."

Keeping low to the tops of the cornstalks for camouflage, Kyle drifted in the direction of town, using the lighthouse as his guide. He sniggered; lighthouses were used to guide ships safely around hazards at sea, and

now he was using this one — which had never been anywhere *near* the sea — to guide himself.

He was so caught up in the irony of his situation that
he missed the big sign looming in front of him until the
last moment. He pulled up, gliding safely over it, and
then paused, hanging in the air. He had come to the edge
of the corn, where a one-lane road wound its way along
the perimeter of the field.

What was a *sign* doing here?

There was just barely enough starlight for him to
examine the sign.

"Oh," he said, his eyes wide with surprise.

"What? What is it?"

"Well, the good news is that the chronovessel worked."

"And the bad news?"

Kyle gulped. The sign said:

BUILDING BOURING'S FUTURE!
SITE OF THE NEW BOURING MIDDLE SCHOOL
CONSTRUCTION BEGINS NOVEMBER 1987.
CLASSES START FALL 1988!

"We're in 1987," he said.

Erasmus was silent for a moment. Then he said,
"You're kidding."

"Nope. I'm looking right at the sign for the middle
school. Which hasn't been built at this time. That's why

the cornfield is still so huge — they haven't cleared the land yet." He looked around and spied some big landscaping machinery on the other side of the road. "They're probably starting soon. We left in November of *our* year and we've arrived in November of 1987. Cool."

"Cool? Are you crazy? We're trapped in the past, years before you were even born. How are we going to get back?"

Kyle paced, gnawing at his bottom lip as he thought. His superbrain wasn't working right, but his plain old human brain was no slouch and it was working just fine. "Don't worry about it. Here's what I'm thinking: You have the schematics for the chronovessel on your hard drive. You can walk me through rebuilding it here and zip — back to the, you know, the present."

"Right. Because the *first* time we used it, we just *zipped* to exactly where we intended to go. We could end up overshooting the present and wind up in the year 3279."

"I wonder what it's like in 3279. Do you think they still talk about my triumph over Mighty Mike that far in the future?"

"Oh, Kyle . . ."

"They would have to. It's going to be a seminal moment in human history, after all. The moment when a human being stands up to the world's first alien invader and kicks his extraterrestrial —"

"Kyle! I just realized something!"

"Settle down. What is it?"

"My charger! My charging cable is still back in the future. The present. Whichever it is. If my battery runs down . . ."

"I can probably put together a charger for you. I'll have to find some stuff. In the meantime —"

"Maybe you should shut me down. To conserve my battery."

"Right." Kyle's fingertip hesitated for a moment at the power button. Was Erasmus maybe . . . *afraid*? Was he worried that Kyle would turn him off and then — for one reason or another — never be able to turn him back on?

Kyle figured *he* would be afraid. And that meant Erasmus probably was, too.

"I'm going to turn you back on," Kyle said. "I'll build a charging cable for you and turn you back on soon. I promise."

"I know," Erasmus said quietly. "I believe you."

Kyle pressed the power button.

He was alone.

Alone in the past.

CHAPTER
THIRTEEN

Kyle listened to the quiet. Bouring wasn't a hub of activity even in his own time, but the twentieth century version of the town was even more deadly dull than the twenty-first-century version. How was that even possible?

He patted his pocket, where Erasmus nestled safely. He wished he had his journal with him — when he couldn't talk to Erasmus, writing in his journal usually helped him organize his thoughts. And organizing thoughts was really, *really* important to Kyle. One of the side effects of being so super-incredibly brilliant was that it was easy to get distracted. Talking to Erasmus or writing helped him stay focused. Heck, if he couldn't have Erasmus or the journal, he would take Lefty — Lefty was great to talk to because he didn't talk back. But this was 1987. Lefty hadn't been born yet. Lefty's parents hadn't even been born yet.

In fact, given the breeding speed of lagomorph generations, Lefty's great-great-great-great-great-grandparents hadn't even been born yet.

That was sort of a depressing thought.

Even though his hometown was right in front of him, Kyle felt very, very alone.

He hid the chronovessel deep in the cornfield, wrapping it first in a plastic tarp he found near the landscaping equipment, then burying it in a shallow ditch. Then he walked along the one-lane road toward the center of town. He realized now that this little road would someday be widened into an extension of Major Street. As he walked, he tried to imagine the buildings and cars that would — more than twenty years from now — exist here. Holding two completely contradictory thoughts in his mind at once was taxing, even for him.

Overhead, the night sky was almost fully dark; he had arrived in 1987 at the same twilight time as he'd left his own time period, but after figuring things out and talking to Erasmus, night had fallen. Kyle ambled down the road, not sure exactly where he would go. He figured he would start at his house — get on the Internet there and find the best place in 1987 to steal some electronic components so that he could recharge Erasmus and repair the chronovessel. And then . . .

He sighed and watched his sigh dissipate in the air. Erasmus thought that he couldn't change the past. Or, if he could, that it wouldn't be useful. Kyle disagreed. There were several possibilities. Sure, Erasmus could be right (although Kyle would never admit it to the AI's "face"), but there was also the chance that Kyle could rescue Mairi in the past, could change the details of his adventure with the Mad Mask. Could make it so that she was never kidnapped, so that she never saw his mask ripped away, so that he never had to erase her memory. . . .

And in that case — if it never happened — then wasn't there also a chance that Kyle would forget, too? That Kyle would finally be able to let go of this guilt . . . ?

Just then, he noticed a figure — a man — standing in the shadows, near the Bouring Middle School sign. When the man realized he'd been seen, he started to sidle away. Suspicious, Kyle was about to step closer when a voice cried out from behind him:

"Hey! Hey!" the voice rang out. "Hey! Give it back!"

Kyle snapped around in time to see two older kids — teenagers — running straight at him, their faces lit with perverse glee. Behind them, making good time, but unable to catch up, was a kid around Kyle's age, lanky and lean, with long legs that ate up the ground.

"Stop!" the chasing kid yelled. "Stop them!"

"Bite me!" one of the runners shouted and put on a burst of speed, giggling as he ran past Kyle.

Kyle wasn't sure whether or not he should interfere. But something in the anguish in the younger kid's voice jostled his sympathy. The first runner was too far now, but the second one had just come even with Kyle, so Kyle stuck out his foot and tripped the kid.

"Ooof!" he complained, sprawling flat on his chest.

"Not *that* one!" the younger kid said. "Stop *him*!" He pointed to the other runner, who was now quite far away, though his laughter floated back to them.

It would be no trick at all for Kyle to grab the kid at superspeed, but he wasn't about to reveal his powers. "Sorry," he said instead.

Frustrated and clearly winded, the younger kid fumed and shook his fist at the retreating teenager. "I know you took it, Maxwell Monroe! I'm telling on you!"

On the ground, the other teen snorted laughter and pushed himself up. He said something, but Kyle didn't hear it — he was in shock. Had the kid said *Maxwell Monroe*? As in *Sheriff* Maxwell Monroe? Had Kyle just seen one of his future enemies as a kid?

"— not afraid of you *or* your parents," the teen said, scrambling to his feet. "So watch it." He rounded on Kyle and pointed an aggressive finger at him. "That goes for you, too, chump. You mess with the Monroe brothers, you get trouble, got it?"

Brothers? The sheriff had a brother?

"Later, ladies." Monroe #2 laughed and trotted off in the same direction as his brother.

"Oh, man," the kid Kyle's age said, and kicked the ground. "Oh, man! My parents are gonna *kill* me!"

"Why?" Kyle asked.

"They just *bought* me that Walkman! They *just* bought it, like, yesterday, and now Max stole it. Sheesh!"

Walkman . . . Walkman . . . Kyle tried to sift through the vast storehouses of information stockpiled in his significant brain, but he got lost in a welter of web pages and images and text. The information was all still there, apparently, but he couldn't fixate on any particular bit. Well, at least his mental hard drive hadn't been erased entirely.

"What's a Walkman?" he finally asked.

The kid stared at him. "Are you kidding me?"

"Let's say I'm not."

"It's a little thing. . . . You carry it around and put music in it and listen with headphones."

"Oh!" Erasmus was settled in Kyle's pocket. "Oh, like an iPod."

The kid raised an eyebrow. "A what?"

Wow. Go figure — only in a town as tiny and useless as Bouring would there actually be someone who didn't know what an iPod was!

"Hey, are you from around here?" the kid asked. "You don't look familiar."

"I'm, uh, new in town." Kyle stuck out his hand. "I'm . . . Theodore." It was the first alias that popped into his head; Kyle forced the image of the Mad Mask out of there.

"Danny." They shook. "Do people call you Theo?"

"Not really."

"Ted? Teddy?"

"Nope."

Danny's nose scrunched up as he thought. "What *do* they call you, then? Dore?"

Kyle gave up. Danny seemed determined to give him a nickname. "Sure. Call me Dore."

"Well, thanks for trying with the Monroe brothers, Dore."

"Sorry I got the wrong one," Kyle said.

Danny shrugged. "Story of my life. The Monroes are always playing pranks on people."

Kyle's jaw dropped. Sheriff Monroe? Playing *pranks*? No way! How many times had Monroe threatened to arrest Kyle, usually for some prank he couldn't connect to Kyle at all? Too many to count.

"You all right?" Danny asked.

"Oh. Yeah." Kyle shook his head to clear it. "Look, I'm, uh, new to town —"

"You already said that."

"Right. Anyway, is there somewhere where I can get online?" In his own time, there was an old Internet café on Major Street, but Kyle didn't know if it had been built in 1987 or not.

"On line?" Danny wrinkled his nose. "Do you mean *in* line?"

"No. I don't want to get into line. I want to . . ." A thought occurred to him. "Never mind. I'll just go to the library."

"Oh! That's where I'm going. That's where I was when the Monroes grabbed my Walkman."

Together, they walked into town. At the town line was the billboard welcoming anyone dumb enough to come here. In Kyle's time, it read YOU ARE ABOUT TO ENTER THE TOWN OF BOURING! IT'S NOT BORING! which was both a pun and a lie at the same time. But in 1987, the sign said WELCOME TO BOURING: THE TOWN FOR "U."

Ugh.

Kyle half listened as Danny chattered on and on (mostly about how depressed he was about losing the Walkman) and checked out the town. It was like seeing a photograph with some spots worn away. Certain buildings and roads were nearly identical to Kyle's own time, but there were also missing buildings, missing floors of buildings. . . . Roads that were too narrow or went only one way instead of both . . . And the town itself was smaller, more constrained — where housing developments and mini-malls had once been, Kyle could see only endless fields.

And there was a column of blackish smoke that rose on the horizon, blacker than the black night sky.

The coal mine. It was still active in 1987.

Kyle felt like he was in the Wild West. If a stagecoach

had thundered by, chased by a posse of deputies firing six-shooters, he wouldn't have given it a second thought.

"Here we are," Danny said, opening a door and gesturing.

The library in Kyle's time was a big, modern, well-lit building at the end of Gordon Road. The 1987 version was a tiny storefront on Major Street. As Danny held open the door, Kyle thought it must be a joke, but a small sign read BOURING PUBLIC LIBRARY — EST'D 1955.

As soon as they went inside, Danny dropped his voice to a low whisper. "I'm gonna get my book bag," he said, and went off toward the back of the building.

Kyle just stood in the entrance for a moment, taking it all in. *This* was a library? In Kyle's time, the library was open and airy. Modern. All bright furniture and chrome accents. There were skylights for natural lighting. A coffee bar. But this place . . . It was small and cramped with old, rickety bookshelves and murky lighting that yellowed the dusty air. A musty smell hung over everything. An old woman stood behind a counter off to one side, but other than that, the place was empty.

"Hey!" Kyle called out to Danny. "Where —"

"Young man!" the woman called sharply. When Kyle looked at her, she pressed her lips together tightly and laid a finger along them.

Was she *kidding* him?

Danny had vanished into the darkness of the stacks, so Kyle instead approached the old woman, who he assumed was the librarian. In his own time, the librarian was a young, pretty woman named Barbara.

"Can you help me?" he started, and she glared again. *Still* too loud? Really?

He lowered his voice to a bare whisper. Feeling like an idiot, he said, "Can you help me?"

"Of course," she whispered back. "That's what I'm here for."

"Where are your computers?"

The librarian glowered at him with a pure outrage Kyle had rarely seen in his life. (Well . . . maybe the time he made all of the clocks at school run backward.) "Computers?" she asked, as if he'd just inquired as to where they kept the dead puppies. "Computers? Young man, this is a *library*. We have *books* here. If you want to play games, I suggest you do so at home."

Oh, so she was one of *those* adults! "But I need to look something up —"

"Of course," she interrupted, and pointed off to a wall of what looked like tiny pull-out cabinets, each the size of an index card. "That's what the card catalog is for."

Kyle didn't know what a *card catalog* was or what it was good for, and he didn't really care. He just needed to track down some electronics and get out of 1987 as soon as possible.

"Look, just tell me where I can get on the Internet," he said.

The librarian blinked rapidly and cocked her head, her lips set in a grim, prissy little line. And then she said:

"What on *earth* is an 'Internet'?"

CHAPTER
FOURTEEN

Mairi squeezed her eyes shut so tight that they hurt, so tight that the skin around them hurt. But she didn't want to see the zombies as they did whatever it was zombies did to their prey. She figured it was going to hurt plenty; she didn't need to see it, too.

After a few moments, the pain started moving back toward her ears. It felt like two tiny but strong men were squatting behind her ears, pulling all the skin on her face backward.

A few moments later, she thought, *This is getting ridiculous!* The zombies had been practically on top of her before. What was taking them so long?

She tried counting to distract herself, but by the time she reached one hundred, she was more annoyed than distracted. What were they waiting for?

Finally, she let one eye open just a sliver.

A zombie stood directly in front of her. Mairi couldn't be sure, but she thought it might be Mrs. Clark, the owner of Clark's Bakery. She always threw in a couple of extra cupcakes when Mairi's mom bought big boxes of them for one of her lighthouse fundraisers.

Mairi opened her eyes. Yes, it was Mrs. Clark.

Standing right in front of her.

Staring right at her.

Mairi couldn't move.

After an eternity of that torture, Mrs. Clark shuffled to one side and walked away.

Mairi didn't realize she'd been holding her breath. She let it leak out slowly.

She counted fifteen zombies on the roof, all of them shuffling around listlessly, as though someone had neglected to tell them what to do once they got up here. Occasionally one of them would wander close to Mairi or look in her direction, but it was as though she was invisible to them.

Were they just not interested in her at all? Was she immune to them somehow?

No, that couldn't be it. They had chased her in the street, chased her into the store, up the stairs, onto the roof. And then nothing.

Why?

More important, was it safe to move? To make a dash for the ladder?

She thought not.

But how long could she stay here, on the roof? With the coming night, it was getting cold up here. Was she going to have to choose between freezing to death and, and . . . whatever it was the zombies did?

She thought again of Sheriff Monroe, of the way he had just collapsed. Was he even alive? What had the Great Nemesis done to him?

"Mairi!" a familiar voice shouted.

Mairi couldn't help herself — at the sound of Mighty Mike's voice, she sat upright and turned around. The zombies — of course! — chose that moment to notice her again. They all made a sort of *Ahhh!* sound at the same time and began moving toward her; she tried to stand, collapsing against the parapet as her twisted ankle barked with pain.

"Mairi!" Mike yelled. "Jump!"

She didn't know where he was. Couldn't see him. But the zombies were almost on top of her now, so Mairi didn't think, didn't cry out, didn't pause. Instead, she pushed off with her good leg, hauled herself over the parapet with straining shoulders, and dropped over the edge into thin air.

CHAPTER
FIFTEEN

Kyle sat on the steps outside the library, his chin in his hands.

No Internet? Really? No *Internet*?

This wasn't the 1980s — it was the Dark Ages! Bouring had always been a backward sort of town, dull and out of step with the exciting world beyond its borders, but this was ridiculous. For no one to have heard of the Internet?

Or maybe . . . maybe it wasn't the whole town in 1987. Maybe it was just that crabby old librarian, the one obsessed with everything being quiet. Book dust had saturated her brain and made her useless. As useless as her superquiet, dark, cramped little place stocked with just books. No computers. No DVDs. Certainly no coffee bar. And Kyle could use a nice, steaming cup of hot chocolate right about now.

What was he supposed to do? He needed the Internet in order to track down a place where he could — ahem! — "borrow" the materials needed to fix the chronovessel.

And then he would skedaddle from this insane time period and never, ever come back.

He glanced up and down the street, hoping for a nice, juicy electronics store. Or an Internet café. But all the stores were closed, the lights out. All Kyle saw was a shadowy figure loitering at the intersection of Major Street and Moldoff Drive. Was it the same guy he'd seen before, near the Bouring Middle School sign? The lamppost there was burned out, so he couldn't be sure, but —

The library door opened just then and Danny came out, a weathered book bag slung over one shoulder. "Are you still here?" he asked Kyle.

As if I have a choice, Kyle thought sourly. "Yeah."

"Do you want to come home for dinner?"

Until Danny said *dinner*, Kyle hadn't even thought about food. But now he realized how hungry he was — practically starving, ravenous. But just walking into some stranger's house? "Um . . ."

"Please, please, come home," Danny begged, to Kyle's surprise. "If you come home with me, my parents might be distracted and not ask where my Walkman is. And even if they notice it's gone, they won't yell too much if we have company. Come on. Please?"

Kyle checked down the road for the mystery man, but he was long gone. His rumbling stomach made the decision for him, and soon he and Danny were walking along Major Street. Kyle recognized some of the buildings and landmarks, but others were either missing or just plain wrong. It felt like some weird cousin of déjà vu — he kept thinking he knew what building or street would be next, but he was only right some of the time.

"So will your parents really not notice the missing, uh" — *What was it called? Oh, yeah* — "Walkman if you bring me home?"

"I think so. My parents are pretty stupid," Danny confided.

Kyle grinned for the first time since arriving in this ridiculous time period. "I know what that's like."

They turned down Kimota Road, which looked pretty similar to the Kimota Road of Kyle's time. The neighborhood had fewer houses than he was used to, but the big old colonial on the corner of Kimota and Batson looked the same. Except its shingles were clean and the paint wasn't peeling and the yard wasn't overgrown with weeds.

Danny led him to a house on Batson and marched inside, calling out, "I'm home!" and tossing his book bag in the corner of the foyer. Kyle looked around. It was a typical Bouring house, which meant it was a typical, boring house. Back in the Stone Age, someone had built a thousand dumb little houses just like this one in Bouring, all of them the same, and they hadn't changed at all between 1987 and Kyle's time, apparently.

"I brought a friend home for dinner!" Danny shouted

toward what Kyle presumed was the kitchen. A woman's voice answered that this was fine and that they should both wash up, so Kyle followed Danny down a short hall to a bathroom, but before he went in, he noticed something and chuckled.

"What's so funny?" Danny asked.

The house was already decorated for the holidays, right down to a small decorative table that held a little porcelain statue of a girl throwing a snowball. Kyle pointed at the statue. "My grandparents have that exact same statue, is all. Except theirs is really old and has a chip in the base."

Danny frowned. "How can they have an old one? This one is new. We had to send away for it because it's only for this year's club members."

"No, no," Kyle said, "my grandparents got one awhile ago. It's sort of worn. . . ." He trailed off.

Danny handed the statue to Kyle. "See? Look."

Sure enough, stenciled into the bottom was MAIL-ORDER EXCLUSIVE, 1987. GIRL PITCHING SNOWBALL.

"But . . ." Kyle looked around. Wait. Wait a second. He knew this house. It was familiar. It was . . .

Oh, no!

"Danny, is your last name —"

Just then, Danny's mom yelled from the kitchen: "I don't hear water running! Wash those hands, Daniel Camden!"

Daniel . . . *Camden?*

He was so shocked that, before he could catch himself, Kyle dropped the statue. Without even looking, he knew exactly how much damage it would take — a small chip in the base. He had seen that same chip, run his fingers over it, many times as a child.

At his grandparents' house.

His grandparents' house!

"I'm sorry," he said. "I didn't mean to drop —"

Just then, Danny's mom — Kyle's grandmother — came around the corner. It was unreal — Kyle had seen pictures of his grandmother when she was younger, but here she was for real. Her hair was reddish-brown not gray, and there was a lot of it. "Did I hear something — Oh. You must be Danny's friend."

"Yes. Yes, I'm Danny's" — son — "friend." Kyle extended his hand. "I'm sorry. I think I broke your statue."

Gramma — Kyle couldn't help thinking of her that way — gasped. "Oh, no. It was brand-new."

"I'm really sorry."

"It was an accident, Mom," Danny/Dad chimed in. "Maybe we can glue it."

"Maybe . . ." Gramma said, now turning the statue over in her hands. Kyle knew that they wouldn't be able to fix it; it was still broken in his own time. He felt bad that the first thing he'd done in 1987 was break something.

". . . my friend," Danny was saying. "His name's Dore."

"Is that what they call you?" Gramma asked, the statue forgotten. "Dore?"

Kyle supposed "they" did. "Yes. Short for Theodore."

"Isn't 'Theo' usually short for Theodore?"

"I'm a little different."

"Well," Gramma said, setting the statue back in its place, "let's go sit down to dinner. Dore, I hope you like lamb."

"Are you kidding?" Kyle's mouth watered at the memory of his grandmother's amazing grilled lamb shanks. "I love your lamb!"

She looked at him quizzically. Danny did, too. "Have you . . . eaten here before?" she asked.

Oops. "Uh, I just mean that —"

"I told Dore about it," Danny said quickly. "And he feels like he's already eaten it."

In the dining room, Kyle had another shock: At the head of the table sat his grandfather.

If seeing his grandmother young and with a head of crazy red hair had been surprising, seeing his grandfather was even more stunning. In his own time, Kyle's grandfather was a slender, weak, quiet man, victim of a stroke when Kyle was just a baby. He'd never fully recovered and at family gatherings he always sat alone, answering questions with a shrug, a grunt, or a single word.

But now . . . today . . . in 1987 . . .

Gramps seemed huge — thick across the chest and through the shoulders, with a thatch of almost-black hair that didn't so much grow on his head as appear to be attacking it. He laughed like a bull, his big, meaty hands smacking the table and making the dishes jump every time he heard something funny or said something that amused himself, which was often, judging by how Kyle's food jerked here and there on its plate. Kyle had been worried about slipping up again and saying something that would reveal he was from his family's future, but that wasn't a problem: Gramps did most of the talking.

The lamb shanks were terrific, better even than Kyle remembered them. The only problem was that there was spinach with them, and Kyle hated spinach. He was a little surprised to see his father avoiding the green stuff, too — in the present, Kyle's dad always ate spinach.

"You're not cleaning your plate," Gramps said at one point, gesturing to Danny's spinach, which by now looked like a pile of congealing moss. "Make that stuff disappear."

"I don't like spinach," Danny said. "Can't I have green beans instead?"

"Your mother made spinach; you eat spinach. End of story."

"But —"

"I said end of story," Gramps said.

Danny started shoveling the spinach in, practically swallowing it whole without chewing. It made Kyle want to gag. From the expression on his face, it made Danny want to gag, too. Kyle watched his father's eyes bug out, watering as he forced the spinach down. He polished it off with a huge gulp of water, as if the spinach threatened to come back up and the water would drown it.

As Danny had predicted, with Kyle present no one asked about the missing Walkman gadget. Gramps held forth at length about his day at the coal mine, where he supervised a team responsible for equipment maintenance. According to Gramps, they didn't have enough brains between them to fill a thimble, and he spent the meal recounting all of their various idiocies in exacting detail.

After dinner, Kyle helped Danny clear the table, stalling. He knew what would come soon, and he wanted to avoid it.

But it happened anyway.

"Danny?" Gramma said. "Isn't it time for Dore to go home? It's getting late."

Problem: Kyle didn't have any "home" to go to. His mother didn't even live in Bouring yet. His father was a kid. And the house where Kyle had grown up either belonged to someone else or didn't even exist.

Still, he had no choice but to leave, so he accepted a hug from his own grandmother and a firm handshake from one of Gramps's enormous paws.

Outside, he stood on the front stoop for a moment. Now what? Where could he go? What should he do?

He couldn't believe that they were just going to let him walk home by himself. In Kyle's time, a kid on the streets alone after dark was cause for half the parents in Bouring to form a special task force to escort the kid two blocks. But apparently in 1987, no one was worried about that.

Just then the front door opened and Danny poked his head out like a thief casing an empty apartment. "What are you still doing here?" he stage-whispered. "You've been standing out here for, like, five minutes."

"I have to tell you something," he said, making a split-second decision that he hoped he wouldn't regret. "I'm not . . . from around here."

"Well, yeah." Danny slipped outside and joined him on the stoop. "No kidding. I know everyone my age around here."

"I sort of . . . ran away from home."

"Really?" Danny's expression said *Cool!*

"Yeah. Really. So I don't have anywhere to sleep tonight —"

"Don't worry about it," Danny said. "I've got an idea. Meet me out back." With that, he went back into the house.

The backyard of the Camden house was like an alien landscape to Kyle. In the present — Kyle's present, the *real* present — it was a well-tended flower garden with two comfortable benches. But in 1987, it was just a flat, scrubby plot of land. The only thing Kyle recognized was the big oak tree, which was a little smaller than he remembered, but otherwise the same.

Right down to the tree house in its branches.

No way, Kyle thought. *There is no way in the world I'm sleeping in —*

"You can sleep in the tree house!" Danny said, having sneaked up on Kyle. He thrust a rolled-up sleeping bag at Kyle. "I do it all the time!"

Kyle sighed. He didn't really have much of a choice, did he?

"Just go up the ladder," Danny said. "You're not afraid of heights, are you?"

Suppressing a chuckle, Kyle wondered what his father's reaction would be if Kyle suddenly soared into the air under his own power. But instead, he just slung the sleeping bag over his shoulder and climbed the boards nailed at intervals into the tree trunk. In his own time, most of them were missing.

He had been inside the old tree house as a child, when visiting his grandparents' house. In the present, his father was too old and too fat to climb the tree, but when Kyle had begged to see the inside of the tree house, Dad had dutifully dragged a ladder over and held it steady as Kyle climbed. Kyle remembered the inside being smelly and moldy and disgusting — warped boards, exposed nails, rotted wood.

But like everything else lately, the tree house surprised him. In 1987, it was brand-new. The boards were straight and true, the nails pounded flush. And it didn't smell at all. There was a little battery-powered lamp in one corner, and when Kyle turned it on, the place filled with warm light. It was cozy.

"I'll leave my window open a crack," Danny called from below, "so if you need anything, just shout."

From the tree house's window, it was a straight shot to the window Kyle knew to be his father's.

"Thanks!" he called down.

"No problem!"

Kyle settled in, propping Erasmus up nearby. This would work out. It would be cold tonight, but cold no longer bothered Kyle — he had flown in the mesosphere with no ill effects. He would get a good night's sleep and then in the morning he would begin his quest to track down the components he needed to repair the chronovessel. He wouldn't be in 1987 for long, and as long as he returned to his own time shortly after vanishing, it would be like he hadn't left at all.

He turned off the lamp just as he caught something from the corner of his eye — the light in Danny's room had come on. Kyle leaned out his own window to say good night.

Sure enough, Danny had cracked the window. Kyle could hear everything in Danny's room.

"I'm not sure," he heard Danny say, and realized he'd tuned in to a conversation already in progress.

"Not *sure*?" Gramps's voice, sounding angry. "What do you *mean* you're not sure?"

"I just mean it's in here somewhere. I just —"

"If you kept this room a little cleaner, you wouldn't have trouble finding things."

"Well, it's in —"

"I want to see it." Even as far away as the tree house, Kyle could feel Gramps's anger, and he knew immediately what was going on: Gramps wanted to see the Walkman.

"I'll find it in the morning when I get up —"

"Find it? So it *is* lost!"

"No, no, it's not —"

"Then show it to me."

Kyle gnawed at his lower lip. He wished he'd tripped not-yet-Sheriff Maxwell instead of his stupid brother.

Danny couldn't stall anymore. Kyle strained to hear and managed to make out a couple of syllables, but nothing more.

Didn't matter. Gramps's reaction told the story: "You *did* lose it! I always know when you're lying! Never forget that. I always know."

"Well . . ."

"You lost it," Gramps said, his voice somehow soft and dangerous at the same time. "You lose everything. You know why? Because you're a *loser*, Daniel. You've always been a loser and you'll always *be* a loser."

"But, Dad —" Even from his position, Kyle could hear the trembling of Danny's voice, a prelude to tears.

"But nothing," Gramps snarled. "I don't know why I expect anything from you. Haven't amounted to anything so far. Why should anything change now?"

Danny started to say something, but Kyle couldn't make it out — his father's voice was clogged and watery. Gramps interrupted, snorting. "Don't you cry. *I* should be the one crying. I drove all the way to Centre City to buy that gizmo for you and you lost it after one day. Do you have any idea how expensive it was? You better learn some responsibility. You better learn how to shape up, or you'll be a loser your whole life."

Obeying his father's orders, Danny didn't cry. Until Gramps left the room, closing the door behind him. And then Kyle heard the sound of *his* father weeping gently and quietly.

The eighties suck, Kyle thought.

CHAPTER
SIXTEEN

In the morning, the eighties still sucked.

Kyle had hoped for at least a moment in the morning when he would wake up and — for just a second or two — forget that he was trapped in his own past and sleeping in his father's childhood tree house, but that didn't happen. From the instant he opened his eyes, he was miserably aware of where and when he was.

He was also miserably aware of the fact that his grandfather was sort of a jerk.

He picked up Erasmus, tempted to switch him on and get the AI's snarky opinion on things. But, no. He had to conserve battery power, at least until he could cobble together a new power cord.

Kyle's first priority had to be repairing the chronovessel and getting back to the present, but he couldn't help thinking that maybe he had another priority now, too: helping his father. . . .

Just then, his dad's childhood voice interrupted him, stage-whispering from below. "Psst! Hey! Dore! You still up there?"

Kyle looked down the ladder. "Yeah."

"I'm coming up. I have breakfast."

A moment later, Danny scrambled up the last rungs of the ladder and into the tree house, barely breathing hard. Kyle couldn't help thinking of his father in the present — the man huffed and puffed just rolling out of bed in the morning.

"Here." Danny shared out some Pop-Tarts and foil-packs of juice. At least *something* about the eighties was familiar!

They ate in silence, until Danny said, "So, uh, where are you running away to?"

"Somewhere . . ." Kyle paused. He didn't want to out-right lie. "Somewhere sort of like here. But bigger. And, uh, more modern." That was a pretty accurate description of Kyle's own version of Bouring, he realized.

"I want to go with you," Danny said with finality. "I want to get out of this town."

"You can't."

"Why not?"

Because if I took you to the present, then you would never meet Mom and I would never be born, which would be a total bummer of a time paradox. Kyle wasn't

100 percent sure if Erasmus had been right about time paradoxes, but he figured maybe it was best to be cautious at this point. "Because I need to travel alone," Kyle said in his toughest, cowboy-est voice.

"Come on, Dore. Take me with you. I hate it here. It's all mean people. Like the Monroe brothers," he added quickly. "Just because you *can* do something doesn't mean you *have* to do it. Just because you're bigger or stronger or smarter doesn't mean you have to treat other people badly."

"No." Kyle rolled up the sleeping bag. He couldn't stick around. The longer he did, the better the chances he would say something to his father that would cause time problems.

"I helped you out," Danny said, hurt. "I gave you a place to sleep, and I brought you breakfast. You owe me."

That much was true. And there was the cruddy way Gramps had spoken to Danny last night, which he couldn't forget, no matter how much he tried. Yeah, this was the past, this was history, but could Kyle really just leave his father in this situation?

"Okay, fine," Kyle relented. He would just have to be careful what he said. "I can't take you with me, but I'll pay you back."

"How?"

Kyle thought for a minute. "How about I get your Walkman back?"

Danny suddenly perked up, all thoughts of escaping Bouring forgotten. "You could do that?"

Maybe. "Definitely."

"Wow!"

"But I'm also going to need some more help from you."

"If you can get my Walkman back, I'll do anything you want!"

"I need to find a way to get on the Internet."

"What's an Internet?"

Kyle sighed. Not this again. Was the entire town of Bouring stuck in the Stone Age?

"Not 'an' Internet — *the* Internet. It's a . . . it's a big network of computers, all connected together."

Danny frowned. "Why would anyone connect a bunch of computers together?"

"Mostly for stupid things like Twitter and YouTube, but trust me — there are some good reasons. I need to get to a computer. At this point, any computer will do."

Danny thought for a moment. "They have a computer at school. I think they use it for attendance."

"That'll do."

"But it's Saturday. School's closed."

Shrugging, Kyle said, "Maybe we'll get lucky and someone left a door unlocked." *More likely, I'll have to kick a door in, but that's okay. It's for science.* "I get back your Walkman and you show me where the computer is."

Grinning, Danny stuck out his hand. "Deal."

After a moment, Kyle shook his father's hand. "Deal."

Kyle clambered down from the tree house after Danny gave the all clear. His parents were busy inside, not paying attention to the backyard and the time traveler living in the tree house.

"So," Kyle said, "tell me about the Monroes." He was still surprised that Sheriff Monroe was such a hellion in this era . . . and that he had a brother. Kyle had never heard the sheriff refer to a brother, and he'd spent an unfortunate amount of time with the sheriff over the years. (Monroe just didn't understand the Prankster Manifesto. Or Kyle. Or much of anything, really.)

"Max and Sammy Monroe. They're bullies. Always playing pranks and practical jokes."

Playing pranks and practical jokes didn't always make someone a bully, Kyle wanted to retort. After all, he was a master of such things, but he never did it to hurt people — just to educate them. To make them more aware of themselves:

THE PRANKSTER MANIFESTO
BY KYLE CAMDEN

1. PEOPLE ARE FOOLISH.
2. SERIOUS PEOPLE ARE DOUBLY FOOLISH. ESPECIALLY PEOPLE IN AUTHORITY: PARENTS, TEACHERS, ETC.
3. PRANKS SHOW PEOPLE HOW FOOLISH THEY ARE.
4. IT'S GOOD TO SHOW PEOPLE HOW FOOLISH THEY ARE BECAUSE THEN THEY STOP ACTING SO SERIOUS.
5. WHEN THEY STOP ACTING SO SERIOUS, THEY CAN UNDERSTAND THE TRUTH.
6. WHICH IS THAT THEY'RE FOOLISH.
7. KYLE CAMDEN IS ALLOWED TO BE SERIOUS BECAUSE HE'S NOT FOOLISH.

In any event, it sounded like Sheriff Monroe and his brother weren't adherents to the Prankster Manifesto. They just sounded like jerks. Which totally made sense, since the sheriff was still a jerk in Kyle's own time.

"And their father doesn't do anything to stop them, even though he's the sheriff," Danny went on. "He just says, 'Boys will be boys' or 'They don't mean anything by it.' Man, I hate that guy!" Danny clenched his fists.

The sheriff's father was the sheriff? That jibed; Kyle

could remember being hauled into Monroe's office one time. There had been a framed photograph of Sheriff Monroe with an old guy also decked out like a sheriff. That must have been Monroe and his dad.

What would turn a punk like Max Monroe into a cop? And maybe more important — how pathetic was it to do the exact same thing as your dad, in the exact same town? Kyle would die of embarrassment if, as an adult, he ended up still living in Bouring, doing the same job as his own father. Ugh.

"So, why did they steal your stuff?" Kyle asked. "What kind of prank is that?"

"I guess it isn't a prank; it's just them messing with me. They know no one will stand up to them because of their father, so they get away with everything."

"Where do they live?"

"Over on Anavis Street."

"Then we go to Anavis Street and we get back your Walkingman."

"It's just *Walkman*," Danny corrected him. "I don't think they would take it home. They're not that stupid — that would be bringing evidence into their own house and the sheriff might eventually catch on."

"Then where?"

"There's been rumors that they have a hideaway out near where the new school's being built. . . ."

Kyle thought. That made sense. The first time he'd

encountered the Monroe brothers, they'd been running in that direction.

"Okay, I think I know what to do," Kyle said, "but I'm gonna need to cover my face. Do you have a mask or anything?"

Danny tapped his foot and stared at the clouds for a moment. "Yeah! I have an old ski mask!" he said triumphantly, then ran off to get it.

While Danny was inside, Kyle risked turning on Erasmus for a moment.

"Kyle!" Erasmus sounded both relieved and worried at the same time. "Are we back in the . . . Oh. No. I guess not."

"We're still in 1987," Kyle told him. "And you're never going to believe this. . . ." He quickly filled Erasmus in on what had happened in the past day.

"Are you crazy?" Erasmus sounded like he'd blown a circuit. "You can't hang out with your own father! You could cause all kinds of time paradoxes and —"

"Chill out, Erasmus. Nothing bad is going to happen. I'm just going to help him get his Walkman back."

"You can't —"

"And in exchange," Kyle went on, "he's going to help us get on the Internet so we can find what we need to fix the chronovessel."

"Internet? Kyle, there *is* no Internet in 1987! Not really. It's more like —"

Kyle heard the door open and switched Erasmus off quickly, slipping him back into his pocket. But not before noticing the battery meter on Erasmus's screen.

It was close to the one-quarter mark. Kyle would have to —

"Here's a mask!" Danny shouted as he jogged over from the front door.

"Not so loud!" Kyle complained. He took the mask and tucked it into his back pocket. "All right, let's go find this hideout of theirs."

Kyle allowed Danny to lead the way to the school construction zone. By daylight, Bouring appeared even stranger to him — the Bouring Bank and Trust clock was the same as in his own time, but the front of the building was shingled, not clad in flagstone. The *Bouring Record* building was bigger, cleaner, more impressive than in Kyle's own time. The comic book store on North Wheeler Street wasn't there at all; instead there was a grubby little place called MARK'S MOD MUSIK MANIA! that advertised CASSETTES AND RECORDS. OUR INVENTORY IS OK! a sign announced. A smaller sign revealed NOW CARRYING COMPACT DISCS!

And from the west side of town, the constant and ever-present black belch of raw smoke from the coal mine, dirtying the sky.

Kyle thought of these things and he thought of Erasmus, his battery power slowly leeching away. Even when shut down, the battery would drain a little bit; that was just how it worked — a trickle-charge kept Erasmus's memory from flushing, kept his clock running. If Kyle couldn't cobble together a charging cable soon, Erasmus would be useless.

Worse than useless . . . What if losing all power like that somehow damaged Erasmus? Would Kyle ever be able to resurrect him?

"How much farther?" he asked Danny.

"Not far, Dore," Danny said. They stopped for a moment in front of the sign announcing the construction of the new school. Kyle couldn't help thinking of his chronovessel, buried not far away. He had to get back to the present.

"Let's hurry up," he told his father.

"It's just over this hill. . . ."

They crested a hill that — in Kyle's time — had been bulldozed flat and looked down on what would some day be a part of the Bouring Middle School parking lot. There was an indentation in the ground a ways off, as if a giant had kicked with the point of his boot.

Carson Cave! Of course! In his own time, the cave had been closed off. It was originally a smallish sort of hole in the landscape, but the Bouring Coal Mining Co.

had gone in there and enlarged it, looking for more coal. When they came up bust, they left it as is and — according to Kyle's dad — kids used to run off in there all the time. But then — a few years ago in Kyle's personal timeline — a kid hiding in there got hurt and couldn't get out. They found him a few days later, clinging to life, and the parents of Bouring went crazy. Since Bouring Mining had been out of business for years, there was no one to sue. Instead, the town parents held a bake sale to raise the funds to dynamite the cave mouth shut, and it had been that way for most of Kyle's memory.

But in 1987, it was a perfect hideaway for two teen punks.

At the entrance to the cave, Kyle pulled on the old ski mask. It smelled faintly of mothballs and there was a tear through which a shock of his black hair poked, but it covered his face and that was all that mattered. "You stay out here," Kyle told Danny. He figured he might need to use his powers at some point and he couldn't afford to have his father see that. "Keep an eye out in case anyone shows up."

"What do I do if someone *does* show up?"

Kyle had been hoping Danny wouldn't ask that. "Go get the sheriff."

"But the sheriff won't —"

"Just do it, okay?"

"All right," Danny said doubtfully. He took up a position near the mouth of Carson Cave as Kyle entered.

136

It was dark inside, but fortunately, with the sunlight from outside, Kyle could see it was a pretty straight shot for most of the way. As the light dimmed, he stretched out his arms and brushed the sides of the tunnel, following the passage's gentle slopes and turns.

Just when he despaired of ever seeing or finding anything, a slight glimmer of light ahead ramped up his hopes. He crept along quietly, closing in on the light, and positioned himself behind an outcropping.

There before him, in a wide, open space lit by a couple of camping lanterns, were the Monroe brothers.

From the looks of the space, the Monroes had been using this as a hideaway for a while. There were piles of candy wrappers, a couple of pizza boxes, and several empty bottles scattered around. There were three big cardboard boxes, and the Monroes themselves sat on what looked like old sofa cushions. Sammy wore an old-fashioned pair of headphones attached to a chunky black box on his belt.

Danny's Walkman!

"Toss me the Billy Joel cassette," Sammy said in the tone of someone used to being obeyed.

"It's my turn," Max said, sounding nothing at all like the sheriff Kyle knew. "You said we each get an hour at a time."

"Stop being such a girl," Sammy said. "I just want to listen to one song and then you can have it."

Max rummaged in one of the boxes and tossed something to Sammy, who opened the Walkman, took out the tape inside, and snapped the new one in.

"What if Camden goes to Dad?" Max asked. "He said if we get in trouble again we're going to military school this time."

"God, Maxie! You're such a baby. Don't worry about Dad." He adjusted the headphones and leaned back, eyes closed, tapping one foot in time to the music only he could hear.

"Don't call me *Maxie*. I hate that. And you —"

Sammy didn't even talk — he just held up a hand to silence his brother.

Kyle had seen enough. He made the sure his mask was on straight. He was going to zip over there and grab the Walkman before they could move. Then he'd be out of the cave at top speed. By the time the Monroes realized what had happened, Kyle and Danny would be halfway home.

But just before he stood up, he heard a sound — rocks sliding against each other. Leaning around the other side of the rock outcropping, Kyle saw stones and gravel tumbling down an incline on the other side of the cavern.

And then a pair of hiking boots came into view as a man carefully picked his way down the tricky incline.

There must be another way into Carson Cave!

The Monroes stood up as the man approached them. Kyle didn't recognize him — he was older, maybe in his forties, with salt-and-pepper hair and a broad, grim face. Thick through the chest and shoulders. A guy you didn't want to mess with.

Not that Kyle was afraid of him, of course.

"Hey, there," Sammy said, pulling the headphones down around his neck.

"Save it," the newcomer snapped. "Do you have it?"

Sammy snorted. "What do you think?"

"I think I paid you a lot of money for —"

"We have it," Max said quickly, and lifted up one of the cardboard boxes. Kyle couldn't see what was under it from his vantage point.

"Piece of cake," Sammy said. "They leave it in Dad's office with no one guarding it. We've been sneaking in there since we were kids."

"It's heavy," Max cautioned. "We had to roll it out on a skateboard."

"Thanks for your concern," the man said with absolutely no sincerity. He stooped down, but Sammy rushed over to him.

"Wait a minute, man! You still owe us the second half."

The man grinned. He reached into his pocket and handed over an envelope. "Go ahead and count it, kid. It's all there."

Sammy shoved the envelope at Max. "Count it, Maxie."

"Don't call me —"

"Count it!"

For a moment, Sam and the man stared at each other in near silence, the only sound the slight, hushed shuffle of bills. "It's all here," Max said after a long moment.

"Great." Sam stuck out a hand. "Pleasure doin' business with you, Mr. Lundergaard."

Lundergaard? Kyle's head spun. Lundergaard? As in Lundergaard Research, the company he and the Mad Mask had attacked just before Ultitron was activated? The top secret think tank that built superpowerful weapons and stuff for the military? *That* Lundergaard? Was it the same guy?

He sifted through the shredded remains of Wikipedia in his mind, picking up a few stray bits here and there. Lundergaard Research had been founded by Walter Lundergaard in the 1980s. It started as a small research firm but quickly catapulted to the top ranks of think tanks and laboratories in the country — the *world* — thanks to some amazing, unprecedented innovations by its founder. That was all Kyle had at the moment. But Erasmus still had Wikipedia memorized; he would know more, once Kyle switched him back on.

Was this man Walter Lundergaard? And what was he doing hanging out in Carson Cave with the Monroe brothers? And what was he buying from them —

Just then, Lundergaard leaned down, grunted, then stood up. He had something balanced on his shoulder.

It took a moment for Kyle to recognize it.

It was a time capsule.

CHAPTER
SEVENTEEN

Mairi's breath whooshed out of her as she plummeted to what would be a messy death, splattered all over the alley next door to the furniture store. She closed her eyes tight, praying that she actually *had* heard his voice, that she hadn't been imagining things, that it hadn't just been her terrified brain giving her ears something to cling to as she stared her own death in the face.

How long would it take to hit the ground? She'd already been falling for a couple of seconds now and if Mighty Mike was flying by, he should have caught her by —

THUMP!

Mairi's eyes flew open at the sudden impact. She recognized immediately the slim, strong arms around her and reflexively settled against Mighty Mike's chest so that he wouldn't drop her.

"Are you KO'd?"

"I'm okay," she told him, though she had been pretty close to being KO'd, too.

"We have to hurry," Mike said, a note of panic in his voice.

Mairi opened her eyes. Mike wasn't flying — he was only five or six feet above the ground, hovering there. Above, the zombies were clustered at the parapet, gazing down, moaning and groaning. Below, a new cluster of them formed.

"What's going on?" she asked. "What are they doing?"

"I don't know." He shifted her. "I can't carry you much longer, though."

What? Mike was superstrong. He had lifted Ultitron, and that robot had been ten stories tall! Carrying Mairi was nothing to him.

Before she could say anything, Mike took off . . . running. Instead of flying away or soaring higher, he actually ran on the air, running at a decent clip, but not nearly as fast as he usually flew.

"What are you doing? Fly away!" She peered over his shoulder and down. "They're following us. Some of them are actually keeping up!"

"Going as fast as I can." Mike huffed and puffed with exertion as he ran, shifting Mairi's weight to make it a little easier.

"What's wrong with you? What's going on?"

"I don't know," Mike said in a tone of voice that told her to please be quiet because he was having trouble talking while running. Mairi shut up and let him run, her eyes peeled for the zombies, who now — whew! — were starting to fall behind.

Mike put on a burst of speed and managed to put more distance between them and the zombies. But Mairi noticed that he was beginning to lose altitude, sinking closer to the ground.

Just then, something caught her attention out of the corner of her eye — a flashing light, a yellow burst that erupted from seemingly nowhere and then faded away. She craned her neck, but it was gone in an instant. . . .

And then it was back, this time lasting longer.

It was . . .

It faded again. Then two more quick bursts of light followed, from the place she knew so well.

"The lighthouse!" she cried, pointing. "Can you make it?"

Mike groaned but nodded, angling so that they headed toward the lighthouse, which was more than a mile away. More irregular flashes of light emanated from the top of the lighthouse. Some were long, some short, but they kept coming. Was someone up there? Someone signaling? And were they signaling so they could help . . . or that they *needed* help?

Either way, it didn't matter. The Lantern Room at the top of the lighthouse, Mairi knew, had a heavy trap-door and a good lock. Her mother had often admonished her against going up into the Lantern Room alone because the trapdoor had a tendency to swing shut and stick.

As best she could tell, Sheriff Monroe had been wrong: The *lighthouse* was the safest place in Bouring right now.

They gained the lighthouse and craned their necks to look up the endless expanse of white brick. The lighthouse had never seemed taller.

"I'm going to have to shift you," Mike said apologetically, and then — without waiting for approval — adjusted Mairi so that she was slung over his shoulder like a sack of potatoes. He took a deep breath and the next thing Mairi knew, they were running *up* the wall of the lighthouse!

To her, hung over Mike's shoulder, watching from behind, it was if someone had suddenly jerked the ground from her. She watched it fall away as Mike's breathing got heavier and heavier, his feet pounding on the wall of the lighthouse and sending jolts and jostles through her.

Just when she thought his strength was about to give out, Mike lunged forward, grabbing the railing that ringed the gallery that ran around the Lantern Room with one hand, steadying Mairi with the other. He heaved her unceremoniously over the railing, dumping her on the gallery floor, and then hung there by his fingertips.

"Mike!" Mairi grabbed at him, catching him by the wrist. She felt incredible strength there, incredible strength that was now flagging.

"I'm KO'd," he assured her, and then between the two of them, they managed to wrestle him next to her on the gallery.

The gallery encircled the lighthouse entirely, bordered on the outside by a railing and on the inside by glass panels that surrounded the Lantern Room. They lay panting on the floor for a while before it occurred to Mairi to make sure they could get inside. She found a glass panel that swung in and hustled Mighty Mike into the Lantern Room. It was small — the tip of a needle — and empty except for the giant lamp and lens.

There was no one there. The great big lantern flashed again, all on its own, as if desperate to guide some invisible ship only it could perceive. Mairi blinked in astonishment. She'd only ever seen the lantern lit during special celebrations, when her mother was at the controls. . . .

Exhausted and still nursing a twisted ankle, Mairi crawled over to the trapdoor, which was shut.

"Does it lock?" Mike asked from where he lay.

"Not on this side, at least. But it should hold. It sticks all the time." To demonstrate, she tugged at the ring that opened the trapdoor and the door swung up easily, revealing the Watch Room below.

Oops. Mom must have finally gotten around to fixing the trapdoor. Great job, Mom!

The Watch Room was empty, too. Mairi had half expected to see her mother down there, working the computer that ran the lantern. Once upon a time, the lantern would have been activated manually by a lighthouse keeper, but Mom had upgraded to the computer so that she could set the lantern to run automatically, if necessary. Had she set a program to run for the time capsule burial? Mairi didn't think so. Mom would have mentioned it. And the lantern wouldn't just be pulsing out random bursts of light — it would be some sort of specific show for the event.

Mike struggled to his feet. "They'll come right up through there. Eventually." He gently guided Mairi away from the trapdoor, then closed it solidly and stared at it. Just as Mairi wondered what he was doing, the black beams of Mighty Vision wobbled from his eyes. Usually, they were strong and powerful blasts of energy, but now they seemed more like limp noodles. Still, as they struck the seam between the trapdoor and the floor, the wood there sizzled and melded into a seal.

Once the trapdoor was totally secure, Mike staggered back, exhausted. "Now . . ." he gasped, ". . . we'll be safe."

"What's going on?" Mairi asked. "What's going on with *you*?"

He shrugged. "I don't know for surety. After I left you and the sheriff, I flew around, trying to see who I could help. I saw some of the bomzies and tried to collect them and take them where they couldn't hurt anyone, but . . ."

"But what? What happened?"

He spread his arms wide. "I don't know. My powers started . . . stopping. My strength. My speed. My flight."

Mairi shivered, and not just from the cold at the top of the lighthouse. She had been counting on Mighty Mike to save her — to save the town — the way he had done so many times before.

But now he was turning into just another kid.

CHAPTER
EIGHTEEN

A time capsule!

Bouring was crazy for time capsules. The town buried one every year around this time, so Kyle knew what they looked like. Time capsules came in all shapes and sizes, but the town of Bouring always used the same kind. And they were identical to the one Lundergaard had just hoisted onto his shoulder. As Kyle watched, the man carefully made his way back up the slight grade he'd come down, struggling a bit with the heavy weight of the time capsule, but soon enough disappearing into the darkness.

That's the 1987 time capsule, Kyle thought. *The one that disappeared. Now I know who took it. But why?*

What should he do about it? Kyle was tempted to fly through the room and go grab the time capsule from Lundergaard. But would that create one of the time paradoxes Erasmus was so worried about? Kyle was no longer certain. And hadn't —

"My turn!" Max said suddenly, grabbing for the Walkman.

"Go put your hair in curlers," Sammy said, dodging his brother's swipe. "I'm not done with it yet."

Right. Danny's Walkman. Kyle had to stay focused. He cleared his throat, stepped out from concealment, and planted his fists on his hips.

"Surrender the Walkman!" he commanded in his deepest, loudest voice. "Now!"

Sammy and Max turned to him in surprise. Then Sammy started giggling. "Is that *you*, Camden? Nice mask."

"Yeah," Max sneered in echo of his brother's tone, "nice mask."

"Last chance," Kyle threatened. "Give it over right now."

Sammy and Max stalked to him and loomed over him, glaring down. "Or what?"

"I'm not Daniel Camden," Kyle intoned. "And you are about to be very, very sorry."

"Oh, rea —"

Before Sammy could even finish the word, Kyle snatched the Walkman from his belt at superspeed, his hand a blur as it moved. Sammy yelped in surprise as the headphones jerked his head forward.

Kyle could have just sped away before they could react, but the opportunity to teach these guys a lesson was too ripe. And for the first time in his life, he had the upper hand on Sheriff Maxwell Monroe. It didn't matter that he wasn't even a sheriff yet — it just mattered that Kyle could finally be the one in power over him.

He clipped the Walkman onto his own belt, then grabbed the Monroes by their wrists . . . and took off!

The cavern was small, but even so, the ceiling was at least ten or twelve feet up, hung with stalactites. He shot up there with the Monroes in tow, then zipped back down to the floor, narrowly missing impaling them on stalgmites. Then he blasted up to the ceiling again. The brothers screamed in terror and struggled to break Kyle's iron grip. It was useless.

"Maybe now you'll learn a lesson about bullying," Kyle told them in a stern voice. "Maybe now you won't make a kid cry again!"

"Cr-cr-cry?" Max stammered as they hovered near a massive stalactite. "We never made anyone cry!"

"Yeah!" Sammy agreed, staring down at the floor in terror. "We never —"

"Shut up," Kyle told them. He drifted down to the floor and dropped them in a crumpled heap on their old sofa cushions. Of course. The Monroe boys hadn't made Danny cry. They'd stolen his new Walkman, but that hadn't made him cry.

Only *Gramps* had been able to do that.

Kyle shook his head to clear it. "Leave Danny Camden alone from now on," Kyle warned them. "In fact, leave *everyone* alone. Got it?"

He took their cowering for a yes.

So. Mission accomplished. But . . .

What was Lundergaard up to? And *was* he the same guy who founded the company? More important, could Kyle finally do what no one else in the history of Bouring had managed to do: solve the mystery of the missing time capsule?

He grabbed one of the lanterns and sped off in the direction Lundergaard had headed, ducking rock outcroppings and twisting through tunnels that sloped gently up, until finally he saw sunlight ahead. Yes — the other entrance to Carson Cave.

Popping up from the ground, Kyle realized he was about a half mile from where he'd planted Danny at the first entrance, right on the edge of the cornfield. A dirt road wound its way through the corn and away from Bouring. In a couple of decades, Kyle knew, that dirt road would end up being an extension of Major Street, connecting Bouring to the main interstate that ran past town. He floated ten feet in the air, looking around. Carrying that heavy time capsule, Lundergaard shouldn't have gotten very far, but he was nowhere to be seen.

And then Kyle spied a pair of tire tracks in the dirt. Lundergaard had had a car waiting.

He fished in his pocket for the tiny Bluetooth ear-piece he'd built, then slipped it into his ear. Switching on Erasmus, Kyle said, "I need information. You still have all of Wikipedia stored on your hard drive, right?"

"Of course I do," Erasmus said in a wounded tone, as if Kyle had insulted him. "Wait a minute. No satellites . . . No cellular . . . We're still in the past, aren't we?"

"Yeah. For now."

"Did you build that charging cable?"

"No," Kyle said guiltily.

"My battery is now at twenty-two percent."

"I know. But look — something strange is going on here. I can't put my finger on it, but it has something to do with Lundergaard. . . ."

"Kyle, I don't care about Lundergaard!" For the first time ever, Kyle heard complete panic in Erasmus's voice. And since Erasmus's voice was patterned after Kyle's, the sound was utterly unnerving. "I only care about making sure I don't fade into oblivion, and getting you back to the present before you totally wreck history!"

Kyle landed near the entrance to the cave. "I'm not going to wreck history," he assured Erasmus.

But was that true? Kyle felt the weight and bulk of the Walkman at his hip. Was Danny *supposed* to get the Walkman back? Or was it a matter of history that Sam and Max Monroe would get away with their bullying and keep the Walkman? Maybe Danny *was* destined to get it back, but some other way — maybe Kyle had only changed the details of history, not its general bend.

Or maybe he was rewriting things as they happened. Did it matter, though?

He decided it didn't matter. The Monroe brothers stealing Danny's Walkman was wrong, whether it took place in 1987 or not. Kyle was just fixing it. What was wrong with that?

"I need you to look up Lundergaard," Kyle told Erasmus. "Something weird is going on here."

"Are you kidding me? You want me to waste processor cycles and battery power on —"

"You could have *done* it already, if you weren't so busy arguing with me."

"Fine. Fine." A moment later, Erasmus said in a very snippy voice: "Lundergaard the company or the guy? I have files on both."

"Start with the guy."

"Walter Lundergaard," Erasmus started, "founder of Lundergaard Research. Now, this is strange: His birthdate isn't listed on Wikipedia. They usually at least have a guess, but there's nothing listed."

"Is there a picture?"

"Now you want me to turn on my screen? In full color? Do you know how much power —"

"Show me the picture."

Erasmus flashed the picture on his screen, at the lowest brightness possible, Kyle noticed. Still, it was clear enough for Kyle to make out. This was definitely the man the Monroes had dealt with, the man who had taken the time capsule.

"When was this picture taken?"

Sulkily, Erasmus answered, "About three years ago."

"Wait. Three years ago as in 1984 or three years ago *our* time?"

"As in 1984. Can I turn off the picture now?"

"Sure, go ahead. No, wait! Do you have a more recent picture? One from our time period?"

"Doing an image search through my terabytes of data —"

"Just do it."

If Erasmus could have rolled his eyes (if he'd had eyes in the first place), he would have done so. Instead, he paused and then, a moment later, flashed an image on his screen. It was a screen-grab from the bouringrecord .com website the day Kyle had left his own time period. He always had Erasmus archive the news, just in case there was mention of Mighty Mike or the Blue Freak. Or maybe even a return of the Mad Mask, who was still out there somewhere.

This particular image belonged to a story that said, "Walter Lundergaard Junior to Attend Time Capsule Burial."

"This is a picture of Junior," Kyle said. "Not Senior. He's the same age as his father is in 1987 in this picture. . . ." He drifted off. "Show me the Senior picture again."

With an astonishing minimum of grumbling, Erasmus did just that, showing the two pictures side by side.

They were identical.

Kyle swallowed, hard. If he still had his supersmarts, he wouldn't even need to ask the next question, but . . .

"Erasmus, what are the odds of a father and son looking exactly the same at the same point in their lives?"

Erasmus said nothing, and for a moment, Kyle thought maybe something had gone kerflooey in the AI's subsystems, but then Erasmus said, "That's a ridiculous question. With genetic variances and environmental factors, a child would have similar features to one parent, but not identical because of the influence of the other parent. Now may I please shut down my screen?"

"Go ahead," Kyle said.

As Erasmus's screen went black, Kyle rubbed his jaw, thinking. Something was wrong. Something was very, very wrong. If the man he had just seen with the time capsule was Walter Lundergaard Senior, then he must have already had his son, in order for his son to be roughly the same age in Kyle's own time. But like Erasmus said —

how could it be that a son would look exactly like the father?

"Something's fishy," Kyle murmured. "Either Walter Lundergaard Junior had some serious plastic surgery in order to look like his father . . ."

". . . or he's a clone . . ." Erasmus said.

". . . or maybe there's just *one* Lundergaard and he's a time traveler, too," Kyle finished.

They were both silent for a moment as that sank in. Could it be possible? Could there be another time traveler?

"What would a time traveler want with the time capsule?" Kyle asked. "That doesn't make any sense. . . ." But wait. Wait. Maybe it *did* make sense.

The time capsule . . . Something about the time capsule tickled a spot in the back of Kyle's brain. What was it? What was it about the time capsule . . .

We left the present when they were supposed to bury the annual time capsule. But then something happened. Something went wrong. And I ignored it. . . .

He thought of the crowd he'd seen in the present, of the way they'd lunged at everything that moved. Like zombies with some sort of hive mind.

"Erasmus, I need you to play back the police scanner audio from the night we left our time."

"Kyle, my battery is —"

"I know. I know. I swear, just play this back for me and I'll shut you down again."

"Battery power is at seventeen percent," Erasmus complained, but queued up the recording. Kyle listened for the second time:

"Received word 2213 at time capsule burial. Sheriff on scene."

"Reporting in, uh, Deputy Travers. On scene at the — What the heck is —"

Babble and confusion and then:

"They're moving too fast! I can't even —"

"— did they come from? Who the —"

At one point: the sound of flesh on flesh, those knuckles. Someone being hit. Hard.

And then someone else.

And then the thing Kyle hated hearing, a sound that chilled his blood: that adult, screaming in absolute terror.

Finally: dead static.

"And what did this prove?" Erasmus demanded. "Battery power at thirteen percent, by the way."

"Lundergaard. He's mixed up in the time capsule somehow. He stole it here, in 1987. And did something to it."

"Something that caused the zombie horde in our own time. I get it. But that isn't helping you build a charging cable for me any time soon. I have a standard 30-pin dock connector. Ground is pins 29 and 30. FireWire power is on pins 19 and 20. You can assemble —"

"Let me think! Maybe it's not a coincidence that we ended up here in 1987. Maybe time travel —"

"Kyle! Charge me up first, then think later!"

"But —"

"No buts! You need my computing abilities to get back home. It's no good if you figure out the time capsule mystery and then never get home!"

"What if there's some sort of quantum entanglement going on? What if our chronovessel was *attracted* to this time period because of something Lundergaard is doing here?"

"It still doesn't matter. We can't interfere. You've already done too much. You have to stay focused on —"

Just then, a police siren screamed, shrill and piercing in the blank air.

CHAPTER
NINETEEN

The siren echoed from over the hill. Kyle ran to the top of the hill, then hit the dirt, flattening himself against the ground. From here, he could see down the gentle slope to the main entrance to Carson Cave, where he'd left Danny.

Danny. Who was now in the clutches of Sammy Monroe!

Sammy held Kyle's father by the collar of his shirt, shaking him. Max was tugging on his brother's arm, trying to pull him away, but Sammy was in a rage, a fury, and nothing could dissuade him, not even the wail of the siren and the slow trundle of the Bouring Sheriff's Department cruiser as it made its way along the dirt road toward the three boys. Kyle wondered briefly why Erasmus hadn't picked up the coming cruiser on the police band, but then realized that the 1987 band must be on a different frequency than the one Erasmus was used to.

The last thing Kyle needed was trouble with the law in 1987. He kept his head down and watched as the police cruiser drifted to a stop, its siren cut off mid-wail. The lights on top kept spinning, though, flashing blue and red along the ground.

"Leave him alone!" Max was saying. "Dad's here! We're gonna get —"

"Tell me how you did it!" Sammy ignored his brother, shaking Danny again. "Tell me!" He started to draw back his free hand, threatening to slap Danny.

But then the door to the cruiser opened and the sheriff stepped out. It was like seeing a fatter version of the Sheriff Monroe of Kyle's time — this Sheriff Monroe had a similar mustache and way of walking, with his thumbs hooked into his gun belt and a swagger that said he was the Law. Max immediately jumped back and stood straight, like a soldier being inspected by a general. Sammy kept screaming at Danny and was about to haul off and smack him when the sheriff barked:

"Samuel Dennis Monroe! Stand down *now*!"

As if waking from a dream, Sammy shook himself and released Danny, who stumbled backward and fell down. Sammy stepped back and stood ramrod-stiff like Max.

"What is going on here?" the sheriff demanded, strutting over to where his sons stood. "I got an anonymous call that something was going on out here. Shoulda known it was the two of you. Causing trouble."

"We weren't —"

"Zip those lips!" the sheriff barked at Sammy. "I didn't ask you a question! You don't open your yap until I give you a reason to!"

Kyle was beginning to see why Sheriff Maxwell Monroe was such a hard case in his own time.

"What's *your* business here, squirt?" the sheriff asked, rounding on Danny, who managed to pick himself up off the ground.

"He grabbed us —" Sammy started, and then broke off, swallowing visibly, when his father fixed him with a deathly glare.

"Tell me what's going on here," the sheriff said. "You first." He pointed at Danny.

Danny stammered, but his voice — while shaky — was clear. "Th-they stole my Walkman!"

"Oh, yeah? Well, why don't we have it, then?" Sammy asked.

The sheriff smoothed his mustache and looked over his sons. "This is true. They don't have it."

"Well, neither do I!"

Kyle slipped a hand to his belt, where the Walkman was clipped. Meanwhile, the sheriff looked over Danny and agreed that the Walkman was not in his possession, either.

"They went into Carson Cave," Danny said. "It's probably in there."

"We were just minding our own business," Sammy lied smoothly, "and then this kid came tearing into the cave and lifted us up —"

"Lifted you up?" The sheriff clearly didn't believe this, and something in his tone of voice told Kyle that he was used to hearing lies from Sammy.

"Like this." Sammy mimed the way Kyle had snatched up the Monroes and hoisted them into the air.

The sheriff looked at Danny — so small and weak compared to the older, bigger Monroe boys — and held back a snort of laughter. "Max?"

Max had been silent the whole time, as if hoping that by saying nothing he could avoid punishment. Now he shrugged. "We don't have the Walkman, Dad. I mean, sir. Simple as that."

"This kid came flying in —"

"Flying?" the sheriff interrupted. "Sammy, I have warned you about making up stories and playing pranks. . . ."

"But it happened! He came in and —"

"It's not the same kid," Max said. "He's wearing different clothes."

Something snapped inside Sammy. Maybe it was being disbelieved. Maybe it was being contradicted by his brother. Maybe it was the fear that the smaller Danny

Camden would win this fight. Or maybe, Kyle thought, Sammy Monroe had been ready to snap for a long time and today just happened to be the day.

Whatever the reason, the older Monroe brother flew into a rage, screaming and ranting. "So he *changed* his clothes! He *changed* them! Big deal!" he bellowed, and charged at Danny, who was too terrified to move. Sammy would have barreled right into Danny and bowled him over, maybe even trampled him into the ground, if the sheriff hadn't reached out and grabbed his son by the arm, yanking him back.

And then Sammy hit his father.

From Kyle's angle, it looked like it was possible that it was an accident, that Sammy's arm just flailed around from being pulled. Or perhaps Sammy was just that angry. Either way, the result was the same, as the sheriff shoved Sammy away so forcefully that even from a distance, Kyle could hear the boy go "Oof!" Sammy grabbed at the air for balance, then fell back and collapsed on the ground. Max ran to his brother's side.

"I have warned you again and again," the sheriff said with barely controlled rage, "about *lying*, about *stealing*, about all of it. And you are making me a laughingstock in this town. The lawman with a *hoodlum* for a son! You've had your last warning. You're going off to military school."

Max gasped. "Dad! Sir! You can't send him —"

"You want to join him?" the sheriff asked. "He's been practically begging for this for years. Get him in the car."

Max helped Sammy get up and make his way over to the sheriff's car. Together, they managed to get in the back. "I don't have time for your nonsense," the sheriff went on. "Someone broke into my office last night and stole the town's time capsule! Another headache I don't need on top of all the other ones. You picked the wrong day to screw up, Sammy."

"What about my Walkman?" Danny asked timidly.

"Don't push your luck," the sheriff threatened, jabbing a stubby finger in Danny's direction. "If you're out here, you must be up to no good just like them. Just consider yourself lucky I'm not hauling you in."

Danny stood in shocked silence as the sheriff climbed into his cruiser, barking to Max to shut the door. Then the cruiser backed onto the dirt road, turned, and drove away.

Kyle waited a few moments to be sure the sheriff's cruiser wasn't going to come back, then jogged down the hill to where his father waited. "Hey, Danny! Hey, look!" He held up the Walkman like a trophy.

Danny turned slowly and didn't move as Kyle came over to him and placed the Walkman in his hands. Kyle watched as his father examined the Walkman as though seeing it for the first time.

"Dore . . ." he said after a moment. "Dore, can you . . . can you fly?"

Kyle cleared his throat. "No. Of course not. No one can fly." He thought of Mairi, of the lies he'd had to tell her, too. And how those lies led to wiping her memory. Why did he have to lie people? Why was he always in this position? Would he always have to lie and hurt people?

"How did you —"

"I went into the cave," Kyle said, falsehoods easily flowing from his tongue, "and the Monroes were leaving. I was in a shadowy part; they didn't see me. I found your Walkingman —"

"Walkman."

"— Walkman in the cave and came out another way." He paused. "Is the sheriff really going to send them to military school?"

Danny shrugged. "Probably. Well, maybe just Sammy. He's the really bad one. He's strong and he's actually really smart, so he thinks that makes it okay to treat other people badly. Max just goes along with him."

Kyle grimaced. Was it *his* fault Sammy Monroe would end up at military school? Sure, Sammy had done other bad things over the years, but it seemed as though his description (his *true* description!) of Kyle's actions in the cave had pushed the sheriff over the edge.

Had Kyle changed history? Was Sammy never supposed to go away? Then again, in Kyle's own time, he'd never known that Sheriff Maxwell Monroe had a brother — maybe Sammy was always destined to go away.

Kyle's head started to hurt.

"Kyle," Erasmus whispered in his ear. "Kyle, my battery power is now at —"

Oh, no. Distracted by the siren, Kyle had forgotten to turn Erasmus off.

"What's that in your ear?" Danny asked, noticing.

"That's my, uh, hearing aid. I have bad hearing."

"You have to do something," Erasmus said urgently.

"I need some wire," Kyle told Danny. "Do you know where I can get some?"

"Well . . . Dad probably has some in the basement. . . . He has all kinds of stuff down there."

"That'll do. Let's go."

Soon, they were back at Kyle's grandparents' house. Kyle almost didn't want to go in — the memory of Gramps haranguing Danny to the point of tears was still fresh. Too fresh.

But he needed to charge up Erasmus.

"I'm home!" Danny yelled to his parents as they entered. "Me and Dore are going downstairs!"

The basement looked almost exactly the way it did in Kyle's time; that was sort of weird. Same old TV in one corner; same old photos on the walls; same old sofa. Except none of it was old right now — it was all brand-new. Kyle's grandparents wouldn't do much with the basement room in decades. Wow.

Danny led Kyle through a door, beyond which Kyle knew lay what his grandmother called "Gramps's workshop." It was a dusty, scary, dark place, filled with cobwebs and the smell of rust.

Or, rather, it *would be* a dusty, scary, dark place. Unlike the other basement room, the workshop in 1987 was completely different than in Kyle's time. Bright, clean, and well-organized. Tools that, in Kyle's time, were piled in jumbles on tables and benches instead hung in perfect order on pegboards in 1987.

"Excellent," Kyle whispered.

"What do you need wire for?" Danny asked, sliding open a drawer to reveal a spool of beautiful copper wire.

Kyle's imagination chose that moment to poop out; he couldn't think of a single good, convincing lie.

"Look, Danny, I hate to ask this, but I need another favor from you, all right?"

Danny nodded.

"I got back your Walkman, right? And I know you really wanted that back. Because your father would be pretty upset if you lost it."

Kyle felt bad saying it; Danny didn't know Kyle had witnessed the argument with Gramps. Still, it had the desired effect, as Danny unconsciously glanced away, ashamed. "Yeah, he would be ticked off."

"So, I did that favor for you. Now I need you to do one for me. I need you to leave me alone down here for a little while."

Danny's eyes bugged out. "What are you going to do? What are you building?"

"Don't worry; I'm not a terrorist."

Danny laughed. "Terrorists are just in movies."

"Well, anyway, I'm not one. I just need to do something and then I'll be out of your hair."

"I thought you needed to see the school computer?"

Oh, right. Kyle had so much going on, he couldn't keep track of it all! "Right. Later. For now, I just need —"

"All right. Don't worry. I'll get us some lunch."

Once he was alone, Kyle slid Erasmus out of his pocket and put him on the workbench. "Here we go."

"Be careful," Erasmus warned. "There are thirty pins in my dock connector. The ones for power are —"

"I remember," Kyle insisted, cutting off a length of wire. The wire was too thick, so he unwound it and selected only two thin strands, one for each of the pins connected to Erasmus's power supply. "I can't build an actual connector," Kyle said. "I'm going to have to solder the wire in place."

"No way! I won't let you go near me with a hot soldering iron!"

"How do you think I built you in the first place?"

"If you solder the wire into place, you won't be able to use the regular charger when we get home."

"We'll worry about that when it happens," Kyle said.

"But —"

"No buts. You don't have a choice. And since you don't have any way of stopping me, I'm just gonna do it." He heated up the soldering iron and then — very, very carefully — soldered the wire into place. "How's that?"

"It might work," Erasmus admitted grumpily. "But until we plug into some power, we won't know."

That was true. Kyle scrounged around and found an old desk lamp under the workbench. He snipped off the plug, then soldered that to the wire attached to Erasmus. It wasn't a pretty sight at all: The sleek, cool lines of the iPod (decked out in Kyle's custom blue-flame paint job) melding into the naked copper wire, which then merged in a blob of silver solder into the black-coated wire of the plug. But it should work.

Should.

Kyle crawled under the workbench and found an electrical outlet. "Ready?" he asked.

"Let's just hope this doesn't blow my circuits out," Erasmus said. Kyle took that as a yes.

He plugged Erasmus in, squeezing his eyes shut at the same time.

A long moment passed.

And then he heard the familiar and very welcome sound of the chime that meant Erasmus was charging.

Whew!

"It's working, Kyle!" Erasmus said excitedly. "It's working!"

"But slowly," Kyle said, noticing the progress bar on Erasmus's screen. "I'm going to give you a little juice now and then top you off when we get into the school. You can charge while I hack into the computer."

"Why not finish me off now?"

"Because Danny will be back any —"

"Hey, Dore!"

Kyle looked out from under the workbench. Danny stood in the doorway, holding two plates. "Are you hungry?"

Kyle realized he was completely famished. "Yeah, I am."

He pushed Erasmus into a dark corner and left him there to charge while he went to eat lunch with his father.

Kyle was surprised to find that the sandwich was tuna made with a little bit of relish, just the way his grandmother made them. Then he remembered that his grandmother had, in fact, made this very sandwich.

"Did you finish what you needed to finish?" Danny asked.

Kyle noticed how his father avoided asking exactly what Kyle had been up to. He appreciated that. "Yeah, I'm done. I just need to clean up in there." He jerked his head toward the door to the workshop — he and Danny had come into the basement room to eat. "Then we can go break into the school. You're not going to change your mind, are you?"

Danny shook his head fiercely. "No way. You got back my Walkman. You saved me, Dore. You're, like, my hero."

Kyle was so shocked he stopped chewing. *My hero.* He'd been called a villain so much that Kyle had never in a million years thought he would hear those words from anyone. Much less from the mouth of his own twelve-year-old father. It had an effect on him that he couldn't have anticipated. His brain whirled; his heart pounded; his chest expanded.

Pride. He felt proud.

I am a hero, he thought. *And when I get back to my own time, I'm going to make sure I'm the most heroic person there is.*

"Let's get going," Kyle said, polishing off his sandwich.

Soon (after Kyle retrieved a now partially charged Erasmus from the workshop), he and Danny made their way to the school. Kyle was surprised to find themselves walking down Freeman Road, toward Bouring Elementary School.

But although the building at the end of the road looked exactly (if a bit more new) like the elementary school Kyle had attended, the sign out front was different, reading instead BOURING JUNIOR HIGH SCHOOL.

"This is . . ." Kyle began.

"Where I go to school," Danny finished. "Well, for another year. Then I'll go to the new middle school they're building. And my dad said this is going to be turned into —"

"— an elementary school." This time Kyle did the finishing honors.

"Yeah." Danny looked around. "Okay, we're lucky it's Saturday. No one's around."

"You can go now," Kyle said. "No point in you getting in trouble if I'm caught." Kyle would never be caught, of course — with his superspeed, he could get away from any situation. Danny wouldn't be so lucky.

"No way," Danny said staunchly. "You helped me and I'm helping you. A deal's a deal. You need me to show you where the computer is."

That was true. Kyle knew where the computers were in Bouring Elementary School decades from now, but who knew what the layout of today's junior high was like?

"All right. But once you show me the computer, you have to beat it."

"Okay."

First they tried the front door, just in case. But it was definitely locked and Kyle noticed chains looped through the handles on the inside. He was amazed that the doors were entirely made of glass — he could see right into the school. In his own time, the doors to every school he'd ever visited were made of heavy steel, with small, reinforced windows.

They went around back. More glass double doors; more chains.

"This is hopeless," Danny said.

"No, it's not. If they have the doors chained from the inside, then there has to be a door *somewhere* that isn't chained. Because otherwise no one could get inside to unchain the other doors."

"Well, yeah, that's true . . ." Danny said.

"You look over there," Kyle said, pointing, "and I'll check over here."

Kyle had already spotted what looked like a maintenance door, a dull green slab of metal with a shiny knob set into it. He knew it would be locked, but he wouldn't let that stop him. He couldn't have Danny around, though.

Danny went off on his own and Kyle quickly dashed to the door. As he'd suspected, it was locked, but so what? He applied a little bit of superstrength to the knob and it came off in his hand. Then he craned his neck to examine the inside of the lock, tripped some tumblers, and presto! The door was open.

"Hey, Danny!" he called. "It's open!"

Danny came running, breathing hard when he slowed to a stop at the door. "Whoa! What luck!"

"Yep. Luck," Kyle agreed, holding the door so that his hand blocked the broken knob. "Let's go." He held the door open and ushered Danny in, then tossed the useless knob far out into the football field behind the school.

Inside, they found themselves in exactly what Kyle had imagined — a maintenance room of some sort. It was dark and gloomy, and it became darker and gloomier as Kyle eased the door shut.

"Hang on . . ." Danny said. "Ah-ha!" A moment later, the room lit up as Danny flicked the light switch. Kyle closed the door all the way.

"All right. Lead me to the computer."

They found another door, this one unlocked, that led into a murky hallway lined with lockers. "This is the eighth-grade hall," Danny whispered. "I don't come here unless I have to."

"Why are you whispering?"

Danny blinked. "I don't know," he whispered.

"Why don't you stop, then?"

"I . . . I can't."

Kyle sighed. "Take me."

As he'd anticipated, the inside of the school had changed a lot since Kyle's days here in elementary school. Or, rather, the inside of the school *would* change a lot between now and Kyle's time in elementary school. A couple of familiar rooms just didn't exist — there were lockers or brick walls where the doors should have been. And one hallway that Kyle remembered leading to the cafeteria instead dead-ended.

Danny lead him out of the eighth-grade hallway, down a large corridor that led to a glass-enclosed office. When Kyle had been in elementary school, this space was for the guidance counselor, his hated Great Nemesis — Melissa Masterton. But in 1987, it was the school's front office.

The door was locked.

"Darn it!" Danny smacked his palm with his fist. "So close! The computer is right through there." He pointed through the glass at a wooden door with a sign that read ATTENDANCE.

Kyle nodded. "Okay. Thanks for your help. It's time for you to go."

"What do you mean?" Danny's eyes grew wide. "Dore! You're not going to break the glass, are you? I didn't help you so that you could break things."

"So breaking *in* is okay, but just plain old breaking isn't?"

Danny fidgeted. "I said I would get you in here and show you the computer. I didn't say anything about causing damage."

Kyle had had no idea that his father was so conscientious. *Maybe that's where I get my good behavior from,* he thought, followed immediately by a weird feeling he couldn't identify. The idea that he'd inherited anything other than eye color from his father was . . . He didn't have a name for it. He didn't know how it made him feel.

"Just go," Kyle said. "I can pick the lock. But you shouldn't stick around, just in case someone shows up. I don't want you to get in trouble."

Danny thought about it, then nodded. "All right. I'll go. But will I see you later?"

Probably not, unless I can't get the chronovessel working. "Of course."

They shook hands and Danny scampered off the way they'd come. Kyle waited until he figured Danny had gotten out through the maintenance room.

And then — without hesitation — he punched through the glass door, shattering it into a million pieces.

CHAPTER
TWENTY

"It was after I started touching the bom . . ." Mike hesitated, then continued, sounding out the word as Mairi nodded along with him, ". . . the *zombies* that I noticed my powers were becoming . . . becoming . . ."

"Weaker?" Mairi supplied.

"I was going to say 'unstronger,' but I think your word is better."

My word is *a word,* Mairi thought.

"I don't know what to do now," Mike admitted. "I couldn't save anyone. I don't know if I can save you."

"That's all right," Mairi said. "We'll save each other, okay?" She smiled reassuringly at Mike, even though the last thing she felt like doing right now was smiling.

He smiled back. "Yes. Very excellent. We'll save each other. That will be very nice."

"Unless we can figure out what's going on," Mairi said, "we might be here awhile. Until the Army comes. Or until your powers come back."

Mike brightened. "Do you think that will happen?"

"It could. Who knows?"

Mike paced the lighthouse. "We need to know."

"Know what?"

"How strong I still am."

"Well, sure, that would be helpful, but —"

CLANG!

Mairi jumped; Mike had delivered a karate blow to the post bolted into the floor that held the massive lighthouse lantern. The entire lamp structure vibrated.

"Mike!"

He did it again, and this time the post bent just a bit. Mairi scrambled out of the way as the lamp structure tilted crazily toward her.

"Stop it, Mike!"

Mike pulled away from the lamp. "I needed to know."

"I didn't know you were still strong enough for that!" Mairi limped over to where Mike stood. The post was crimped and dented. It would have been hugely impressive if Mairi didn't know for a fact that Mike *should* have been able to punch through it with one shot. "I didn't think you could still do that."

And then she noticed that his knuckles were bleeding.

Mike stared at it as though he'd never seen his own blood before. And Mairi thought that maybe he hadn't. Unwrapping her scarf, she offered it to him.

He flexed his fingers, testing his hand. "It's not broken. I will be KO'd."

"It's actually 'okay,' " Mairi finally told him.

Mike nodded grimly. "Yes. Of course. I knew that one already. Stupid of me to forget it."

"Don't worry about it. Here" — still holding out the scarf — "For the bleeding."

He took the scarf and wound it around his hand carefully. "This is strange," he said.

"You've never been really hurt before," Mairi said. "At least not since you got your powers and your amnesia. You should —"

"That's not what I mean." He pointed to the lamp, which still flashed despite the abuse he'd dished out to it. "It keeps doing the same thing, over and over."

"Right. It's flashing."

"But I mean . . ." Mike sounded puzzled. Well, more puzzled than usual. "It's not always flashing the same way."

She realized Mike was right — the light would stop for a moment, then start up again. She watched it, almost hypnotized by it, and realized that what had appeared to be random was actually a pattern. There were two kinds of bursts — long ones and short ones — and they were *repeating.* . . .

"It's Morse code," she whispered. Kyle had taught her Morse code years ago, and they used to use it at school to tap out messages to each other during class.

"Who is Moore and why should we care about his code?" Mike asked.

"Not Moore's code," Mairi said. "*Morse* code. It's the way people used to communicate, before phones and e-mail and stuff. It's like a system of dots and dashes, and depending on how you combine them, you get letters and words."

"I see no dots." Mike peered around. "No dashes, either."

"You don't have to *literally* have dots and dashes. Just something shorter and something longer. A dot and a dash. Or a short sound and a long one. Or . . ." She gestured to the lantern, which pulsed out a long burst of light, followed by a quick blip.

"Oh," Mike said. "I get it."

A moment later, he actually *did* get it, and his face lit up without any help from the lantern. "What does it say?" he asked.

Mairi squinted at the light as it dotted and dashed away. "I don't know. I don't remember it well enough. But I know someone who *will* know." She turned to Mike, her eyes fierce. "Do you think you can fly just a little more?"

"Where are we going?"

"We have to find Kyle Camden."

CHAPTER
TWENTY-ONE

"We're about to make a move," Kyle said, switching on Erasmus.

"It's about time," Erasmus said through the earpiece. "We can't keep delaying. We need to get back to our time."

"We can just set the machine to bring us back a few seconds after we left," Kyle reminded him. "It'll be like we never left."

"You'd like to think so," Erasmus said, "but there's no guarantee we can fine-tune it that well. Not with the technology in this era."

"You're such a bummer." Kyle stepped through the frame of the door. The room marked ATTENDANCE was unlocked, so he went in.

It was a small room, lit by sunlight streaming through slatted blinds over a single window. If Danny had just pointed out the window, Kyle could have saved a lot of time. And a glass door.

Oh, well.

The room was packed with shelves and filing cabinets. Against one wall was a smallish desk with a boxy computer on it. The computer looked like something out of the old movies Kyle's parents watched — it was positively ancient.

"Whoa," Kyle breathed. "Old school." He chuckled, looking around Bouring Junior High. "Literally."

"Where are we?" Erasmus demanded. "You know I can't see and without Wi-Fi and cell signals and GPS to guide me, I can't tell where we are or —"

"We're at Bouring Junior High," Kyle told him, slipping into the chair at the desk. "We're going to get online, find a place where we can get the stuff we need to fix the chronovessel, and get out of this time period."

"But I tried telling you before that —"

"Quiet. I need to think."

"But —"

Kyle popped out his earpiece and put it on the desk. Let Erasmus chatter away if he wanted to. Kyle had things to do.

There was no mouse for the computer and the keys were stiff and clunky. Kyle found the power switch and the computer screen powered on with a dull beep. A glowing green rectangle blinked in one corner for a moment, then vanished, only to be replaced by blocky, green text:

LOGON? < ▌

Kyle stared at the screen. What the heck . . . ?

Ah. Wait. A password. That's what it wanted.

He pawed through some papers on the desk and found nothing. But when he opened one of the drawers, he found a slip of paper with several words crossed out . . . and one word that wasn't: *lunchroom.*

You're kidding me. Not only are they stupid enough to write down the password right next to the computer, but they also make it something easy like lunchroom? *Really? Have these people* never *heard of phishing or malware?*

Kyle typed *lunchroom* at the prompt and hit ENTER. The computer made another dull beep and then the screen flashed. Kyle grinned, ready to launch a web browser. . . .

But all that showed up on the screen was more text:

MAIN MENU
ATTENDANCE
GRADES
FACULTY
ADMINISTRATION
COUNTY
PLEASE ENTER SELECTION: ___

Kyle stared at the screen, which glowed back at him with that weird greenish text.

No mouse. No trackpad. No windows or icons or *anything*. This was the most useless computer in history!

He tried entering one of the underlined letters, but that only took him to more useless submenus — a grade book, a roster, stuff like that. Each one had an option to back out to the Main Menu, so he always ended up back at the original screen.

"Erasmus," he said, slipping the earbud back in, "I need your help."

"Haven't you been listening to me?" Erasmus fumed.

"Not really. This computer is all —"

"I tried to explain it to you before. There *is* no Internet in 1987!"

"What?" Kyle couldn't believe it. How could that be possible? How could people live without the Internet? "You mean no Internet in Bouring, right? They haven't been hooked up yet?"

"No, Kyle. No Internet. Period. The TCP/IP protocol that runs the Internet in our time is barely a decade old at this point in history. There are various government and military systems connected by some old-fashioned 56 Kbps backbones —"

"Fifty-six kilobytes per second!" Kyle gasped, horrified. That was so *slow*! How could anything get done at that speed?

"— but the term *Internet* is only being used in some very specific organizations. Here in 1987, we're on the cusp of global hookup, but it hasn't happened yet. There's NSFNET, ARPANET, NSI . . . a bunch of strung-together networks out there, but nothing remotely like the Internet you're used to. Heck, Tim Berners-Lee and Robert Cailliau won't even build the first prototype of the World Wide Web for two more years."

Kyle sank low in the chair, deflated and defeated. "We're out of luck, then," he moaned. "How else am I supposed to find a place to get the components we need in order to repair the chronovessel?"

"Think it through," Erasmus encouraged him. "We've managed to do so much together — we can get through this, too!"

"Yeah, we did all of that stuff when my brain wasn't scrambled by time travel." Kyle almost brought his fist down on the desk, but decided against smashing it to pieces. "Now I'm so messed up that I couldn't even remember when the Internet was invented. Pathetic."

"That is pathetic," Erasmus agreed, "but you've always been more than just sheer brainpower, Kyle. As much as I hate to say it, even before you built me, even before the plasma storm gave you your powers, you were a smart kid. And you pulled some exceptional pranks, back in the day. Be creative. Think."

"You're smarter than I am now," Kyle said morosely. "And you have my creativity — I programmed it into you. You don't even need me."

"Wrong. You can see — I can't. You can find something that might help us."

"At this point," Kyle snarked, "the only way we're getting back to our time period is if we stuff ourselves into a —" He broke off, staring at the useless computer screen.

"Stuff ourselves into a what? Kyle? Kyle?"

Kyle thought back. To earlier in the day. Carson Cave. The Monroe boys. And Walter Lundergaard, taking the —

"— time capsule," Kyle finished.

"You couldn't fit in the . . . Oh. Oh! I see what you're thinking!"

"If — *if* — Lundergaard is a time traveler, too, then he'll probably have something we can use to fix the chronovessel!" Kyle jumped up from the desk. "All we have to do is go to Lundergaard Research and —"

"Lundergaard Research wasn't founded until 1989, Kyle. There's nowhere to go."

Kyle paced the office. "He must be nearby, though. He was at Carson Cave. He knew the Monroes — he hired them to steal the time capsule."

"That's true. He must have a hideout or a lab or something nearby. How do we find it?"

"I don't know . . ." Kyle roamed the confines of the office, swinging his arms. *Think! Think!* "If I could be on the Internet for just two minutes! I just need to go

187

to, like, WhitePages.com and —" He stopped, staring. "Hey, Erasmus? Where did they get the name for WhitePages.com?"

"The name? It comes from the olden days, when there was a book that contained the same information."

"And the book was called *White Pages*?"

"Yes."

With a cry of triumph, Kyle snatched up a heavy book from one of the bookshelves. BOURING AND SUR- ROUNDING AREAS WHITE PAGES, it said on the cover.

"Ah-ha! Definitely old school!" He flipped through the book until he found a listing for Lundergaard, W. Not far from here, actually: over on Thorul Court.

"We've got him!"

First, they went back to the spot where they'd hidden the chronovessel. Kyle wanted to examine the thing thoroughly. If he was going to swipe stuff from Lundergaard, he wanted to make sure he got everything he needed the first time out.

He pulled off the tarp and whistled a long, low whistle.

"What is it?" Erasmus asked.

"It's, uh, worse than I thought."

And it was. When they had first arrived in 1987, Kyle had been disoriented, and it had been nighttime. He hadn't really been able to examine the chronovessel. Now, in the light of day, he had the complete picture, and it was an ugly one.

Scorch marks scarred the sides of the motorbike, and there were new dents and dings all along its body that Kyle knew hadn't originally been there. The wheels — which were really just for balance, since the thing didn't run anymore — had melted to the rims. The whole chassis appeared to have been caught in a shoot-out somewhere and then gone over with a flamethrower. It was a miracle that the video camera and control board were still in good shape.

"This is not gonna be good. . . ." Kyle muttered as he pried open what had once been the gas tank, where he'd installed the components for time travel.

What he found was a melted, fused, burned hunk of circuits, wires, and motherboards. It was as though he had thrown it all into a microwave. It was ten times — a thousand times — worse than he had imagined.

"We're in trouble," he told Erasmus, and rolled up his sleeves. Time to get to work.

An hour later, he had most of the chronovessel disassembled and spread out before him in a rough sort of triage system: broken parts that could be fixed, broken parts that were hopeless, and parts that could still be used.

Sadly, the third category was almost bare.

For that matter, so was the first.

"Okay, walk me through this again," Kyle said to Erasmus. "And don't lose your patience this time. The antimatter production disks . . ."

". . . need to be made of titanium or better," Erasmus said, exasperated. With Kyle's superintelligence still not fully active, he was relying on Erasmus to remind him how they had originally built the chronovessel, and it was wearing on the AI's patience. Kyle suddenly realized how other people probably felt around *him* . . . and he didn't like it.

"And then the conduits from the dark energy collector —"

"*To* the dark energy collector!" Erasmus exploded. "The conduits run *to* the dark energy collector! Or maybe you *want* to create a superdense black hole in the middle of Bouring and suck half the solar system into oblivion!"

"Right. Right. I remember now. You don't have to be so mean."

"You're right. I should be kinder and take your feelings into consideration and let you blow up the planet when you reverse the power flow from the neutrino combiner and back up chronons into the storage matrix."

"Point taken." Kyle still didn't like it, though. "I think we have a complete list. Do we?"

Erasmus sniffed, an impressive feat given that he didn't have a nose. "Well, assuming you've reported accurately the status of all the components, yes."

"I have," Kyle said, offended. Maybe his intellect wasn't firing on all neurons right now, but that didn't mean he was an idiot. Wasn't it Erasmus himself who pointed out just a little while ago that Kyle was pretty darn smart even without the plasma-powered buffing? "You need to chill out and trust me."

"I'll trust you when you get us home and get this wire out of my dock connector." Erasmus wasn't backing down.

Kyle shrugged, a motion totally lost on Erasmus, and stood up, dusting off his knees. "Let's go, then — next stop, Thorul Court!"

It was getting dark, but not yet dark enough to risk flying, so Kyle took a roundabout route to Thorul Court, running at superspeed through the woods and open fields that surrounded Bouring. He made it in less than five minutes, a world's record in 1987 or any other time.

Walter Lundergaard's house was a nondescript three-story Colonial at the very center of Thorul Court. In Kyle's own time, Thorul Court wasn't a pleasant place to live — there were only a couple of homes anyone lived in and the rest were unoccupied.

Including, Kyle realized now, Lundergaard's. At some point between 1987 and the present, Lundergaard's house would be gutted by a fire. No one would ever reclaim it or repair it, so it would just sit for years and years, decrepit and unloved, in a permanent state of disrepair that would drive other homeowners from the court.

But that was at some point in the future. For now, Thorul Court looked like any other part of Bouring, and Lundergaard's house was whole, its shingles a sparkling pearl gray, with bright, freshly painted white trim and shutters. You could hardly believe a time traveler lived there.

"Kyle!" Erasmus said suddenly. If Kyle didn't know better, he would say his partner was out of breath. "You're not going to believe this!"

"Try me. I believe a lot these days."

"I'm picking up a Wi-Fi signal!"

"What?" That should be impossible. Wi-Fi wasn't even invented yet.

"We're at the very edge of the signal's range. It's on the experimental Q band, but it's strong. Origination point is roughly thirty-two meters due east."

Kyle was facing due east. And thirty-two meters in front of him was smack in the middle of Lundergaard's house.

"He's definitely a time traveler. Has to be. How else could he have Wi-Fi in 1987? Can you get into his system?"

"No. He's using top-grade quantum encryption. Not even available commercially in our time. It would take me roughly three thousand years to hack his system, assuming no microscopic degradation of my circuitry in that time."

"Well, I'm not waiting three thousand years to figure out what this guy's up to. I'm going to find out the old-fashioned way." Kyle marched forward. There was no car in the driveway, so Lundergaard probably wasn't home. He would have the run of the place.

The front door was locked, as expected, and Kyle didn't want to draw attention by knocking it down, so he crept around the side of the house to the backyard. There was an old batwing cellar door set in the ground against the rear wall. A heavy chain and padlock kept it secure.

"Well, well," Kyle murmured. "That's interesting. I guess the ordinary lock just wasn't enough, eh, Walter?"

He took the chain in both hands and pulled it apart like shredding cotton candy.

Once opened, the door revealed a set of concrete stairs descending into darkness. Kyle took Erasmus out of his pocket and had him crank up his screen brightness to use as a flashlight.

"This is going to —"

"— drain your battery. I know. Complain about something else for a change; I have a charging cable now."

"How could I forget? It's grafted to me like a tail."

Kyle fiddled with the cord, wrapping it around Erasmus's shell to keep it from dangling. "You can't feel it. Stop being a baby."

He crept down the stairs, shutting the doors behind him so that no one would see anything out of the ordinary, should they happen to look in Lundergaard's backyard. Erasmus's screen only lit up a few feet in front of him, so Kyle moved slowly, mincing along, one hand outstretched along the wall to feel for a light switch.

"How's that Wi-Fi signal?"

"Stronger. We're very close."

By the light of Erasmus's screen, Kyle could tell that he'd gone from a short corridor into an actual room, but he couldn't make out much in the way of details, just shadowy, blocky shapes. Desks? Workbenches? He felt on the wall to his left, then his right, finally locating a light switch.

Revealed in the lights that flickered to life along the ceiling was the most magnificent workshop Kyle had ever seen. It was the workshop of his dreams. He wanted *his* basement to look like this someday.

All along one wall were gigantic flat-screen monitors, six of them tiled to take up the entire wall. On another wall were mounted two large whiteboards — each covered in multicolored marker script — and several corkboards, which were studded with tacked-up papers and drawings. And along the third wall were rows and rows of filing cabinets.

In the middle of the room were desks and workbenches, all neatly organized and arranged, piled high with all the gadgets and gear any budding genius could ever want . . . including a sleek and slim laptop computer. The room felt cool, despite all of the computer equipment, and Kyle realized that air conditioning vents blew frigid air from the ceiling, even though it was November.

"Wait a second," he muttered.

"The Wi-Fi is coming from close by, Kyle. Only a few yards —"

"Flat-screen TVs weren't this big in 1987. And that laptop is from our time. Lundergaard is *definitely* a time traveler."

"How is that possible?" Erasmus asked. "We invented time travel."

"Technically, I invented it. You helped."

"We're stuck in 1987 and in the basement lab of someone who shouldn't even exist, and you're really going to argue technicalities with me?"

"Facts are facts."

"Just poke around and see if what we need is around here."

Kyle chuckled. "Trust me, Erasmus. *Everything* we need is around here."

Peering around again, looking beyond the wealth of electronic treasure gathered in the basement, Kyle noticed a flight of stairs leading up, into the house itself, no doubt. There was also a door made of steel — riveted and reinforced with bands across it, and a massive lock that might as well have had a sign reading KEEP OUT! SERIOUSLY.

"I wonder what you have hidden in there, Walter?" Kyle murmured.

"Stop wondering and start gathering up the stuff we need to fix the chronovessel," Erasmus complained.

"Sure, that makes sense." But Kyle couldn't help himself. After being stuck in the primitive 1980s, seeing all these signs of civilization made him almost dizzy with homesickness. He made a beeline for the laptop and tapped its space bar. The screensaver flickered off and the current project window came to life. Kyle blinked. It looked familiar.

"Are you getting what we need?" Erasmus asked.

"Wait. Give me a second." Kyle clicked around a little bit, popping open some other windows. Various technical drawings and schematics appeared on the screen. "This all looks . . ." He drifted off, thinking, then turned to look at the whiteboards and their multicolored scrawl.

Equations. Heady stuff — black hole event horizons and neutron star densities . . .

"What are you up to, Lundergaard?"

Back at the computer, Kyle stared and stared at the windows until suddenly he realized why it all looked so familiar — it was the onboard telemetry circuit design for the chronovessel.

It was Kyle's own design, decades before he'd invented it!

"He *is* a time traveler," Kyle whispered. "It's the only explanation. In the present or maybe even in our future, he must have gotten his hands on my chronovessel and come back to the 1980s. That's why Lundergaard Research is so advanced in our time; he started off with *our* technology in the past and had decades to improve it. But why?"

"Money," Erasmus said. "World domination. Any of the standard villainous reasons for executing a nefarious plot. Does it really matter? Lundergaard is a bad guy, but he has the equipment we need to repair the chronovessel. Take it and run."

"We don't know he's a bad guy, though. He could be a good guy."

"He was working with the Monroe brothers. He stole the time capsule."

"But that's not necessarily —"

"Not necessarily what?" asked a new voice.

Kyle knew even before he turned around that it would be Walter Lundergaard.

He turned.

Sometimes he hated being right all the time.

CHAPTER
TWENTY-TWO

Lundergaard stood at the bottom of the staircase that led to the rest of the house. He held some sort of gadget in one hand and a gun in the other, pointed at Kyle. Normally guns didn't scare Kyle — he knew from experience that he was bulletproof. Not to mention bomb-proof, fireproof, and bazooka-proof.

But this gun didn't look like an ordinary, run-of-the-mill pistol. It was a dull silver color and the barrel was bulbous, as if it had tried to swallow something too big to get down in one gulp. For all Kyle knew, that gun could hurt him very badly. He thought of the Mad Mask's force field — it was definitely still possible to hurt Kyle, with the right science.

"Finish your thought, young man," Lundergaard said in a very calm voice. "Not necessarily what?"

"I . . . uh . . ." Kyle's mind raced and his eyes flicked over to the way he'd come in. At superspeed, he could make it before —

"Ah, ah, ah!" Lundergaard said, and clicked the gadget in his hand. A shimmering field of energy blocked the exit. "A force field. I assure you passing through it will —"

Kyle didn't let Lundergaard finish. He moved, quickly. Not at the exit and the force field, but at Lundergaard himself, reaching out at superspeed for the gadget with one hand and the gun with the other.

He never made it.

A strange pain — strange both because it was pain and also because it was somehow familiar — buzzed through Kyle like a whole fleet of bees with steel stingers. He collapsed backward, stumbling away from Lundergaard and crashing into a workbench, which promptly fell into pieces at contact with his superstrong, super-resistant body.

"He's *definitely* a bad guy," Erasmus commented as Kyle shook his head to clear it.

"How on earth can you still be standing?" Lundergaard marveled. "That burst should have rendered you unconscious or —" He broke off and gasped, his entire expression changing to one of amazement, his eyes filled with sudden recognition.

"You . . . You're Kyle Camden!" Lundergaard cried. "You're Kyle Camden *as a child*! Of course! I should have known I would encounter you in this time period. It makes perfect sense."

"Not to me," Erasmus admitted.

Not to Kyle, either, but he didn't care. "Turn off the force fields, Lundergaard. I'm taking what I need and leaving."

"I don't know if I can let you do that." Lundergaard paused for a moment, confused. "But . . . I also . . . I don't know if I *can't* let you do that. The time paradoxes . . ."

"I *told* you there were time paradoxes!" Erasmus said.

"Not now." To Lundergaard: "Look, we can do this the easy way —"

"Or the hard way. Yes, yes, I under —"

"No, I was going to say that we can do this the easy way *or* the way where I break every bone in your body. Your choice."

He had expected Lundergaard to be intimidated or scared, but instead the older man just sighed and shook his head. "Oh, Kyle. You haven't outgrown your childish bluster yet, have you? You told me that you were a smug, petulant child, but I didn't believe you."

"What do you mean *I* told you?" Kyle thought for a second. "And I am *not* smug and petulant!"

"Well . . ." Erasmus started, and Kyle shushed him.

Lundergaard, safe behind his force field, went on talking, as if to himself, as though Kyle weren't even in the room. "So it's . . . it's 1987. Which means this is your first trip through time. Which means you're only twelve years old . . ." He drifted off for a moment, thinking.

Kyle wanted to rush him at superspeed again, push through that force field, but he was paralyzed by shock: *first* trip through time?

"Kyle," Lundergaard said, "I suppose I should have expected this all along. I don't know why I didn't." He lowered the strange-looking gun and his face relaxed. "Believe it or not, I'm not the 'bad guy.' I'm not your enemy at all. I'm going to turn off the force field in a moment . . . and then I'm going to invite you upstairs for something to drink and tell you what I know." Lundergaard smiled. "Is that all right?"

Kyle nodded, knowing that as soon as the force field was down, he could race over there at superspeed and . . .

But his curiosity got the better of him. Lundergaard clicked the button and turned to go up the stairs.

Kyle followed.

After the modernity of Walter Lundergaard's basement workshop, his kitchen was a second shock — it was just as boringly ancient as every other part of the 1980s Kyle had seen. The microwave oven, for example, was *huge* and actually had a dial on it, as well as an analog clock.

"I can't upgrade the whole house," Lundergaard said, as if he could read Kyle's mind. He had put the gun and the other gadget on a shelf near the fridge, as if he didn't care for them anymore. For some reason, that gesture made Kyle want to trust him. "Sometimes people come over. I have to keep all of the future stuff down in the basement, under lock and key."

"What about that big steel door?" Kyle asked. "More future stuff?"

Puttering at the stove, his back to Kyle, Lundergaard shrugged. "No. I, well, I'm building a reactor. To power my own time machine. Very radioactive and very dangerous." He turned around to face Kyle. "We can't all be supergeniuses like you, Kyle. I can't construct my own zero-point energy filtration system out of the guts of a PlayStation. For one thing, the PlayStation hasn't been invented yet. For another, well, I'm just not that smart. Really smart, sure. Kyle Camden–smart? Nah." He dropped a wink. "I'm making coffee for myself. What can I get for you?"

Kyle was surprised to find that he was thirsty. "Do you have soda?"

"Sure do." Lundergaard rummaged in the fridge and brought out a nice, cold can of soda for Kyle. Moments later, the coffeemaker chirped and Lundergaard sat at the kitchen table, gesturing for Kyle to join him.

"Tell me what's going on," Erasmus demanded as Kyle sat.

"Later," Kyle murmured, covering the sound with the snap-hiss of opening the soda can.

He covered the *sound* of the word, but not the motion of his lips. Lundergaard's eyes lit up. "Are you talking to Erasmus?" he asked excitedly.

Kyle blinked. "You know about Erasmus?"

Lundergaard reared back his head and laughed, a long, honest burst of laughter so infectious that Kyle almost joined in. "Do I know about Erasmus? Oh, Kyle . . . I keep forgetting. . . . Even though you're only twelve, you seem so much like the Kyle that I already know. Knew. Will know." He frowned. "Time travel really messes up verbs, doesn't it?"

"Yeah! Exactly! I was just thinking that yesterday."

"Is that how long you've been here in 1987? Since yesterday?"

"Yeah."

Lundergaard nodded and sipped at his coffee, then grimaced. "I've been here considerably longer. And trust me when I tell you that the worst part of being stuck in the past is that it's impossible to get or make a decent cup of coffee."

Kyle knew from previous experience that there was no such thing as a "decent cup of coffee," even in the twenty-first century, but he couldn't be bothered to explain this to Lundergaard. It was as though something happened to adults' taste buds when they grew up, something that made them think coffee was "good." He kept quiet and drank his soda.

"You're probably dying to ask me a bunch of questions," Lundergaard said. "So fire away."

"How did you get here?" Kyle asked. "What are you up to? Why did you take the time capsule? How do you know me? How do you know about Erasmus? What is —"

"Whoa! Whoa!" Lundergaard held up his hands in surrender. "Whoa, there! Let a fella collect his thoughts!" He grinned again and saluted Kyle with his coffee cup before taking another reluctant sip of the sludge within. "Let me try to explain this to you. . . .

"Many years in the future — in *your* future, Kyle — you and I will meet. You'll be older when we meet. In your twenties."

Kyle tried to imagine himself that old, and found that he couldn't do it. "How did we —"

"One at a time," Lundergaard admonished, waggling a finger. "Let me tell the story the best way I can. It's confusing enough, with all the time travel stuff.

"Anyway, by the time I met you, you had already traveled in time. Obviously." He gestured across the table at Kyle. "You and Erasmus were working on a way to perfect the system, though. The biggest problem was that only someone indestructible — like you, for example — could survive the time travel process. You wanted to make it so that anyone could travel through time."

"I did?" That didn't really sound like something Kyle

205

would be bothered with. But who knew what he would be like when he was older?

"Yes, you did. I volunteered for one of the tests." Lundergaard shrugged. "As you can see, it worked. Sort of."

"So . . . you're stuck here? Because of *me*?" The soda suddenly felt thick and viscous in Kyle's throat, and he pushed the can away from him. "It's all my fault?"

"Don't blame yourself. Remember: I volunteered. I knew there was a chance I could be stuck in the past, or even worse. But it was worth it, to help you with your project. Of course, now that you're here in 1987, you can help me figure out how to get home."

Lundergaard's smile was so wide and joyous that it killed Kyle to tell him, "I don't know if I can do that. I can't even figure out how to get *myself* home right now." He explained how the chronovessel had burned up and melted down during its maiden voyage and how his own superintellect was on the fritz. Lundergaard's smile faded with each word until the man was staring down into his coffee cup as though it were an endless pit of blackness and sourness. (Which, really, coffee was, but Kyle realized it wasn't helpful to point this out at the time.)

"Then I suppose," Lundergaard said at last, "I'll have to fall back on my original plan." He sighed.

"What's your original plan?"

"Well, you saw the tech down in the basement. I scavenged from what was left of *my* time machine when I first arrived here in the 1980s. I think I've gone about as far on my own as I can. My original plan was to use my advanced technology to form a sort of research company."

"Lundergaard Research," Erasmus piped up. "We're witnessing its formation."

"By getting a jump start on technology with the futuristic tech at my disposal, I estimate my think tank should be able to re-create time travel technology in a reasonable amount of time."

A reasonable amount of time! And then Kyle could go home, too!

"How long will it take?" Kyle asked.

Lundergaard shrugged and finished off the dregs of his coffee. "Probably about twenty or thirty years."

CHAPTER
TWENTY-THREE

"Why Kyle Camden?" Mike asked, clearly unhappy with the proposition.

"I know you guys don't get along all that well —"

"It's not *that*."

"— but Kyle's the one who taught me Morse code —"

"Not *exactly* . . ."

"— and I know he'll still be able to read it. I'm only picking up a couple of letters. I think there's an O or maybe two. I think I remember O. It was three long."

"Three dashes," Mike clarified.

"Yeah." Mairi reached into her pocket for her video camera, miraculously intact after everything she'd been through. "I'm pretty sure I didn't see him in the crowd at the time capsule site, but I want to make sure. . . ." She set the video to run at double speed and watched the crowd mill and mingle and zip by as if they'd been given a fraction of Mighty Mike's old superspeed. She knew

Kyle like she knew her own reflection in a mirror — if he'd been at the burial, she would recognize him.

But after watching all of the footage she'd shot, she didn't see him at all.

"Is this good or bad?" Mike asked.

Mairi shrugged. "I'm not one hundred percent sure, to tell the truth. It means he probably wasn't zombified like everyone else, but who knows where he could be?"

Even as she said it, though, she thought she had the answer. Kyle would be home, of course. Home, alone. Sulking. Just like he had been ever since the Mad Mask and the Blue Freak and Ultitron attacked Bouring.

She led Mike through the open windowpane back out onto the balcony that ringed the lighthouse. From here, she could see the entire town of Bouring. All that moved were occasional batches of what she couldn't help thinking of as zombies. Or even "bomzies," as Mike had called them. She scanned the topography for a few minutes and then pinpointed her target.

"There," she told Mike, pointing. "Can you carry me to that house?"

"It will be easier and faster if I don't take you," Mike said apologetically.

"I think I need to go anyway," she told him. "You might need help. No offense or anything, but you're not quite as supery-dupery as you used to be."

"True. But you are pretty un-super-dupery yourself."
He gestured to her bleeding arm and her twisted ankle.

"Well, maybe between the two of us, we can make it work. How about that?"

Mike drew in a deep breath and let it out slowly. "Very well, then." With an unfamiliar grunt and a slight buckling of his knees, he swept Mairi up into his arms. And without even giving her a moment to catch her breath, he jumped off the lighthouse and into naked space.

Mairi screamed as they hit the open air, but even though they plunged rather than soared, they did so slowly, and sooner than she expected, they were riding the air currents, having only dropped about ten feet from their launch point. It was better than she'd expected.

She clutched Mike tightly. For the first time ever, she could feel sweat dampening the back of his neck and seeping through his costume. "Are you all right?" she asked, feeling stupid for even thinking the question.

Surprisingly, he said, "It's not as bad as I thought it would be. We were so high up, I'm mostly just gliding. It's easier than flying."

Now a million new questions flooded Mairi's mind. Crazy questions that had nothing to do with their current predicament, but the kinds of questions she couldn't help having anyway. Like: Was it normally difficult for Mike to fly? Even when he wasn't "bomzie"-sapped? It always seemed so effortless, but did he strain to do it under normal circumstances? And how much did he know about his own powers? For the first time, she wondered: Was it possible Mike knew things about himself that he hadn't told anyone?

She never got the chance to ask any of those questions. Before she knew it, Mike had unerringly glided them right into Kyle's backyard. All was still and quiet here, but she couldn't help looking around for zombies. There were none to be found.

The basement door was the sort made of heavy glass that slid open. Mairi looked around for something heavy to break it with. She figured if she ended up saving the world, the Camdens would forgive her. And if she didn't end up saving the world, well, a broken door wouldn't really matter, would it?

Mike surprised her, though, by just tugging on the door. It slid open easily.

"Mighty Strength," she mumbled.

"No, it was just unlocked," he said. "I barely had to pull at all."

Together, they crept into the Camden basement. The lights were out and Mairi fumbled about for a switch. She hadn't been down here in forever and couldn't remember where one was.

"I see stairs," Mike said. Of course. He could see in the dark. "Follow me." He took her hand and led her across the dark basement, steering her this way and that. "Be full of caring, Mairi. There are strange machines and pieces of machines everywhere."

Mairi was pretty sure all Mr. Camden kept down here was his lawn mower and some gardening equipment, but if Mike thought that was strange, whatever.

They made their way up the stairs. She could see a bit now — there was some starlight and light from the lamp-posts coming in through the windows. But all the indoor lights were out, which made Mairi wonder if Kyle really was home or not. She knew his parents had been at the time capsule burial — she'd seen them there and they'd also shown up on the video she'd shot. But if Kyle wasn't there and wasn't here, then where . . .

"Kyle?" she called softly, hoping to be just loud enough to get his attention, but not loud enough attract any zombies in the area.

"KYLE!" Mighty Mike bellowed at the top of his lungs, shaking the walls.

Mairi turned and stared at Mike, who regarded her with an innocent "What? Me?" expression.

"Mike!" she admonished.

"You were being very quiet," Mike said. "I doubt he could have heard you."

Mairi slapped her own forehead. Now she just had to hope and pray that nothing shambling and moaning and all zombie-ish had heard Mike's Mighty Shout.

They sneaked around the Camden house. Mairi had been here a million times — it was practically her second home — but with no one else around, it felt like she was breaking and entering. Suddenly, Mike stopped her and cocked his head.

"I hear something," he said. "Upstairs."

Upstairs. The bedrooms. What if Kyle was hurt?

Mairi raced up the stairs, Mike behind her. She knew exactly where she was going, so she turned down the hall, tore past Mr. and Mrs. Camden's room and the bathroom, and burst into Kyle's room without even knocking.

It was empty.

Except for Lefty, angrily pulling at the bars to his cage.

"Is that what you heard?" Mairi asked.

"Yes."

Sighing and thinking of Sashimi, Mairi opened the cage lid and stroked Lefty to calm him down. Kyle left the rabbit food and treats on a shelf above the cage, so she also refilled his food bowl and tossed him some treats. She drew the line at emptying his litter box.

"Now what?" Mike asked, looking around. "Kyle does not seem to be here."

"I know. I know. . . ." She gazed around the room. The closet was partly open and she thought she could see the edge of a flat-screen TV there. Where the heck had *that* come from?

"Mairi?" Mike asked. "Mairi, what do we do now?"

"I don't know," she said. If only Kyle had been here . . . Where *was* he, anyway? Off being all emo . . .

Just then, she noticed: Kyle's computer! She flipped open the laptop lid and the computer lit up. "We don't need Kyle," she said. "We just need a Morse code cheat sheet."

Soon, she had a page on the Internet showing which groups of dots and dashes corresponded to which numbers and letters in the English alphabet. She grabbed a piece of paper and a pen from Kyle's desk, then stood at his window, looking out at the lighthouse.

A long burst of light, follow by two more. Then two quick ones. Then two long. And three short.

Mairi checked her guide. "Eighty-seven," she said. "Seven . . ." She blinked. "That's it. It stopped."

"Wait!" Mike said. "Look! It's beginning again."

Of course! The message would end and leave a gap of time before starting up again. Mairi watched carefully, jotting down each character long and short burst — each dot and dash — as it came up. Then, when it ended and restarted the cycle, she looked down at what she'd written and compared it to the cheat sheet. What . . . ?

"What does it say?" Mike asked.

Mairi held up the paper so that he could see what she'd written:

LOOK IN 1987.

CHAPTER
TWENTY-FOUR

"So we met another time traveler," Erasmus said, exasperated, "and he can't help us at all."

"At least he let us have some of his spare parts," Kyle said.

They were back at the site of the ruined and wrecked chronovessel, where Kyle now spilled out the contents of the garbage bag Lundergaard had given him to carry the parts. "I wish I could do more for you," the older man had said, "but I need everything else to start my company and get working on my own time travel solution. With any luck, twenty years from now, I'll be able to return to where I belong, to *your* future."

"But you'll be twenty years older!" Kyle had protested.

"At least I'll be back where I belong," Lundergaard had said sadly.

Now Kyle inspected the parts laid out before him. "I think this is everything we need. Well, except for some tools to put it all together. But I know where I can borrow them."

"Steal them, you mean."

"No, Erasmus. I'm just going to ask nicely."

Kyle sat in his father's tree house, waiting for the bedroom light to come on. It was close to bedtime, so Danny would have to come in soon.

Just then, the light flicked on. Kyle had a pebble in his hand he was going to throw at the window to get Danny's attention, but he held off. Gramps was coming into the room with Danny.

Kyle gritted his teeth. He flew to the bedroom window and hovered next to it, pressed close to the house.

"— *told* you!" Danny said.

"Don't back talk me," Gramps warned.

"Here it is. Like I said." Kyle realized Danny was showing Gramps the recovered Walkman.

"Well . . . good. But you shouldn't have lost it yesterday."

"I didn't lose it. I just couldn't find it."

"It's the same thing," Gramps said in an annoyed tone, a tone very close to the one he'd had the night before. "We work hard to give you nice things. You need to be responsible. If I ask to see something of yours, you show it to me, got it? If you're not responsible, there are consequences. Understand?"

"Yes, sir," Danny said.

There was a pause and then Danny said, "Dad?"

"What?" Gramps sounded farther away. He must have been leaving the room.

"You shouldn't have called me a loser," Danny said with the slightest tremble in his voice. Kyle couldn't believe what he was hearing. He risked moving a bit so that he could peek into the window.

"I shouldn't have lost the Walkman, but you shouldn't have said that to me. It's not right."

Gramps breathed in deep. "Go to bed," he said.

Danny folded his arms over his chest.

"Go. To. Bed."

Gramps shut off the light and closed the door, leaving Danny alone in the dark.

Kyle couldn't believe it. He was actually proud of his father.

He hated to ruin the moment, but he needed to. He sped back to the tree house and tossed his pebble. Danny opened the window. "Dore? Is that you?"

"Yeah. Can you let me in?"

Soon, he was sneaking into the basement with Danny.

"Your clothes are getting a little . . . ripe," his father said.

"I just need to borrow some tools and then I'll be out of here."

"You're really leaving, huh? Really running away."

Kyle paused as he gathered up the tools. "Yeah. I wish I could take you with me —"

"Don't. It's okay. I'll be all right here."

Kyle thought about it. "Yeah. I bet you will." He put the tools into a sack that Danny provided and told him where he could find them tomorrow.

"Wait," Danny said. "Before you go." He ran off and came back with a shirt and a pair of jeans. "Here. These are old. Mom won't notice they're missing."

Kyle took the clothes and tucked them into the sack. "Thanks, Dad," he said before he could stop himself.

"Dad?"

"Dan. I said, 'Thanks, Dan.'"

"Oh."

"He *believed* that?" Erasmus said into Kyle's ear as they left. "Your father really *is* an idiot!"

"Don't talk about my father that way," Kyle said, and they headed off to the chronovessel . . . and to their own time.

Hours later, deep in the thick of the cold, November night, Kyle realized he wouldn't be returning to his own time after all.

"I can't believe it," he said, sitting back on his haunches in the cornfield. All around him were rebuilt and reassembled components made with parts taken from Lundergaard's workshop.

The chronovessel itself stood before him, its chassis patched to the best of Kyle's abilities. It needed a couple of coats of paint and a ton of bodywork, but it was otherwise as good as new.

Except for one thing.

The computer.

The computer that controlled the whole thing.

They had all the pieces they needed to make the chronovessel run, but not the computer that could control it. That had been a custom-built component Kyle assembled in his basement, using parts only available in the twenty-first century. The technology to make microprocessors that small and that powerful hadn't been invented yet.

Kyle thought of the laptop in Lundergaard's basement. It wasn't perfect, but it was pretty close. He knew Lundergaard needed it, but maybe . . .

"Maybe I could just borrow it. . . ."

"It would be destroyed when we went to the future," Erasmus said. "And anyway, how would you send it back to him from our own time?"

That was true. Kyle knew it was true.

"Go through everything else you saw in his basement," Erasmus said, "and maybe I can jury-rig something."

It was frustrating — before his trip through time, *Kyle* would have been the one to "jury-rig something."

Before the trip through time, Kyle had a perfect memory, too. Right now, just trying to recall the details of a stupid basement was taxing Kyle's brainpower. Even though his normal intelligence was still higher than most people's, compared to his superintelligence — compared to *Erasmus* — he was an idiot. He hated being an idiot.

Kyle described the basement as best he could, right down to the big flat-screen TVs on the wall and the steel door with its lock.

"If you've described the room to me accurately," Erasmus said, putting an emphasis on the word *if* that Kyle didn't like, "then there's something wrong. Lundergaard said that the door concealed his reactor."

"Right. He's trying to generate power for time travel the old-fashioned way, with nuclear —"

"Did you see a Wi-Fi router in the basement anywhere?"

Kyle thought back. Wi-Fi routers were pretty small and not terribly noticeable. "I don't remember."

"Because, again, assuming you have the rough layout of the basement right . . . You're sure that the steel door was to your left as you entered the basement from outside?"

"Yes, Erasmus! I'm sure!"

"Because *that* is where the Wi-Fi signal I picked up was coming from. It was just a few yards in that direction."

"That's ridiculous," Kyle said. "Who puts their Wi-Fi router inside a reactor?"

"Unless there's no reactor . . ."

Kyle didn't pause to think. He didn't even pause to say something snarky. He just took off right away, blasting up into the atmosphere, high enough that no one could see him, then arcing down to Thorul Court at a blistering speed. It was night by now, and unless someone looked at him at exactly the right moment, no one would see him.

"Kyle, what are you —"

"He lied," Kyle growled. "Lundergaard lied." He was in the backyard of Lundergaard's house again. He could see a light on in a top-floor window, and he yearned to fling himself through the air, through that window, into whichever room Lundergaard was in, and then beat some answers out of the man.

But, no. That would come later. He still remembered the lingering pain of Lundergaard's force field. "First, we see what he's hiding," Kyle murmured. "Then we confront him."

"Be careful," Erasmus said as Kyle snapped off a shiny new chain and lock that had been put on the batwing door. Lundergaard had wasted no time.

Kyle crept back into the basement. Everything was as it had been before. He licked his lips at the sight of the laptop, but then told himself, *Later. First, we see what he's been hiding.*

The steel door had a truly massive lock on it, and the hinges were triple-reinforced. It took Kyle all of three seconds to wrench the lock free from its housing, complete with a loud, screeching sound that he was sure Lundergaard could hear three stories above. But nothing happened, so he went to open the door. "This is where the Wi-Fi signal is coming from?" he asked.

"Yes, but you do realize," Erasmus said, "that if there *is* a nuclear reactor in there, there's a chance you'll let loose enough radiation to kill half of Bouring?"

"I'd bet my life it's not a reactor."

"It's not *your* life you're betting," Erasmus said drily.

Kyle paused just a moment, then he opened the door. It was a thick and heavy slab of steel — six inches at least. Heavy, but the hinges were well-oiled, and the door swung open more easily than he would have imagined.

If it was a nuclear reactor, it was the darkest one Kyle had ever seen — the room beyond the door was utterly black. There was no way even to tell how big it was.

Under protest, Erasmus allowed Kyle to use him as a flashlight again, and the space lit up.

Kyle swallowed. Hard. He had imagined a lot. He had pictured many, many secrets Lundergaard could be keeping back here.

But not *this*.

A small room lurked behind the steel door, no more than six feet in any direction. More like an old root cellar, maybe. It smelled faintly of rot and dirt and sweat.

And there was a man.

A man chained to the wall.

Kyle was certain the man was dead, but then he blinked and lolled his head and looked directly at Kyle and said, in a voice cracked and hollow with disuse, "Help. Me."

CHAPTER
TWENTY-FIVE

For the first time in his memory, Kyle could not move, could not speak, could not even *think*. He simply stood there in the tiny room, frozen in place, unable to do anything but stare into the man's bloodshot blue eyes. Something familiar lurked in them, something that Kyle associated with pain. . . . It was on the fringe of his memory when Erasmus spoke up in his ear.

"Kyle! Kyle! You've been silent and motionless for thirty-seven seconds! What's going on?"

"I . . . I don't know," Kyle whispered.

"The Wi-Fi signal is directly in front of you. What do you see?"

The man licked his lips and took a deep breath. "Please," he whispered. "Please, help me. Hurry."

"It's a man," Kyle said. "I don't —"

"A man? What? That doesn't make any —"

"Oh, Kyle," said a voice from behind him, and Kyle knew it to be Lundergaard before he even turned around. This time, he didn't even give Lundergaard a chance to say anything else — he launched himself right at the older man at top speed.

CRACK! Kyle screamed as the force field sparked and zapped around him, throwing him back into the small room, the room he now realized was really a prison cell for the chained man. He shook spots from his eyes and shuddered through the pain, hurling himself at Lundergaard again.

FA-ZAMMMM! The force field did its dirty work again, and Kyle found himself writhing on the floor with pain.

"Did you really think I didn't have an alarm hooked up down here?" Lundergaard asked. "Did you really think I wouldn't turn on my force field before I came down here?" He made a clucking sound with his tongue. "You really *have* lost your superbrain, haven't you?"

"Kyle!" Erasmus screamed in his ear. "Kyle, are you all right? Talk to me! Kyle!"

"I'm . . . okay. . . ." Kyle said, forcing himself up onto his hands and knees. He glared at Lundergaard with pure hate, and Lundergaard just smiled an evil smile. "It feels like . . ."

And then Kyle understood. Understood everything. He looked back over his shoulder at the chained man, then whirled back to Lundergaard. "You have —"

"It's over, Kyle," Lundergaard said.

"But —"

"I thought I could let you live. Feed you some lies, the kind of lies a child would believe, and let you go on your way. Maybe you would find your way back through time and maybe you wouldn't. I don't care either way. But now you've found my little secret. I can't have that. I have the time capsule; that's all that matters. Good-bye, Kyle Camden."

"The time capsule!" Kyle had completely forgotten. "What do you want from it? What are you going to steal —"

Before Kyle could finish, Lundergaard lifted a hand — in it, he held the strange-looking pistol.

"Jack!" Kyle screamed. "Jack, turn it off!"

Lundergaard pulled the trigger and a burst of energy slammed into Kyle, hurling him back against the far wall, barely missing the chained man. Dirt exploded from the wall at the point of impact, and Kyle thought that maybe one of the chains loosened a bit. Not that it would matter. It was Jack, all right. He was sure of it. In no shape to do anything, really.

"It's Jack," he told Erasmus quickly. "Try to get him to shut everything off. Especially that gun."

"Jack? Jack who?"

But Lundergaard was already aiming the gun again. Kyle's body ached in anticipation.

At superspeed, Kyle slipped his earbuds out and slid them into Jack's ears instead, leaving Erasmus hanging around the man's neck, then he launched himself through the air.

Lundergaard chortled as he pulled the trigger again. But this time Kyle was ready for it — at the last possible instant, he arced up into the air, smashing through the ceiling of the basement, crashing through the floor of what looked like a living room, and immediately dived back down through the floor a few feet away.

It worked. He caught Lundergaard off guard, coming through the basement ceiling right behind the older man. He grabbed Lundergaard —

ZZZZZKKKLL!

The force field!

Kyle spun away from Lundergaard, twisting and groaning in pain. He knew where the force field had come from. He knew why it hurt so much.

Lundergaard spun around and fired his gun. Kyle dodged and the energy beam caught only the edge of his shoulder. Kyle grabbed a nearby table and hurled it at Lundergaard, who instinctively held up his arms to shield himself. The table wasn't alive — it could go through the force field . . . and it did, knocking the gun from Lundergaard's hand and — even better — knocking Lundergaard to the floor.

Kyle zipped over there, but first he paused for half a second to rip the steel door out of the wall. He stood over Lundergaard, the massive door held over his head like he was ready to squish a cockroach.

"I'm not dumb enough to try to touch you again," Kyle said, "but I will take great joy in breaking every bone in your body with this door if you don't start talking."

Lundergaard's eyes darted back and forth in panic. "Now, Kyle, you need to —"

"I need to give my arms a break because this thing is getting heavy," Kyle lied. "I'm thinking about dropping it on your head. I know that force field is only keyed to a plasma-powered body. Like mine."

Lundergaard reached into his pocket. Kyle drew in a deep breath. He couldn't stop Lundergaard without actually crushing the man to death with the door . . . and he wasn't willing to cross that line, even for a lying, time-traveling bad guy like Walter Lundergaard. It just wasn't right.

Besides — he still had questions he needed answered, and Lundergaard was the guy to answer them.

"I will squash you like roadkill," Kyle growled in his most threatening voice.

Lundergaard called his bluff; he pulled a gadget from his pocket and pushed a button.

And everything exploded.

✳   ✳   ✳

Sirens.

The sirens woke Kyle from what had been a hard, black sleep. More accurately, a complete unconsciousness. He wondered how long he'd been out cold.

He also wondered how long he'd been on fire.

Kyle shouted, beating his body with his invulnerable hands to put out the fire. Flames couldn't hurt him, but he didn't want to be running around Bouring naked, clothes burned off. He figured even in 1987 people would frown on that.

All around him, the workshop was in flames. Sparks spat into the air. The big TVs were melting and the air smelled like burned plastic. The lights had gone out, but the fire made the room a moving sculpture of light and dark.

Lundergaard was nowhere to be seen.

Kyle hit the ground and rolled to put out the last of the flames licking at him, managing to maneuver his way back into the small prison room at the same time. The fire hadn't moved here yet, but it was only a matter of time.

Jack — it really *was* Jack, Kyle was certain of it — leaned against the wall, unconscious. Kyle crawled over and reclaimed Erasmus.

"— not sure *why* I'm telling you this," Erasmus was saying, "but for the forty-second time: Jack, please turn everything off. Can you hear me, Jack?"

"It's me, Erasmus. I'm back."

"Kyle!" Erasmus actually sounded relieved. "What's going on? There was an explosion and then three minutes went by and I kept talking to this person who never responded —"

"Three minutes? And the fire trucks are already here? Let's hear it for the Bouring FD," Kyle said.

"We need to get out of here," Erasmus said.

"Yeah," Kyle said. "Fire can't hurt me, but it can hurt Jack." He snapped the chains holding Jack to the wall and slung the man over his shoulders. "Still, we might be able to scavenge *some*thing. Even with the lights out, I can see well enough to grab a few more . . . Ack!"

As he spoke, Kyle had stood up, directly into a cloud of acrid smoke that blinded him and sent him into a choking spasm. It felt like it would never end, as though he'd sucked a pound of sand down his throat and into his lungs. He doubled over and collapsed to the floor, gasping.

He was fireproof, but his lungs, it turned out, weren't smoke-proof. A minor detail, but an important one. Past experience had proven that Kyle didn't need to breathe for long stretches at a time, but when he *did* breathe, he was just as susceptible to smoke inhalation as anyone else, apparently.

"Kyle? Kyle, are you all right?"

"Yeah." He coughed and spat out a wad of something thick, black, and gross. "But I think I just need to get us out of here."

"Indeed. The temperature is rising. Clearly, Lundergaard wants to destroy all evidence of the lab."

Kyle held his breath and fumbled in the smoky darkness. He had what he needed to repair the time machine, but he wanted more.

But he wouldn't get it.

Then he launched himself through the hole he'd made in the ceiling before and kept going at an angle, smashing open the ceiling of the first floor with his fist, then the second floor, then through the back wall of the house, exploding into the open air. A massive gout of flame followed him, a huge fireball roaring at him like a dragon from its cage. Kyle hovered in the night sky for a moment, wondering if he should try to put the fire out. But below him, the Bouring Fire Department was already on the scene, and Kyle knew they would extinguish the blaze before it could spread. After all, that's how it was in his own time.

He was starting to get the hang of being in the past.

Under cover of smoke and night, Kyle flew away, still cradling Jack, who was breathing evenly.

"Were you able to grab anything else from the lab?" Erasmus asked.

"No. Just Jack."

"And what's *that* about?" Erasmus asked. "Jack *who*? Why did you have me talking to him? Who *is* he?"

Feeling the weight of the man in his arms, Kyle drew in a deep breath. "It's Jack Stanley, Erasmus. It's the Mad Mask."

CHAPTER
TWENTY-SIX

" 'Look in 1987'?" Mighty Mike said. "What's a 1987?"

"It's not a thing," Mairi said. "It's a year."

"Oh. Right. Of course." Mike scratched his head. "I still don't understand." He looked at Mairi hopefully, as though assuming she could figure it out, or already had.

Yeah, right — she wished. It made no sense to her whatsoever.

"You're bleeding," Mike said, pointing.

Mairi looked down at her arm, which still streamed with blood. In all the running and flying and racing away from zombies, she'd completely forgotten about it. "It's not that bad," she said, even though she knew it was. It should have stopped on its own by now.

Mike held up his own bandaged hand. "I disagree. I think it's probably bad. Here." He ripped off the edge of his cape and wrapped it around her arm, tying it tightly to keep it in place. "That will stench the blood loss."

"Stanch," Mairi corrected him automatically. 1987 . . . What in the world could that mean? Were they supposed to go look in a book about 1987? Her dad had a shelf of old almanacs in the basement — would the one for the year 1987 have some kind of information in it? And who had left this message? And why? What on earth was going on here?

"Mairi?" Mike interrupted. "I'm just wondering if you have any thoughts or ideas . . . ? My brain is sort of empty right now."

Mike's expression was open and honest and utterly clueless. He was the most powerful kid on the planet (or had been, at least, until the zombies came), and now he was just as helpless as she was. What were they going to do? How could they get help?

A new thought occurred to her: It was possible that she and Mike were the last non-zombified people in all of Bouring. Meaning that any help would have to come from the outside. But what if the zombies spread? What if they moved on to other towns, other cities? If Mighty Mike couldn't stop them, then maybe *nothing* could stop them. And then . . .

She took a deep breath and leaned against the wall to collect herself. She couldn't panic. Not now. Not even though she really, really wanted to panic and figured she deserved it after everything she'd been through.

"What do they want?" she murmured.

"What does who want?" asked Mike.

"The zombies. They were chasing me. Us. Why? What do they want?" As long as she kept talking and thinking, her arm and her twisted ankle didn't hurt so bad.

Mike frowned, his brow furrowed in deep thought. "I saw a documentary once," he said, "which explanationed that zombies like to eat human brains."

"That wasn't a documentary, Mike. It was a movie. It was fake. Made up."

Mike tilted his head like a confused puppy. "Really? Truly?"

"Yes."

"It seemed very real."

"Trust me."

Mike leaned in close. "Why would someone invent something that horrible?"

He seemed genuinely concerned, as though he just couldn't imagine why someone would want to make a horror movie, forgetting for the moment that he was actually *living* in a horror movie.

"We can talk about that another time," she said. "Right now we have to figure out the deal with these zombies so that we can stop them. If we can figure out what they want, maybe that will give us a clue."

"They want people to slow down," Mike said confidently.

"What do you mean?"

"Well, I noticed right after the extrusion that the zombies all went after the people who were running away." He shivered. "There were a lot of people running. I tried to help them all, Mairi." He grabbed her arm — the uninjured one — and squeezed urgently. "I really tried. I tried, but I couldn't —"

"I know, Mike. I know. It's all right." She peeled his fingers away and took his hand in her own. "I know you tried. This isn't your fault. The town would have opened that time capsule even if you hadn't. What else did you see?"

"Every time they caught someone, that person would stop running and fall down. That's all."

Just as she'd witnessed with the Great Nemesis and the sheriff. One moment, Sheriff Monroe had been moving just fine, the next — flump! On the ground.

"And once people stopped moving, the zombies lost all interest in them," Mike went on. "Which makes sense now that I know that they don't actually eat brains. Before, I was confused."

So, Mairi thought, *they stop people from moving and then move on. . . . But why? What are they trying to do?* "None of this makes any sense."

"Especially since we've already looked in 1987," Mike said.

Mairi waved him away. "One mystery at a time, Mike. We'll figure out who sent that message after we figure out how to stop the —" She broke off and now it was her turn to look confused. "Wait. What did you mean by 'we've already looked in 1987'?"

"I . . ." He looked like he was afraid he'd done or said something wrong. "I just meant . . . The capsule I opened . . . At the ceremony? That one? It said '1987' on it. But you're right. That's nothing to worry about right now. The zombies are more important."

Mairi waved him quiet again. 1987 . . . The time capsule that had started all of this *was* the 1987 capsule. And now they were being told to "look in 1987." That couldn't be a coincidence. Could it?

"It has to be connected," Mairi said. "Someone's sending us a message."

"But we already looked in 1987. That started all of this." He gestured beyond the walls, beyond the house. Once again, Mairi wondered how many normal people — if any — were left in Bouring.

She licked her lips.

And then she surprised both Mike and herself when she said, "I know what we need to do."

CHAPTER
TWENTY–SEVEN

"The Mad Mask?" Erasmus yelped for the umpteenth time. "Are you *serious*?"

By now, they had returned to the site of the partly reassembled chronovessel. The useless chronovessel, without its supercomputer core. Jack Stanley — the Mad Mask — lay unconscious and breathing evenly on the ground, one arm curled around a cornstalk as if even in dreams the Mad Mask feared falling.

"Yeah," Kyle said. "It's him." He crouched down next to his old foe. A shiver ran through him as he remembered — mere weeks ago in his personal timeline — thrashing his way through a small army of look-alike MadDroids in order to finally turn the brain-wave manipulator on his enemy and end Ultitron's rampage through Bouring.

And to save Mairi . . .

Kyle sighed. He'd been forced to wear the Mad Mask's mask, and when he'd taken it off, Mairi had seen . . .

"He's older than the last time we saw him," Kyle went on, tamping down the memories. "And he looks terrible. Underfed. Exhausted. He must be from some point in *our* future."

"This is getting ridiculous," Erasmus complained. "Is *everybody* a freaking time traveler?"

Kyle chuckled. "I should have realized it the first time Lundergaard used that force field against me — it's the exact same force field the Mad Mask used."

"Kyle, if this is the Mad Mask, then you can't trust him. You need to —"

"He's been chained up in a dungeon by Lundergaard for who knows how long. Haven't you ever heard the expression 'The enemy of my enemy is my friend'?"

"Yes. I've also heard the expression 'There is no honor among thieves.'"

"Well, I —" Kyle broke off as Jack mumbled something and then woke up as if he'd been set on fire, jerking into a sitting position and nearly ripping the cornstalk out of the ground.

"I'll do it! I'll do it!" the Mad Mask screamed. "Don't hurt me! Don't . . ." He stopped, looking up. "The stars . . ." he whispered in amazement. "I'm *outside*. . . ."

"Jack." Kyle took the Mad Mask's chin and turned his face so that their eyes met. "Jack, listen to me. How long have you been chained up in there? What was he doing to you?"

The Mad Mask blinked once, very slowly, then several more times, very quickly. It was as though something deep within him had broken and was now repairing itself. "Kyle?" he asked after a long moment of silence. "Is that you?"

"Of course it's me. But how did you get so old?"

The Mad Mask laughed, his head thrown back, and for just a second or two, Kyle thought he detected some of the old bravado of the enemy he'd once known. But it faded quickly, replaced by the new, humbled, broken man before him.

"That's funny," Jack said. "I was about to ask *you* how you got so *young*. But it must be the time travel, right? We're both in the same time period right now, but we're both *from* different time periods. Right?"

Kyle nodded.

"So I'm from your future."

Kyle nodded again.

Jack took a deep breath. "I think I need something to eat. It feels like it's been years. And then, oh, boy, have I got a story for you. . . ."

Kyle felt bad about doing it, but the Mad Mask *did* seem to be starving — Kyle thought he could see Jack's ribs right through the holes in his old, ripped-up shirt — so he moved at superspeed and snagged a sandwich, a soda, and a couple of bags of chips from a convenience store on Major Street. The convenience store itself was no longer around in Kyle's time — it was a bank — and he wondered if the mysterious disappearance of some of its inventory back in 1987 had contributed to it going out of business.

Jack tore into the sandwich as if he'd been starved for days. And maybe he had been.

"How long has Lundergaard been holding you like that?" Kyle asked.

"Pretty much since we got here," Jack said around a mouthful.

"How long have you been here in 1987?" Kyle asked.

"1987?" Jack almost choked on his food. "It's 1987? We've been here *years*, then. It's been so long and I've been locked up, but I know it was much earlier than that when we arrived."

Kyle swallowed hard, as if trying to gulp down a steel ball. Years? He'd been trapped in the past for a day or so and it was already driving him nuts. How could anyone have tolerated being in the past for so long . . . and being locked up and tortured and made a slave on top of all that?

"Lundergaard has a lot to answer for," Kyle said.

Jack nodded knowingly. "He's some sort of . . . He's some kind of time-traveling bandit," he said. "I don't know where in the timestream he comes from, to be honest. At this point, maybe *he* doesn't even remember anymore. I don't know. He's crazy, so who can tell? At first I thought I could trust him. He said . . ." Jack shook his head. "I should start from the beginning. Or *my* beginning at least."

"In my future," Kyle said.

"Yes."

"This is crazy," Erasmus said.

"Be quiet and listen," Kyle scolded.

Jack grinned. "Talking to Erasmus, huh? Hey there, Erasmus."

Kyle had almost forgotten — in his own time, the Mad Mask had learned about the existence of Erasmus. And now — at some point in his future — he would let Walter Lundergaard in on the secret, too. Why?

"I'm not talking to *him*," Erasmus said. "I don't trust him. His superpower to make electronics do whatever he wants is dangerous to me."

"He probably doesn't trust me," the Mad Mask said, even though he couldn't hear what was in Kyle's earbud. Or could he? Did his power let him eavesdrop on Erasmus's digital voice?

"Just tell me what happened," Kyle said. "Tell me how you got here." *Because maybe that will help me get home.*

Jack nodded. He looked down at the sandwich as though he didn't know what it was, as though it had

243

turned into a hamster in his hands. Kyle realized that Jack had been stalling — he didn't want to talk about the future. He didn't want to *think* about it. He wanted to forget everything that had led him to this moment.

And maybe part of that is my fault. After all, I did erase part of his memory with the brain-wave manipulator. Kyle shivered with guilt. Was this broken man in front of him the result of the brain-wave manipulator? If so, what fates awaited his parents?

What would happen to Mairi?

"There was a battle . . ." Jack began, his eyes haunted. He stopped himself, blinked one supremely slow, endless blink, then shook his head. "A war," he emended. "There was a war. *Will be* a war, I guess, is the right way to put it. In the future. Your future."

"There's always wars —"

"No. This one is . . ." Jack paused to think. "There was you. And me. And Mike, of course. And the Giggler —"

"The Giggler?"

"Never mind. He doesn't matter. You won't meet him for a while. But there was Lundergaard, obviously, and it was all tied up in the Heroes' Club and the secrecy and —" He babbled on and on, his words slurring together as he spoke, as though he had to speak them as quickly as possible. Kyle finally reached out and took his hand to guide him back into the moment, into the real and the now.

"Jack, talk to me. What's going on here?"

"I . . . I don't know how much of it I can tell you. Time paradoxes . . ."

"Forget about time paradoxes. Just focus. Tell me how you got to 1987."

The Mad Mask nodded. "Okay. Right. During the war . . . Let's just say there was a betrayal, okay? And Lundergaard and I ended up thrown back in time. Together. And he swore he'd get us back to the present, but then . . ."

"Another betrayal," Kyle guessed.

Jack sighed. "Yeah. He was obsessed with my superpower. And it made sense — he was a genius. He *is* a genius. So I listened to him and I did what he told me to do. I thought it would get us home. At first it was just, like, 'Help me get this computer running, Jack.' 'See if you can make this laser more powerful, Jack.' 'Make this toaster generate a Wi-Fi signal, Jack.' But the next thing I knew, he'd had me create a gadget that gave him *control* over me. . . ."

"And then used you to create more gadgets."

"Yep."

Kyle sat back on his haunches, thinking.

"You can't trust him," Erasmus said. "He's insane. Remember Ultitron? Remember how he kidnapped Mairi?"

"That was a long time ago," Kyle murmured, hoping Jack couldn't hear.

"It was only a couple of weeks ago!"

"To us. To him, it was years ago. More than fifteen, from the looks of him."

Jack opened one of the bags of chips and pawed around inside it. "You don't trust me, do you?" he asked idly, as if unoffended by the idea.

"You have to admit —"

"I did some crazy stuff to you when we were kids," Jack admitted. "I don't blame you for being suspicious."

"Well, there's that," Kyle said, "and also, since the time travel, my brain's been kind of on the fritz —"

"Don't tell him that!" Erasmus cried.

"— so I'm thinking extra hard about things."

Jack frowned. "Your brain . . . ? Oh, right. I remember now. I remember you telling me how the first time you traveled through time, it affected your intelligence. I can fix that."

"What?" Kyle and Erasmus said at the same time.

"Sure. Piece of cake." The Mad Mask dropped the chips and scrounged around the spare parts Kyle had strewn around the chronovessel. He started snapping pieces together, humming a little under his breath as he did so.

"What are you doing?" Kyle asked.

"Just building a little gadget that will restore your intellect. It's easy. Remember: The electronics don't actually have to work. My superpower *makes* them work."

He brandished his device, a motley collection of twisted wires, screws, bolts, and a single burned-out circuit board.

"That won't do —" Kyle stopped speaking as Jack's brow furrowed, his mouth tightened in a thin line. . . .

And the device flared to life! A burst of light erupted from the dead circuitry and zapped Kyle right between the eyes. He jerked back, but there was no pain.

It must have been an electrical neuron burst piggybacked on a neutrino carrier wave, he thought. *That could pass through me harmlessly and still —*

"I have some good news," Kyle announced to Erasmus. His memory of Wikipedia was nearly complete now, and when he glanced at the sky, he found that not only could he identify each star, but he could also remember when it had been discovered and by whom. "My thoughts are more complicated. I think my superbrain is back online."

"Great. Use that superbrain to figure out if we can trust the Mad Mask. I doubt it, though."

Kyle looked over at his old nemesis, who looked twice as exhausted now. "Sorry," Jack whispered. "He's been pushing me so hard lately . . . I just need some rest. . . ."

He started to lie back down in the corn, but Kyle couldn't let him crash on the cold ground again. "Hang on, Jack." He gathered up the Mad Mask in his arms and took to the night sky.

Soon, they were in the backyard of the Camden house. Kyle scouted quickly and when he was sure no one was looking, he darted into the tree house. The sleeping bag was still there, and he tucked Jack into it.

"Thanks, Kyle," the Mad Mask mumbled. "You're a good friend. . . ."

Kyle watched him drift off into a smooth and untroubled sleep.

A good friend . . . to my enemy? Maybe. But what about to Mairi? I have to make up to her what I did. Somehow. I have to get back to my time.

Kyle eyed Erasmus's power reading. He'd been able to charge up the iPod during the day, but his battery power was pretty low again. "Let me fill you up. Then we'll see what we can do now that my brain is back online."

Dressed in his father's hand-me-downs, Kyle headed back into town and looked for a twenty-four-hour gas station or convenience store. Only . . . no such thing existed in Bouring in 1987, it seemed. The place where he'd swiped Jack's sandwich and chips was now closed and dark. So he went back to the junior high, since he knew he could get in. In the Attendance office, he plugged Erasmus into the wall and waited as he charged, strumming his fingers on the keyboard to the ancient computer.

"I bet I know what you're thinking," Erasmus said.

"Given that our brains are nearly identical, that's a pretty bad bet for me to take."

"You're wondering if Jack's superpower could fix the chronovessel."

Kyle shrugged. The movement was lost on Erasmus, but sometimes you just need a good shrug. "I don't know. I wasn't really wondering it. I was more thinking in that direction."

"I don't trust —"

"It's a moot point. He's so weak and his power takes so much out of him that I doubt he could handle something that big at this point. And besides, he'd need to make a —" He broke off and sat up straight. "Hey, Erasmus!"

"Yes?"

"We need a supercomputer to run the chronovessel, right?"

"Right."

"What if we *had* a supercomputer, but it was really big, not really small?"

Erasmus pondered. "How big?"

"As big as the world," Kyle said, grinning.

CHAPTER
TWENTY-EIGHT

Kyle's fingers pounded the keyboard before him, bringing the computer to life.

"Kyle, what are you talking about?" Erasmus demanded. "A computer as big as the world won't fit in the chronovessel."

"It doesn't need to!" Kyle exclaimed. "We just need the computing *power*, not the computer itself. If I can calculate all the possible vectors and odds of our trip, I can preload them into the system before we leave. It'll be slower, but we *should* be able to make it!"

"That won't work! First of all, it's *too* slow. It's like counting from one to a million by ones instead of by thousands. And second of all, you don't *have* a supercomputer to begin with."

"Yes, I do! It's called the Internet."

"The Internet doesn't exist —"

"— yet," Kyle finished. "*Yet*. But all of the infrastructure is there. You said it yourself. There are 56 Kbps backbones in place. Military and government and academic networks already connected. It's just a matter of getting them to talk to one another."

"But they don't know one another!"

"It doesn't matter!" Kyle crowed. "Have you ever heard of six degrees of separation?" Before Erasmus could say, "Of course I have," Kyle went on, typing as he spoke. Talking through this out loud helped him.

"Six degrees of separation is a theory that everyone on Earth is interconnected, that I know someone who knows someone who knows someone else and three more someones in the chain until you can reach any other person on the planet. The president, the pope, the guy who washes cars in New Zealand. Anyone.

"This computer is just sitting here in this office," Kyle went on, "but it knows the county school board computer." At the Main Menu, he typed *C* for *County*. "Now I'm logging into the county computer. And the county computer knows the state board of education computer. And *that* computer knows a bunch of other computers. And eventually one of them — *one* of them is all it takes — will know a university computer. And that computer knows a bunch of other university computers, and one of *those* computers will know a military computer because the military does a lot of work with colleges. Get it?"

"Kyle . . . the security . . ."

Kyle laughed. "*What* security? Computer security is a joke in this era." He typed furiously. "I just hacked into the governor's computer from the state board of education. Computer viruses barely even exist at this point. No one's even really seen a dangerous Trojan horse. And encryption is weak, weak, weak!"

Kyle kept typing, connecting to more and more and bigger and bigger computers out there in the world. "I'm hacking the entire Internet!" he chortled. "This is the greatest prank ever!"

"You're not hacking the Internet," Erasmus whispered. "You're *inventing* it."

Around the country — and then around the world — computers began misbehaving. No one knew why. No one could figure it out. It seemed to be a hacker attack, but on a scale no one could imagine — it would have to be thousands of hackers, all working at the same time. . . .

Or one superintelligent twelve-year-old with all the knowledge of the next few decades.

In missile silos in Nebraska, soldiers panicked as they lost control of their systems. Banks in Switzerland were suddenly unable to calculate balances. In Moscow, airlines shut down as their computerized control systems began calculating physics problems that no one could understand.

There was no Internet in 1987, but that didn't mean Kyle couldn't create one for himself.

There was only one problem: It wasn't enough.

Even with all the processing power of thousands of computers around the world, Kyle couldn't attain his goal. The systems were too weak, their connections too tenuous and slow. It was like swimming in tar. By the time one computer was ready to hand off its conclusions to another, the next computer in the chain was just coming online due to slow data transmission speeds. Kyle tried to compensate, but nothing he did worked. He could type at his top speed and it didn't matter — the computer in front of him could only receive those keystrokes so quickly. Kyle was too fast for it. Too fast for the slow data backbones.

Too fast and, paradoxically, too late.

There was nothing he could do.

He'd failed.

Kyle slumped in the chair, not moving. He didn't know how much time had gone by. It felt like days — like weeks — but the sky was only now beginning to lighten to the east, so he knew it had only been a few hours.

He had done his best. No one could say otherwise.

With a few keystrokes, he disconnected from the proto-Internet he'd created. Poof. It was like it had never existed. In a few years, though, an even better version would come into existence, and this time it would stay.

With a sigh, he said, "Lundergaard said this was my first trip through time. Looks like it's my last, too."

"But if he knows for sure that you travel again . . ."

"Sorry, Erasmus. You have the schematics yourself. The chronovessel isn't going anywhere. Er, any*when*, I mean."

"Then we've created a time paradox. Lundergaard remembers you traveling again, but you can't. So . . ."

"So what?"

Erasmus said the three hardest words an AI can ever say: "I don't know."

Kyle stared out the window. "Yeah. Neither do I, pal."

He had never felt this way before. All his life, he'd been able to accomplish just about anything he set his mind to, whether it was outwitting his parents, making his teachers look like fools, or pulling the wool over Sheriff Monroe's eyes. Yes, he had had setbacks before, but never had he failed so completely, so abjectly. What was his next step? What should he do now?

"I guess we should trash the school," Erasmus said.

Good point. Kyle couldn't risk someone figuring out why he'd been in the school. There was a slim chance that someone could see what he'd done on the computer and trace it back to Danny, which Kyle could not abide. So he tossed the computer on the floor, where it popped into a somewhat disappointing display of sparks.

Then he went and wrecked the school so that it would look like vandals had come through and randomly trashed the place. He ripped open lockers and scattered their contents down the hallways. Broke into the cafeteria freezer and hauled frozen food out into the classrooms to melt there. Spilled gallons of paint and cleaner from the maintenance room on walls and floors.

It wasn't nearly as much fun as Kyle thought it would be.

He flew off in the predawn light. But where could he go? He was an exile here. He wouldn't even be *born* for years and years and years.

Off to the west, the smoke column from the coal mine rose, a thick, black, twisted pillar of choking carcinogens and pollution. His nose wrinkled. Ugh. This was his fate. Trapped in a primitive age of coal mining and no Internet and televisions that were big and boxy and pixelated. What a tremendous pile of garbage his life had become.

He looked north — the Bouring Lighthouse stood against the lightening sky. Kyle put in a burst of speed and soon was at the top of the lighthouse. He landed on the balcony that ran around the structure and leaned against the railing, gazing down at Bouring. He heaved out a tremendous sigh.

"So, trashing the school didn't make you feel any better?" Erasmus asked.

"Not really." As a younger kid, he'd fantasized about wrecking the place, but now that he'd done it, it lacked something. It wasn't sophisticated. It wasn't pranksterish. It was just random, wanton destruction.

Like the "zombies" he'd seen in his own time, wandering the town, destroying everything in their path.

"But wait," he mumbled. "They *weren't* destroying everything in their path."

"What are you talking about?"

"Be quiet for a second, Erasmus." Kyle thought. The zombies hadn't been *destroying* things. He remembered now, flying over Bouring the night he'd left the twenty-first century — they had been attacking things that *moved*. Even windblown street signs. They weren't destroying things at all. It was more like they . . . like they wanted things to be still . . . ?

"That doesn't make any sense. . . ."

"Kyle, talk to me. That's why you built me."

Kyle quickly filled him in on what he'd realized about the zombies. "But I'm not sure what it means."

"Don't you see, Kyle? It's all about the time capsule. Lundergaard stole it."

Kyle smacked his forehead with the heel of his palm. "Of course! I'm an idiot! I was thinking he wanted to steal something *from* it. But he put something *into* it."

"And then he buried it in the plot for the year we came from," Erasmus went on, "and when it was dug up —"

"It caused the zombie plague."

"But why? Why would he do that?"

Kyle didn't have an answer to that. "I'm not sure it matters. If Lundergaard is doing it, it can't be for a good reason. He's up to something —" And then it hit Kyle. He knew exactly what Lundergaard was up to, and he launched himself from the top of the lighthouse and flew as fast as he could.

"Darn it!" Kyle exclaimed.

"Nothing?" Erasmus asked.

"Nothing," Kyle agreed.

He knelt down on the grass at the burial site for the Bouring time capsules. Twenty yards away was the hole for the 1987 capsule, dug a few days ago by deputies, then staked and roped off for safety. Nothing would ever be buried there, now. The time capsule was with Lundergaard.

And would — in the future — be unearthed from the very spot where Kyle now knelt.

He had hoped to come here and dig up the time capsule, thereby foiling Lundergaard's plans and saving the future, but there were no signs at all that the dirt here had been disturbed. The time capsule wasn't buried. Not yet.

"He could bury it any time between now and the day it's dug up," Kyle realized.

"We'll have to check," Erasmus said. "We'll check every few days, and see if the ground is disturbed. . . . We'll keep checking. . . ."

"Yeah, for the next few *decades*," Kyle said. "If we could only find Lundergaard . . ."

"He blew up his own house to get away from us. I think he'll be difficult to find."

"Maybe there's a clue back at what's left of his lab. . . ."

"Or maybe you should just talk to his accomplice," Erasmus said drily. "Assuming he's still in the tree house."

Duh! In all the excitement of hacking the Internet, Kyle had completely forgotten that the Mad Mask was sleeping peacefully in his father's tree house. Bouring was waking up, so he stuck to the ground, moving quickly, using trees and parked cars for cover. In the backyard, he looked up at the empty window of the tree house.

"I bet you a million dollars he's already gone," Erasmus grumbled.

"I'll take that bet," Kyle said. "I have a feeling."

"You and your 'feelings.' "

Kyle scrambled up the ladder and poked his head into the tree house. He had a moment of panic when he didn't see the Mad Mask, but then he realized that Jack was still here — he'd just turned around in the sleeping bag, facing away from Kyle.

"You can deposit that million bucks any time you want," Kyle said.

The Mad Mask rolled over to face Kyle, rubbing his eyes. A good night's sleep seemed to have done him a world of good — his eyes were brighter, his expression less downtrodden. He visibly perked up at the sight of Kyle.

"Kyle! For a minute there, when I woke up, I thought maybe I was dreaming that I'd escaped. But I really did, didn't I?"

"Yeah, with a little help," Erasmus snarked.

Kyle chose not to relay that message. "You're free of Lundergaard, for sure. But we need to talk some more."

"Of course."

It had been risky enough planting Jack in the tree house overnight in the first place; Kyle wasn't about to compound the risk by hanging out when everyone in the Camden house was awake. He flew the two of them to the top of the lighthouse for privacy. In his own time, there was a chance Mairi's mom would be puttering around up there, but in 1987, the lighthouse was abandoned. They stared at each other for a moment. It was unreal — Jack Stanley, so much older (and saner!) than the last time Kyle had seen him, three weeks ago, running like a lunatic through the sewers of Bouring, raving about his deformed face. . . .

"So," Kyle said, "I, uh, see that pimple of yours has cleared up."

The Mad Mask leveled a quizzical look at Kyle, then memory flashed in his eyes. "Oh, right. Right. I really *was* crazy, back in the day, wasn't I?"

"You referred to yourself in the third person. All. The. Time."

"Was that annoying?"

"You have no idea."

"Sorry." A shrug.

"You can make up for it now. I need you to tell me everything you know about Lundergaard's plans," Kyle said. "I have to get back to my own time, and once I do, I'll need to know how to stop him."

Jack sighed and rested his chin in his palm, gazing out over the 1987 Bouring skyline. "I wish I could tell you everything, Kyle. But I don't know much. I was basically his slave. And his computer. A combination of the two. Once he had me create a sort of functioning brain-wave manipulator, he could erase and restore my memories whenever he wanted. He kept me just aware enough to build things for him, to power them."

Kyle's guts squirmed at the thought of being so enslaved. Yes, Jack had done something horrible — he'd built Ultitron and nearly destroyed Bouring — but no one deserved the torment he'd been undergoing at the hands of Walter Lundergaard.

"There's nothing you can remember about his plan?"

"I just know that a couple of days ago, he got really excited. He told me we had a guest coming."

"A guest?"

"What guest?" Erasmus asked.

Jack shrugged. "Yeah. His exact words: 'We need to be ready, Jackie-boy.' He called me that all the time. I hated it. 'We need to be ready, Jackie-boy. Our guest is coming.'" Jack frowned. "And then he said something like, 'Exactly on schedule.' And he had me create a gadget for him that could collect zero-point energy —"

"Kyle!" Erasmus shouted at top volume.

"Yeow!" Kyle yanked his earbud out. "Keep it down!"

When he reinserted the earbud a moment later, Erasmus was at the tail end of a halfhearted apology. ". . . be able to handle a little shout anyway. But listen, here's the important thing, Kyle — *you* are the guest!"

"Of course. . . ." Kyle whispered. It made perfect sense. "That's why we ended up here in 1987. Lundergaard knew we would be here." Kyle smacked a fist into his palm. "There was someone watching us when we 'landed' here, someone who followed me all the way to the library with Danny. It must have been Lundergaard all along. He knows us in our future, so he knew exactly when we would land in 1987. And he had Jack build a gadget to suck up the zero-point energy from the chronovessel —"

"— to power whatever nefarious plot he has going on," Erasmus said, picking up the thread. "And since he was siphoning our energy —"

"— the chronovessel pooped out and we ended up in 1987!" Kyle finished.

Jack stared at him. "It's really strange watching you have half a conversation with yourself."

Kyle waved it away. "Not now."

"But I remember something else, Kyle. It wasn't just the zero-point energy collector."

"Uh-oh," said Erasmus. "This won't be good, I bet."

"It had to do with *you*!" Jack said in horror, his expression guilty and terrified at once.

"I told you," Erasmus singsonged.

"He wanted to be able to . . . to *scan* you. He had me build a device that recorded everything about you as soon as you walked into his house!"

"Say that again?" Kyle's head was spinning.

Jack jumped up, speaking rapidly. "It was his special

project. We collected the zero-point energy and then . . ." Jack stomped his feet in frustration. "I'm trying to remember! I really am!"

"I know, Jack," Kyle said gently. "Take your time."

"Don't coddle him!" Erasmus demanded. "He helped get us into this situation!"

"And now he's going to help us get out," Kyle said with confidence. "Talk it out, Jack."

"His plan . . . Somehow it's tied into you." Jack shook his head. "No, not *you*. Your powers. The way they work. He gathered — he had *me* gather — all this information about your biology and physiology. About your powers, Kyle. How they work. How the plasma storm altered you on a quantum level, making you superhuman."

Kyle rocked back on his heels. Incredible! With the Mad Mask's help, Lundergaard had managed to study Kyle without Kyle being aware of it.

"And — oh. Oh, Kyle . . . I can't remember it all, but . . . something to do with a time capsule. I remember that part really well. Because I assumed it would have to do with a time *machine*, but he specifically said time *capsule*."

"So . . ."

"He has your journal," Jack said. "I just remembered. I couldn't read it — it was in some kind of code —"

"A symmetric polyalphabetic cipher," Kyle said with justifiable pride. "I created it myself."

"Well, at some point, Lundergaard got ahold of it. He cracked your code. That's how he knew . . ."

"That's how he knew everything," Kyle whispered. "It's how he knew I would time travel. . . ."

"It's how he knew we would leave the day of the time capsule burial," Erasmus added. "That's why he planned whatever-it-is for that day. Because he knew you'd be out of the way, trapped in the past."

"Whatever Lundergaard did to the time capsule, it had something to do with your powers," Jack said.

"What?" That made no sense at all! Unless . . . Unless the "zombies" weren't really zombies after all. What if they were just plasma-powered drones? What if Lundergaard had done something to them and then sent them out to . . . to . . . "To what?" he asked aloud.

"Maybe if we knew his ultimate goal," Erasmus offered, "we could figure out what he was doing with the time capsule."

"Well, if I had a time capsule," Kyle said, "I would put a message in it, telling someone to get me back from 1987. But there's no one in 1987 smart enough to —"

He broke off because in that instant he figured it out. Erasmus did, too, because they started talking at the same time:

"He's building an endpoint — !"

"— figured out how to time travel without a chronovessel!"

They babbled over each other for a moment until the Mad Mask finally shouted, "Stop it! I can only hear half the conversation!" and when Kyle stopped to take a breath, Erasmus said, "He can't build a chronovessel in *this* time period, but he's figured out how to time travel without one."

Kyle quickly filled Jack in on what he and Erasmus had figured out. "Look, it's simple, once you have all the pieces. Lundergaard's making a puzzle, and the final solution to the puzzle is going to send him through time. The zombies are the key. He created them in our time by putting something in the time capsule, something that uses the same plasma science that gave me and Mighty Mike our powers. Heck, the same plasma that gave *you* your powers, Jack. When I saw the zombies before we came back to 1987, I thought they were after *motion* but they're not; they're absorbing *time* from things. Stealing it. Movement is just a function of time — you move because you have the time to do it. The zombies are freezing things in time with some kind of artificial super-power created —"

"— created by the same phenomenon that gave us our powers!" Jack said, catching on. "And when they absorb enough of it —"

"— they'll create a time-dense endpoint in our time. Dense enough to pull Lundergaard through time and transport him back to the twenty-first century. He's from there, too — he's trapped in 1987 like we are. He wants to go home. And he needed me in 1987 to do it."

"Wait, wait, wait!" Erasmus chimed in. "Wait! You're not thinking straight. Lundergaard is *already* in our own time. He already exists there. If he succeeds in this plan, there will be *two* of him at the time capsule site."

Kyle pondered this and relayed it to Jack, who shrugged in a non-super-genius way. "Look, I told you — Lundergaard time travels. It's what he does."

"But if there are two of him at once —"

"He doesn't care."

"Kyle, there's a chance that all of that plasma energy, combined with the zero-point energy of time travel, could have some bizarre side effects," Erasmus warned.

"Like what?" Kyle held up a finger to hold off Jack while he listened to Erasmus.

"Well . . . my calculations aren't perfect because we don't have access to all of Lundergaard's data, but there's a chance that the 1987 version of Lundergaard would pop into our present and push *that* version of Lundergaard out of the way, knocking him into the timestream, probably propelling him into the future."

Kyle told this to Jack. "That doesn't sound like a big deal," Jack said, and Kyle agreed.

"But depending on what the version of Lundergaard is doing in our own time . . . Depending on what he's set up to do . . . There's a chance that both Lundergaards will end up in the same space and at the same moment in time. Both of them supercharged beyond belief, existing in the same quantum configuration."

Kyle's stomach went sour. "Oh, man. If that happens . . ."

"What?" Jack asked.

"If that happens, then there's a good chance Lundergaard will split the universe wide open," Erasmus said to Kyle. "He'll rip space/time from end to end. He might survive and be tossed into a parallel universe, but every other living thing in the universe will be wiped out."

In halting phrases, Kyle explained this to Jack. "But that can't be his plan, can it?"

Jack sighed. "I've been trying to explain to you — he's crazy. And obsessed with time travel. He's been trying to perfect it forever. If he has to blow up a universe to do it, he will. It's all one big experiment to him, all one more step toward his ultimate goal: the ability to go anywhere, any*when*, and do anything he wants to anyone."

"And he's gonna use my technology and data about my superpowers to do it," Kyle said grimly.

"I don't get that part," Jack admitted. "Why not just use *my* powers?" Jack asked. "He's had me as his slave for years now, and he never scanned *my* biology."

"Tell him, Kyle," Erasmus said. "Tell him how your situation is unique. You were directly exposed to the plasma energies. The Mad Mask only got a residual whiff days later. His biology isn't as intimately mutated."

It was true. Kyle explained this to Jack and even as he did, he realized something. "I can handle my powers. Because I got a direct dose of the real plasma. But Lundergaard can only fake the plasma. So when the zombies finish absorbing all of that temporal energy, they'll turn on each other and start absorbing each other for the final burst Lundergaard needs."

The Mad Mask gulped. "That can't be good."

"It isn't," Kyle said grimly. "Bouring will become nothing more than a town full of statues. They won't be dead, but it'll be worse — they'll be frozen in time, forever! We have to stop him!"

Jack was thunderstruck, speechless. Erasmus, of course, wasn't. "How do you plan to do that?" Erasmus asked. "He has *years* to bury that time capsule. And we have no way of finding him. Besides, in our time, the time capsule *was* buried, which means we didn't stop Lundergaard."

Kyle rolled his eyes. "Don't start with me about time paradoxes again. There's no evidence —"

"Lundergaard himself said that time paradoxes could happen."

"You're gonna trust *Lundergaard*? About *anything*?"

"Kyle, think about everything that's happened since

we arrived in 1987. Has anything we've done changed the past? Or has it just reinforced it?"

Kyle grudgingly took a moment to think . . . and realized that Erasmus was right. Everything he'd done in 1987 had only confirmed his own present. In his own time, he'd never known Sheriff Monroe had a brother — boom, Sammy Monroe ends up going to military school, leaving Bouring because of Kyle's actions. In his own time, his grandmother's Christmas snow statue was chipped; what was the first thing Kyle had done upon walking into her house? He'd chipped the statue. The house on Thorul Court, the one that had never recovered from being burned — it had burned just hours ago thanks to Kyle's presence in 1987. Everywhere he turned his mind, every memory he filtered through his massive intellect, screamed out one thing to him: He could not change the past.

"It's too dangerous even to try," he concluded.

"There could be a way around time paradoxes," Jack said. "Lundergaard used to talk about it . . . I don't remember the details," he added, sheepish and ashamed.

"No, no. It doesn't matter. Even if there's a way around it . . . Even if the parallel universe theory is right and we stop Lundergaard here and now, that means there's *still* a parallel universe out there where the people of Bouring are frozen in time. What about *them*?"

"True . . ."

The three of them sat there (well, Jack and Kyle sat — Erasmus loafed in a pocket) and pondered the problem. And then an idea exploded like fireworks in Kyle's mind. "I've got it!"

"Got what?"

"We can't stop Lundergaard in 1987, right?"

"Right," both Jack and Erasmus agreed at the same time.

"That means we have to stop him in *our* time!"

"Well, duh, genius," Erasmus said. "But we can't *get* to our time!"

Kyle grinned. "We don't *have* to. . . ."

CHAPTER TWENTY-NINE

"We both need to go," Mairi told Mike, even though he was once again being all superheroey and noble and telling her that it was too dangerous for her to go with him.

"I do not know if I can fly all the way back to the burial spot while carrying you," Mike said. And if anyone else had said it, Mairi would have thought they were lying in order to protect her. But Mike didn't seem capable of lying, and his face was open and naked with anguish as he spoke.

"You need to take me," she insisted. "I won't let you go alone. You're hurt and your powers are going away. You'll need me to watch your back." Inspiration struck. "You were able to glide all the way here from the lighthouse without using a lot of your powers, right? Maybe if we went up on the roof and jumped from there, you could get some gliding in, too. Make it a little easier on you."

Mike pondered, then nodded gravely. "Very well, Mairi. I will let you accost me."

"Assist, you mean."

"That's not a bad word?"

"No."

"Hmm. All right, then. Let's go."

With that, they opened the window and climbed out. Mike went first, digging his hands into the side of the house to form handholds for Mairi. She tried not to look down, but she couldn't help it. For a moment, she felt dizzy and nauseated, but then she closed her eyes and forced herself to keep climbing. Soon, Mike was hauling her over the storm gutter and onto the roof.

"Are you ready?" he asked.

Was she? Heck, yeah!

He lifted Mairi and heaved her over his shoulder. It was disconcerting to hear him grunt as he did it, one more indication of how weak he'd become.

"Hold tight," he told her, something he'd never had to say before. She thought she heard worry and maybe a little fear in his voice for the first time ever. Mairi grabbed the collar of his cape and gripped it with all her strength.

"Ready?"

"Ready."

He raced forward as fast as he could . . . so much slower than he used to be able to. When they got to the edge of the roof, at the last possible instant, Mike leaped.

Mairi's breath caught in her chest.

And they fell.

Wind whipped past Mairi and she was so shocked that she forgot to scream as the ground rushed up at them, huge and fatal.

Just when she thought they would smash into the ground and splatter into a million pieces, Mike groaned and they slowed. They weren't flying — not really — but they were hovering about ten feet off the ground.

"Let me . . . catch my . . . breath . . ." Mike panted.

"Take your time."

He nodded and gulped in air, then began to run, climbing a little bit as he did. Soon they were running two stories straight up, making a beeline for the site of the time capsule burial. On the streets below, she noticed clusters of zombies, shambling along toward the same place. As they ran overhead, the zombies took notice and moved more quickly, unerringly following them along the streets and alleyways of Bouring toward the burial site.

"Faster," Mairi urged, feeling guilty for even saying it.

"I'll try," Mike said, making her feel even more guilty. And did — he tried and he succeeded, putting on a little more speed so that they could outpace the trailing zombies.

As they ran over and past Mairi's neighborhood, she was seized by a sudden, crazy urge to ask Mighty Mike if they could go check on Sashimi. Just to make sure her cat was safe. She knew it was foolish. She knew the world was ending around her. For some reason, though, Sashimi was suddenly the most important thing in the world to her.

Maybe because it was something she felt she could control.

Stop being silly, she thought. *You have something more important to do.*

Namely: getting to the site of the time capsule burial. Mike had been right and wrong at the same time. Yes, they had already looked in *one* 1987, the 1987 time capsule. But there was a *second* 1987 — the plot of land where that time capsule was supposed to have been buried all those years ago. Mairi was willing to bet that something else had been buried there, something that would give them a clue as to the zombie plague rampaging through Bouring. Maybe even something that would stop the zombies.

She hoped. She hoped and hoped and hoped it was true. Because if not . . . well, if not, then maybe she and Mike should have just run out of Bouring and tried to get help from the government.

Too late to change her mind now. They were coming into view of the site, and . . .

And oh, wow.

It was like half the town of Bouring was there. A lot of people were collapsed on the ground, as she'd seen before, most of them piled around a single point. Walter Lundergaard. He stood on the dais near the open time capsule, his arms outstretched to the sky, his head thrown back. He did not move, but there was a menace about him nonetheless. Through his clothing, lines of glowing light pulsated, as though he wore some kind of circuitry there.

Bodies arrayed around him like flower petals that have fallen off a tree.

There were still some zombies, stumbling around, now touching one another. Mairi watched as each touched zombie crumpled to a heap. Occasionally, a moving one would break off from the pack, lurch toward Lundergaard, and then . . .

And then a burst of light would explode from the zombie, washing over Lundergaard, and the zombie would join its motionless buddies in a heap on the ground.

What were they *doing*?

As they closed in, Mairi fumbled for her video camera in her pocket. She almost dropped it, but caught it at the last second and aimed it at Walter Lundergaard. His eerie, glowing form. His expression was almost satanic, his grin so evil that Mairi could barely abide looking at it . . . but she zoomed in anyway. Zoomed in on his insane face.

And then he spoke to her:

"Record what you like, girl. Soon, none of this will matter. Soon, I will be lord and master of all time and space!"

Okay. Right. Mairi didn't know if she should laugh her head off or run screaming.

She didn't have time to decide — that's when the zombies noticed her and Mighty Mike. They looked up and they began to fidget, like cats pawing at mice behind clear glass. As the zombies following them along the streets poured into the area, the ground below Mairi became thick with sluggish moving forms, all of them now grasping upward.

"There's the 1987 plot," Mairi said, pointing. There weren't too many zombies in that area. Not yet.

Still, Mairi knew what she had to do. Mike was weak — she could feel his muscles trembling with the effort of carrying her. He wouldn't be able to hold off the zombies and dig out the 1987 plot before being overwhelmed by the horde.

"Put me down over there," she said, pointing to a spot far from the 1987 area. "I'll move around and distract them. Run as far as I can. I'll give you time to dig out whatever's down there."

Mike said nothing, but moved in the direction she'd indicated. She kept filming, getting a good sweeping shot of some zombies headed for Lundergaard to "drop off" their supply of . . . whatever. She didn't like the idea of becoming one of the zombies — it was inevitable that they would catch her eventually — but it was a sacrifice she was willing to make if it meant Mike could somehow stop them.

Tears rolled down her cheeks. She would never see her parents again. Or Sashimi. Or her friends from school.

Kyle.

That was all right, though. She focused on the video camera screen. She would film while running, she'd decided. So that someone else could see the video later and maybe learn from it. She had to do this. She had to —

Hey, wait! Why where there suddenly tree branches in her video screen? She looked up. What was Mike doing?

"What are you doing?" she demanded. "Put me down over *there*."

While she'd been distracted, Mike had air-run over to a tall tree. Now he was lifting Mairi off his shoulder, planting her securely in some of the high branches.

"What are you doing?" she asked again. "Put me on the ground."

"I'm sorry, Mairi," he said with real regret. "It's my job to protect Bouring and I failed at it. At least this way, I protected you."

"Mike!" she shouted, and reached out for him, but he had already stepped back and she had to cling to the branches to keep from falling out of the tree and breaking her neck.

"Mike!" she screamed again as he ran off to the 1987 plot, and the army of zombies waiting there for him.

CHAPTER
THIRTY

Kyle explained to Erasmus what he needed designed. Jack listened in. "That's not a problem," he said, catching on. "I can make something like that out of a spool of wire, a bowling ball, and some electrical tape."

"Sorry, Jack, but this is going to have to work even if you're *not* around. But I *will* need something else from you." He explained quickly. Jack arched an eyebrow, then grinned in such a sinister way that Kyle was worried he might have to punch out the Mad Mask.

But the sinister intent behind the grin was clearly aimed at Walter Lundergaard, not Kyle. "I like it," Jack said. "I like it a lot. And I can do it. I'll need to rest a little first." He told Kyle what he would need, and Kyle added it to his mental shopping list. There would be two gadgets built — one by Kyle and one by Jack. Kyle let Erasmus get started on some schematics as he sped down from the lighthouse, leaving Jack for the moment.

Bouring was awake now, in that 1987 way. Even in Kyle's time, Bouring was a quiet place, but in 1987, it was even quieter. Still, there were people out and about, so Kyle couldn't risk flying around. He would have to take the sidewalks and roads like everyone else.

He jogged to the other side of town, where he'd hidden the tools for Danny. Fortunately, his father hadn't come to get them yet. He would need these.

Then he made his way back to Thorul Court. Lundergaard's house fire had been put out and looked more like the way Kyle remembered it now. The area was roped off, but Kyle slipped under the ropes. The air in the house steamed. Kyle knew that even after a fire has been put out, a building can remain dangerously hot for a while. But he was indestructible. It didn't matter.

As the epicenter of the explosion that had wrecked the house, the workshop was a disaster. Very little had survived the original explosion intact, and what had didn't survive the ensuing fire. Kyle nearly wept at the sight of so many beautiful, beautiful computers, now reduced to useless slag.

Well, *almost* useless.

He couldn't use any of the detritus to build his own supercomputer for the chronovessel, but he *could* scavenge the raw components to build something else. He was going to defeat Walter Lundergaard all those years in the future without ever touching the man. Or even seeing him again, for that matter.

"Think you're so smart, huh?" Kyle asked no one in particular. "You don't know who you're messing with, Lundergaard. Erasmus, how's that schematic coming along?"

"It's ready for you."

Kyle nodded and wiped some sweat from his upper lip. He had everything he needed spread out on the floor before him. "Walk me through it."

With Erasmus's instructions, Kyle began assembling . . . the LuBKiG!

"It stands for 'Lundergaard Butt-Kicking Gadget,'" he informed Erasmus.

"Whatever," said Erasmus. "Make sure you don't build the central core out of aluminum — it'll catalyze the reaction early and blow up in your face."

Oops. "Okay, done. Thanks."

The LuBKiG was simple. And the best part of it was that it used Lundergaard's own information from his personal hard drive to ruin his plan.

If Lundergaard could put something in the time capsule that made a plasma burst to turn people into powered zombies, then Kyle could use the same data to build something that did the opposite — a gadget that would reverse the process, sucking the powers out of everyone who had them. Theoretically, once that happened, all of the stored-up temporal energy in the zombies would be released and go back where it came from.

The one problem, of course, was that Kyle couldn't be in the twenty-first century to use the gadget. But he realized that that didn't matter, and Lundergaard, in a way, had given him the answer. Or maybe Kyle had said it before: Everyone in the world is time traveling into the future. One second at a time.

Walter Lundergaard's time capsule was traveling into the future, waiting for someone to dig it up.

Kyle would do the same with the LuBKiG. Bury it and let someone in his own time dig it up and use it against the zombies. Just to make sure it would activate, he cobbled together a crude timing device and a heat-sensor. When the LuBKiG was touched by anyone on the right date — the date of the zombie plague — it would automatically activate, reversing the process begun by Lundergaard's gadget.

"But how can you be sure someone will dig it up?" Erasmus asked.

"Already thought of that," Kyle told him, putting the finishing touches on the LuBKiG. "It's all taken care of. That's where Jack comes in."

He held the LuBKiG before him and grinned proudly. "Now we'll go re-hide the tools for Danny and then wait until night."

"I hope you know what you're doing."

"Don't I always?"

"You *really* don't want me to answer that question, do you?"

"Probably not."

Night fell in 1987 for the third time for Kyle. He flew back to the time capsule burial site and was relieved to find that no one had yet filled in the hole for this year's time capsule.

"This is gonna get dirty," Kyle said under his breath, and dove into the hole.

It went down a little more than six feet. Kyle dug down another two with his bare hands and placed the LuBKiG there, then covered it up with a foot of dirt. In a day or so, he knew, the deputies would give up their search for the time capsule Lundergaard had stolen. Nineteen eighty-seven's burial would be called off and the hole would be filled in.

"Now to leave a clue," Kyle said, and flew back to the lighthouse.

"Why the lighthouse?" Erasmus asked. "No one goes here. Not in 1987, not in our own time. It's a crazy place to leave a clue."

"It's the *best* place," Kyle said, touching down near

Jack, who was staring up at the stars. "I know it's the one thing in Bouring that will be exactly the same until our time. It stood abandoned like this until Mairi's mom started up the museum. And she cleaned it up and did basic maintenance, but she also wanted the lighthouse to be as close to its original construction and features as possible, so she only made one serious change. A computer, to run the lantern."

"That computer is still decades in the future. It can't help us now. We can't leave a message on it."

Kyle grinned. "No. But we *know* it will be here. The location of the lighthouse won't change between now and our time." He gazed up at the sky. At the stars. And at the things that weren't stars at all. Planets. Comets. Satellites.

"Can you do it, Jack? Can you do what I asked?" He handed over a pile of electronic junk.

The Mad Mask nodded slowly, looking at the components in his hands. "It only needs to work once, right?"

"Yes."

"It'll tax my powers," Jack said soberly. "But I can do it."

"Do what?" Erasmus demanded.

"I know you can't read them," Kyle said to Erasmus, "but there *are* satellites up there. I could fly up and see them. You're just looking on the wrong frequencies. But right now, I'm building something that Jack will turn into a gadget that can see those older frequencies."

"What will *that* accomplish? And what does that have to do with the lighthouse?"

"It's nice to be supersmart again," Kyle commented. "I like being smarter than you."

Erasmus was shocked into rare silence.

Kyle continued. "I'm going to fly up there into the exosphere. Get within sight of the satellites. Start logging the location, velocity, and direction of a bunch of them. And then I'm going to use Jack's widget to send a signal."

"To do what?" Erasmus's curiosity overwhelmed his outrage at being called less intelligent than Kyle.

"Well, that signal is just going to bounce around for a couple of decades. From satellite to satellite, ricocheting all around the planet." Kyle smiled when he thought of it — a single beam of encoded photons, shooting around the world in invisible silence for decades. "And since we're going to calculate the angles perfectly, I can guarantee that the day of the zombie attack in Bouring, that signal will return here, right to the lighthouse, and activate the lighthouse computer."

"I get it," Erasmus said. "You're going to use the lantern as a beacon, to guide people to safety. The lighthouse is the safest place in Bouring! Especially if you're running from a zombie horde."

"Well, yeah, that's part of it. If Mighty Mike has any brains at all, this is where he'll go."

"That's a mighty big if."

Kyle grinned again. "Yeah, but if he doesn't think of it, Mairi will. But we're not just going to light the lantern, Erasmus. We're going to use it to send a message. In Morse code. Something short. Something simple."

"What should the message be?"

Kyle shrugged. "The easiest one possible: Look in 1987."

Later, Kyle soared into the air, moving faster than he'd ever moved before. He would have to fly higher than ever.

The temperature extremes would probably destroy anything with him, so he'd left Erasmus with Jack for safekeeping. The AI was *not* happy about being left in the hands of an old enemy, but Jack was harmless enough now. Kyle truly believed that.

He flew higher. And higher.

Ice crystals began to form on him as he hit the upper reaches of the troposphere, water vapor in the air clinging to him and freezing in the icy cold. He had Jack's gadget protectively tucked under his arm, shielding it from the temperature changes with his own indestructible body. He hoped Jack was right, that he could extend his power this far. Usually, the Mad Mask had to be relatively close to an electronic device to make it function. Kyle would be five hundred miles straight up when he needed the gadget to work.

"I'll make it work," Jack had promised. "Even if it causes my head to explode, I'll make it work."

"Can we get both?" Erasmus had snarked, and then Kyle had handed him off and leaped into the air.

Suddenly, the winds that buffeted him ended. He'd entered the calmer stratosphere. There was little water vapor here, too, so he shook off the ice crystals that had formed on him and watched them drift down, down, down, vanishing into the clouds below.

It got even colder as he entered the mesosphere, down to −148°F. The cold couldn't hurt Kyle, but his breath froze as soon as it left his nose, so he held it instead.

And then — just when he thought he could stand the cold no more — he burst into the thermosphere, where the thinner gases absorbed ultraviolet radiation directly from the sun. The temperature soared to thousands of degrees in an instant, but Kyle couldn't feel it — those same thin gases meant that the air pressure was so low that the heat wasn't a factor. Still, knowing that he was surrounded by such heat caused Kyle to grimly set his jaw, praying that he'd shielded the device well, praying that Jack still had a connection to it. . . .

Up he flew! Ever more up, where radio waves bounced and danced, broadcasting all over the planet. His own signal would live here for part of the next few decades as it made its slow, yet faster-than-light path from outer space to the future computer at the Bouring Lighthouse.

And then, finally, the exosphere, where there was almost no gas at all. Nearly no oxygen. Kyle kept holding his breath, mostly because there was nothing to breathe, but also because he wasn't sure if Jack's gadget would work or not.

He pulled it out from under his arm. If it was still connected to the Mad Mask, a single LED light would be illuminated.

Kyle almost wept when saw that the light was on.

He pressed the only button on the device and waited a moment. It would have been nice if something dramatic had happened, like a light show or something like that. But the signal beam was invisible and silent.

Kyle tossed the gadget into space and dropped back down to Earth, plunging through the cold, the heat, the cold again, the sudden impact of weather, the planet rushing up at him like a bullet.

✻   ✻   ✻

Later, Kyle sat once again at the top of the lighthouse and stared up at the stars, where his encoded message now lived. It was up there, so tiny and so concealed that even the satellites it used to relay itself around the world wouldn't know it was there.

An exhausted Mad Mask lay next to him, asleep. Kyle smiled. Jack was sleeping a lot lately. He deserved it.

Kyle remembered lying out near where the plasma storm had transformed him, hanging out with Mairi and the Astronomy Club right before the ASE attacked. He had showed Mairi how to find Pegasus in the stars. It was a happy moment for him. With his best friend.

He would never see her again, he realized. Well, unless he stuck around Bouring for the next couple of decades. Then he would be there when she was born. But by then Kyle would be old — over thirty! — and he doubted young Mairi would want to be friends with an old guy.

Besides, she would be better off without him. He had saved her life more than once, true, but he had also done that thing no best friend should ever do: He had lied to her.

And he had erased part of her memory. Best friends shouldn't do that, either.

Pegasus was bright tonight. Kyle stared at it until his vision blurred. He should have been tired — it had been at least thirty-six hours since he'd slept — but instead he felt only a quiet peacefulness. Contentment.

Marred by only one thing.

"I'm sorry, Erasmus."

"For what?"

"For stranding us here. It's all my fault. I should have listened to you and just gone back to the night Mighty Mike arrived, like we planned. Then we wouldn't have ended up here. Stuck here."

"You didn't know. And I can't believe I'm saying this, but it probably wasn't even your fault. Maybe we were destined to come here. To learn about Lundergaard's plan and foil it. You mentioned before that maybe there was some kind of quantum entanglement that drew us here. Based on what the Mad Mask told us, maybe Lundergaard's machines and experiments attracted us to this time period. Maybe it would have happened no matter what. Think of it that way."

Yeah, maybe . . . "I just wanted to help Mairi. That's all. I couldn't stand looking at her, being around her, talking to her, knowing what I did to her. It was wrong."

"You didn't have a choice."

Silence. For a long time. Kyle watched the stars and the planets. Mars. He could see Mars. He wondered: Could he *fly* to Mars? Maybe that would give him something to do in the boring old days of 1987. . . .

"Maybe not." Kyle lay back on the roof of the light-house, his hands behind his head. "Maybe not. But just because you don't have a choice doesn't make the thing you do right."

"Hey, Kyle?" It wasn't Erasmus speaking — it was Jack. Kyle turned to the Mad Mask.

"I thought you were asleep."

"I was. I just woke up. I overheard, well, *your* part of the conversation. I hope you don't mind."

"Not really."

Jack bit his lip. "Kyle . . . what if I told you there was a way back to your time?"

Kyle sat upright. "What? What do you mean?"

If Erasmus could have gasped, he would have. "What's he talking about?"

"What are you talking about?"

"Let's go to the chronovessel."

"There's no point. Even if I put it back together —"

"What do you have to lose?" Jack asked.

True.

With the Mad Mask in tow, Kyle flew to where the chronovessel and its pieces waited for him. "Now what?"

"Put it all back together."

"But —"

"Just do it."

Kyle relented. After all, he had nothing else to do with his time, right? Until he could figure out what sort of life to live as a refugee in 1987, he might as well do *something*. And once the chronovessel was back in one piece, it would be easier to hide it somewhere.

It took him a couple of hours, but soon he had the chronovessel completed. He had enjoyed the work, actually. Working with his hands on such a complicated project forced him to focus on what was right in front of him. It left him no time to feel guilty about mind-wiping Mairi or stranding Erasmus.

"Okay, it's done," he told Jack. "And I appreciate the distraction. I really do. But it's still pointless. There's no computer in this time period sophisticated enough to run the chronovessel."

"Yes, there is," Jack said.

Kyle blinked. That was impossible. He had hacked into every major computer that existed in 1987. None of them was powerful enough to do the chronometric calculations, much less small enough to fit in the motorbike. "There's no such supercomputer. We checked."

The Mad Mask grinned. "Well, what if I told you you don't actually *need* a supercomputer?"

Erasmus made a pretty decent digital imitation of a snort. "He's really lost his marbles, hasn't he?"

"You," Jack went on, "just need something that *thinks* it's a supercomputer."

Kyle's eyes widened. "No way. Look, you're weak.

And it's so complicated . . . I wondered before, but I didn't want to ask because of everything. . . ."

"Because of everything I've been through. I know. But, Kyle —"

"Can you really do it?"

"I think I can. While you were up in the exosphere, I talked to Erasmus a little bit. About your chronovessel. I think I can put together a machine that will function long enough to get you back to the present."

"You *think* you can?" Kyle shivered at the thought of being lost in time. Again.

"This might be our only chance, Kyle," Erasmus said. "In the words of the original Erasmus: 'Fortune favors the audacious.'"

"I thought it was 'Fortune favors the bold.'"

"I dislike that particular translation," Erasmus said officiously.

"Of course you do."

"Well, in the original Latin, it's —"

"Enough. I don't care." He tapped his foot, thinking. The Mad Mask stared at him, steadily, unnervingly. "Okay, okay," Kyle said at last. "Fine: Let's give it a shot."

"Excellent!" The Mad Mask rubbed his hands together. "Give me a little while with some of the spare parts."

"Okay, and while you're doing that, I have something I need to do. Before we go."

He took off, flying toward Bouring.

When Kyle was little, his father used to enjoy telling him about the Bouring of his own childhood. "It was so safe here," Dad used to say, "that half the time people wouldn't even lock their doors at night."

Kyle figured that was just Dad being hyperbolic, trying to make some kind of point about the good ol' days. But as he stood at the front door to his grandparents' house, he realized it wasn't just hyperbole — it was midnight and the door really was unlocked. He went in, quietly.

Upstairs, he paused in the hallway to slip on the ski mask he'd borrowed from Danny. Then he stole into his grandparents' bedroom.

Gramps was snoring loudly on his back. Gramma was wearing a sleeping mask and earplugs, poor woman.

Kyle took a deep breath. A part of him wanted to play the worst, meanest prank possible on his jerk of a grandfather. Maybe haul him out of bed at superspeed, race down the stairs, out the front door, and then into the sky.

At a thousand feet straight up, maybe Gramps would gain a new perspective on how he talked to his son.

And then . . . back to bed? Leave him hanging on a tree somewhere? Drop him off at the peak of Mt. Everest for a couple of hours? Lots of nasty things could be done with superpowers, after all.

But in the end, instead, Kyle crept into his father's bedroom. Danny slept peacefully, the Walkman clutched in his hands.

"Thanks, Dad," Kyle whispered.

CHAPTER THIRTY-ONE

"Last chance," Kyle said. "Are you sure about this?"

The Mad Mask stood up from where he'd been crouched down by the motorbike and brushed his hands on his pants. Inside the open gas tank was a tangle of wires and circuits that Kyle knew would only work because Jack Stanley believed they would.

"Am I going to lose my superintelligence again?" Kyle wondered aloud, not really expecting anyone to answer.

"No way to know," Jack said. "But I don't think so. I think Lundergaard's interference caused that particular problem. He won't be messing with your trip this time." Jack touched some of the rat's nest of wiring he'd shoved into the chronovessel. "All systems online," he said. "Everything is green. You're good to go."

"You mean *we're* good to go, right?"

Jack said nothing. He just closed up the gas tank.

"Jack. *We're* going back to the present, right?"

"Kyle . . . first of all, your present isn't even my present. In your time, I'm still a fourteen-year-old supervillain

with a bad attitude and a partly erased memory. I probably just got out of the Bouring sewer system and started
planning my revenge on you." He stopped for a moment.
"Um, about that . . . Be on the lookout for me, will you?
My memory's a little hazy, but I'm pretty sure I did some
nasty stuff to you to get back at you for destroying
Ultitron."

"Look, even if my present isn't *your* present, wouldn't
you rather be there than here?"

"It's a moot point, Kyle. I'm not invulnerable like you
are. I wouldn't survive the rigors of time travel. Not in
this version of the chronovessel. Now, the one you'll
build as an adult is a whole different . . ." He shrugged.
"I *have* to stay here." He shoved Kyle at the motorbike.
"Now stop arguing with me and get going."

Kyle had so much to say . . . but in the end, there was
nothing to say. Nothing at all.

He held out his hand. After a moment, the Mad
Mask — Kyle's betrayer, Kyle's foe, Kyle's friend —
shook it. "Good luck, Kyle. We'll meet again."

"I'll find a way to rescue you. Someday."

Kyle swallowed hard and straddled the motorbike.
"Coordinates in?" he asked Erasmus, who was wirelessly
plugged into the system.

"Coordinates in."

"Okay. I trust you, Erasmus."

"Of course you do. Hit the activation button."

Kyle hesitated only half a second before hitting the button. The motorbike's strange fusion of gadgets whined.

"Kyle! Wait!" Jack shouted.

"Kyle, you need to hit the priming button now. We need to travel before the zero-point energy collectors overflow."

"Hang on —"

"We can't hang on —"

"What is it, Jack?"

Screaming above the noise of the chronovessel, Jack shouted, "I just remembered something! About your future!"

"Kyle! Hit the priming button!"

"One second, Erasmus! What, Jack? What?"

Some dust and smoke kicked up. Corn silk flew in the air. The Mad Mask held up a hand against it all. "There was a weapon! That's the last thing I remember before Lundergaard pulled me through time and brought me back here! When you were betrayed in the future, you sent a weapon into the past! To help your younger self!"

"I did *what*?"

Erasmus screamed in Kyle's ear. Kyle's finger hovered over the priming button. He needed to time travel *now*, but he also needed to hear what the Mad Mask had to say.

"You had a name for it!" Jack yelled. "It was Project Something-or-Other. Something metallic. Project Steel. Or Steely. Or Brassy. Something with a *y*."

"Kyle! Now!" Complete and total panic in Erasmus's voice, and before Kyle could allow himself to think about it any further, he thumbed the button and suddenly the Mad Mask vanished, the corn field vanished, everything vanished.

Once again, a pattern of shapes and colors exploded before Kyle's eyes. It happened again. And over and over, just like last time. He couldn't keep up — the colors and lights kept coming, kept erupting and glowing and flaring before him, so fast, so beautiful, and so tragic. No one else would see this. No one else would ever see this.

AndthensuddenlyeverythingwentsofastthatKylecouldn't evenseeitandtheworldbecamenothingmorethanablurof motionandactionandpatternsoflightanddarkthatbuffeted himlikehighwindsonaplainonlythesewindsweremadeof colorsandtheyassaultedhimoverandoverandhestruggledto stayonthemotorbikeandhescreamedtoErasmusbuttherewas notimeforthescreamandnoairandnosoundandhisscream diedassoonasitwasbornandthen —

Kyle's scream choked off in his throat as the menagerie of moving colors came to a halt. He was gripping the motorbike so tight that he'd twisted and bent the handles.

"Erasmus? Erasmus, did we make it?"

For a heart-stopping moment, there was nothing in his ear. Then: "We definitely traveled in time. Not sure where . . . Systems are down. . . ."

"We did it! When are we?"

"Check the readout. I need to reboot some things."

Kyle glanced down at the readout in front of him; his jaw dropped. It was *the* night! The night of the plasma storm! Jack's fake supercomputer had dropped him at exactly the right time and place to witness Mighty Mike's arrival on earth.

And . . . to record it. Kyle checked the video camera. It was fine. He got off the bike and rolled it to the edge of the cornfield. Going by his memory of that night, he aimed the camera at the spot where Mighty Mike would touch down, then switched on the camera. He waited. As he watched, he saw another version of himself walk into frame. A thrill of excitement went through him. He remembered this so well — coming to the field to set up the prank. And then the light from the sky . . .

"Kyle, we have a problem."

"What do you mean? It worked. We make one more jump and we're home."

"Check the chronovessel."

Kyle opened the gas tank. A cloud of noxious, noisome smoke poured out. The Mad Mask's makeshift supercomputer was nothing more than melted slag.

"Oh, man . . ." He gnawed at a fingernail for a moment. "Okay, let's see. . . . Look, we're almost back in the present. We could just wait a few weeks and we'd catch up to present, right?"

"That's probably not a good idea. Right at this instant, there are two of you. Who knows what kind of time paradox that could create?"

"Okay, then I go steal some stuff and build another supercomputer to replace the missing one. We're almost back to the present — we'll be able to get the components we need."

"No. That could cause another paradox. The stuff you steal might be needed elsewhere down the line."

"But if our trip to the past has taught us anything," Kyle said, "it's that everything I did back then was *supposed* to happen anyway. So if I go steal some stuff now —"

"If our trip to the past taught us anything," Erasmus chided, "it's that we got lucky. Maybe you were always supposed to be the cause of Sammy Monroe leaving Bouring or your grandmother's statue breaking. Who knows? Maybe it was supposed to be something else, though. There were *decades* for those things to happen. If you hadn't dropped the statue, there were twenty years and more for someone else to do it. If you hadn't gotten Sammy in trouble, he had plenty of time to do it to himself. But right now, time is short. Literally. There's only a few weeks between right now and our present. If you screw something up, there's no way for the timestream to fix it."

"Then what am I supposed to do? It's not like there's a supercomputer just lying around that I can use."

"There's one," Erasmus told him, his voice more serious than Kyle had ever heard before. "Just one."

And then Kyle realized what Erasmus meant. "No!" he shouted. "No *way*! You'll . . . !" He thought of the twisted, melted wreck of circuitry he'd hauled out of the guts of the chronovessel. He couldn't let Erasmus . . . "There's no way I'm going to let you do that! I won't install you in the bike. No."

"Kyle, it's the only way." Erasmus's voice was gentle.

"Well, tough. Because you don't have hands and I won't do it."

"You have to. It's the only way to get you back home. I know you have a lot of faith in Mairi, but what if she doesn't get to the lighthouse? What if Mighty Mike won't help her? What if they don't find the clue or figure out the clue? You need to be back in the present so that you can stop Lundergaard's plan and save Bouring."

"Not if it means you die."

"You made me based on yourself, Kyle. As long as you're alive, I can't die."

Kyle thought he felt a tear or two coming on and frowned until the feeling went away. Crying wasn't going to help anyone right now. Erasmus was right. Kyle knew he was right. But he wanted more than anything for Erasmus to be wrong. To be so, so wrong. He had already lost so much. Ever since that plasma storm transformed him, Kyle had lost his standing as the most popular kid in Bouring, his best friend, his own time period . . . and now he had to lose Erasmus, too?

He screamed. Just once. Just one loud, anguished scream to the heavens.

And then he said, very quietly, "Okay. I'll do·it."

"Good. Wire me in," Erasmus said.

Kyle crouched down by the motorbike and opened the gas tank. He nestled Erasmus in there as gently as he could, then took a deep breath and made the wiring connections necessary.

"You good?" he asked, shutting the tank.

"All systems online. Everything is green. I'll stay in touch with you via your earpiece for . . . well, for as long as I can."

"Can't we —"

"No. Now. I'm losing a lot of power. If we don't go now, we don't go at all."

Kyle threw his leg over the chronovessel and said, "Okay, I'm ready."

"Activate in three . . . two . . ."

Kyle hit the button as Erasmus said, "One."

As the world exploded again, Kyle thought he heard Erasmus say, "Good-bye."

The chronovessel sizzled and crackled with electrical sparks as it dropped out of the timestream and back into normal reality. The first thing Kyle saw was the video camera mounted on the handlebars — it had finally surrendered to the rigors of time travel. It looked like a wax version of a video camera that had been left out in the sun.

The second thing he saw was the readout screen. Which told him that he was back in the present, mere hours after he'd left. It was more than the seconds he'd planned, but hopefully still in time to save Bouring.

"We did it, Erasmus!" he shouted. "We did it! We're home!"

No answer.

Kyle tapped his earpiece to make sure it was still working.

Oh, no.

He dismounted from the motorbike and ripped open the gas tank.

The circuitry there was a melted mass of shiny copper and plastic. Erasmus's blue-flame paint job had cracked and peeled.

"No," Kyle said. "No, no, no, no, no!"

He pried Erasmus out of the mess, only to find that half of the AI stayed behind, fused to the other useless junk inside.

Erasmus was gone.

Kyle dropped to his knees. He couldn't believe it. Erasmus was gone. And what did Kyle have to show for it? Yes, he'd traveled in time. But he hadn't been able to change his history with Mairi. And the video camera was destroyed, so his original idea to videotape Mighty Mike's arrival was dead, too. He had traveled in time for nothing.

All he had left was revenge.

He clenched his fists. Lundergaard. He would stop Walter Lundergaard. No matter what.

He soared into the air and flew at top speed to the other side of town. Below him, Bouring seemed frozen, more like a photograph of a town than an actual town. All that moved were the zombies, which seemed to notice him high up in the air, sensing his movement more than actually seeing him. As he flew overhead, they streamed into the streets, following him.

At the time capsule burial site, all was chaos. Throngs of zombies packed the area, stepping over and around the stiff, still bodies of those who were stopped in time. There, in the middle of it all, was Walter Lundergaard, his clothing burned away now by the power of the special circuitry-suit he wore beneath. Collecting all of that energy. Kyle could barely look in his direction. So much power, collected in one place. And this, Kyle knew, was only one end of a pipeline that stretched back to 1987, where another Lundergaard waited for the moment that would yank him through time.

And possibly destroy the universe.

Okay, Kyle, enough thinking. Time for action.

With a bird's-eye view, Kyle quickly spotted the area reserved for 1987. It sported the largest cluster of zombies, with more and more of them flowing into the area.

In the middle of them was Mighty Mike. Kyle could just barely make out the shine of his cape and suit. He was struggling against the zombies as he stood in a deep hole. For every zombie he flung back, he would get a few seconds to dig a bit deeper before more would attack him. He looked bad — not nearly as strong or as fast as he usually was.

It looked like Mike had gotten the clue Kyle left behind in 1987. He was digging for the LuBKiG as fast as he could.

The zombies get their powers from the same energy as Mighty Mike — they're sapping his superpowers! When his powers are all gone, he'll freeze up like anyone else.

Furthermore, Kyle realized, even if Mike survived the zombies, the LuBKiG would destroy his powers. It was designed to remove the zombie powers; it would do the same to Mike's . . . and to Kyle's, if he was in range.

Kyle looked around. Once Mighty Mike got to the LuBKiG, everything would be fixed. And, hey — Mighty Mike wouldn't be so mighty anymore, either. Score! In the meantime, before Kyle got out of range, he had to find . . .

Mairi! There she was — in the high branches of a nearby tree, struggling to climb into lower branches. Kyle's lip curled. What was she doing? She should stay where it was safe!

But of course not. Not Mairi. She wanted to help Mighty Mike. Even though a single zombie touch would — as far as she knew — freeze her forever. But Mairi wouldn't just think of herself. She was too good for that.

Just like Erasmus hadn't thought of himself, making the ultimate sacrifice to get Kyle home. Just like Jack Stanley had volunteered to stay in 1987 and grow old by now, all to help the people of the present.

Just like Danny had helped Kyle steal those tools and break into the school, even though he could have gotten caught and gotten another chewing out from Gramps.

Heck, even Max Monroe had tried to stop Sammy from beating up Danny.

Fortune favors the audacious.

So, what's it going to be, Kyle? he asked himself as he watched Mighty Mike dig down a little farther. *Does everyone get to be a hero except for you?*

More and more zombies poured into the burial site. It looked as though almost everyone in Bouring was here.

Mairi was halfway down the tree.

Erasmus turned out to be a hero. And he was based on me. So maybe that means . . .

Now or never, Kyle thought.

He pulled on his dad's ski mask and dove as fast as he could, before he could change his mind, barreling right into the mass of zombies surrounding Mighty Mike.

The numbing effect hit him immediately. His top speed dropped and it was only the force of gravity that kept him going. His strength, sapped, was no longer as super as it had been mere moments ago.

Mike seemed shocked to find Kyle in the hole with him. Kyle spun quickly, tossing several zombies out of the pit. "Get out of here," he snarled at Mike. "Hurry."

Mike's eyes widened. He couldn't recognize Kyle in his father's hand-me-downs and ski mask, but he knew that voice. "Blue Freak . . ."

"It's the Azure Avenger. Make sure they get it right on my statue," Kyle said with a bravado he didn't really feel. From all the zombie touches, he felt weaker than he'd felt since getting his powers. He still had a little ways down to dig, too.

"What are you doing here?" Mike asked. He was breathing hard and heavy, having difficulty catching his breath. Kyle felt bad for him for the first time ever.

"Saving your butt," Kyle said. "And the world. Because you can't seem to get it done."

"I —"

"I don't have time to argue," Kyle said. He grabbed Mike by the arm and lifted him up. Then, with all the strength in his body, he hurled Mike out of the pit and as far to the west as he could. He was pretty sure he'd gotten Mike out of the impact area of the LuBKiG. And he was pretty sure Mike had just enough invulnerability left to survive.

Pretty sure.

He dug into the dirt, his muscles sore and aching for the first time in so long. It was a good thing Mike had already dug down so far. Kyle wouldn't have been able to make it these last couple of feet, not with the zombies draining his powers. He hated to admit it, but he and Mighty Mike had made a pretty good team.

Zombies dived into the hole and every touch of their fingers and palms and feet sapped his strength, made him feel like he was walking through hip-high snowdrifts.

But then he saw it.

The LuBKiG.

He could barely make out the top of it, covered now in only a scattering of dirt and loose pebbles. Kyle reached out for it, fighting against a tide of zombie bodies sapping his strength, his speed, his movement, his life.

And then he thought, *What if it doesn't work?*

He imagined Erasmus saying snarkily, "Well, *you* built it, so I'd say the odds are about fifty-fifty."

Kyle laughed to himself, even though he was trapped in a pit with zombies. His hands brushed away the dirt and touched the top of the LuBKiG.

And the world went violently white and loud.

Kyle blinked. Spots chased other spots before him, obscuring his vision, making it almost impossible to see. A great roar filled his ears.

Eventually, the roar quieted. He heard moans instead.

As his vision cleared, he saw that he was still in the pit. The zombies weren't zombies anymore — they were all groaning and trying to pull themselves away from one another. Kyle looked up from the pit, to the sky, and told himself to fly away, but he knew even as he thought it that it wouldn't happen.

His powers were gone. Strength. Invulnerability. Flight. Superintellect.

Gone.

He was just Kyle again.

And his back was killing him. Wow. Pain. His whole body was sore, strained, like he'd just done way too many push-ups in gym class.

Before anyone else in the pit could react, he clambered over them — apologizing for the occasional foot in someone's face — and hauled himself out of the pit. He looked around. The entire town of Bouring was here, basically looking like a bunch of people who've just woken up from the same bad nightmare. Kyle pushed a few people aside, knocking them over. It wasn't polite, but he had to get out of here. His ski mask wouldn't hide his identity from anyone who knew him well. Like Mairi, for example.

Mairi who was now almost out of the tree.

Kyle ran off, but suddenly he heard a voice call out, "Help! Help me! Please!"

He stopped. Looked around. Off to one side, there was a young woman stuck under a light pole that had fallen. It was on her leg and she couldn't move it. With all the chaos, it could be hours before someone got to her.

Well, hero? What are you going to do about it?

Kyle sighed and ran over to her. She stared at his mask, but said nothing as he pushed and strained and heaved against the light pole. Five minutes ago, he was strong enough to pick this up with his pinky and toss it a mile. Now . . .

After much grunting and sweating, he managed to move it just enough that she could pull her leg out from under. "Thank you," she said. "Thank you so —"

But she couldn't finish — Kyle had already run off into the darkness.

CHAPTER
THIRTY-TWO

Mairi took a deep breath and held it as the doctor stitched up her arm. She didn't need a lot of stitches — just ten — and he'd numbed the arm already, but even the mere thought of someone sewing her skin made her a little squeamish. Not very squeamish. Just a little.

Oh, this is ridiculous, she thought. *You just survived a plague of the world's most bizarre zombies. You can handle a little stitching.*

She blew out her breath.

"There," the doctor said after a moment. "Good as new." He taped a bandage over the area. "Keep it clean and dry. Bring her back in a week," he said to her parents.

Mairi's mom nodded, and her dad gathered her up in his arms, even though she was *way* too big and too old for such childish nonsense. "Dad, come on. I'm fine. *I'm* not the one who was turned into a zombie."

"We almost lost you," he told her.

"No, *I* almost lost *you*, but I saved the day."

Mairi's mom shook her head. "Darling, we've talked

about exaggerating the truth before. Mighty Mike saved the day."

Mairi fumed and struggled until her dad put her down. Mighty Mike wouldn't even have known where to go for help if it hadn't been for her! He wouldn't have been able to . . . to . . .

What *had* he done? It had been several hours since the zombie plague suddenly ended. No one could get close to the 1987 time capsule burial site, so Mairi didn't know what Mike had found down there that rescued everyone. But it was *something*, she knew. She had watched him flail his way through the zombies and dig up the 1987 plot. And then she'd lost track for a moment while she negotiated a particularly tricky set of branches on her way down from the tree, and the next thing she — or anyone else — knew, there was a white flash of light and suddenly everyone who'd been "frozen" by the zombies was unfrozen and all of the zombies were dazed and staggering around as if they'd just been slapped with bricks.

So Mike had saved everyone. Again.

"With my help," Mairi insisted to her parents.

"Of course, dear," Mom said, thinking Mairi couldn't see her rolling her eyes.

But Mairi could see it. And she didn't like being patronized. She had done something heroic and dangerous, but got no credit for it. No one else could possibly understand how that made her feel.

from the top secret journal of
Kyle Camden (open text):

Since I no longer possess the capacity to cipher my journal, this entry — my last — will have to be in open text. As a result, I will be speaking obliquely about certain matters.

Well, I'm back from my . . . trip. It's strange to be here and to feel so normal. It's been a long time since I felt normal.

Once again, Mighty Mike is receiving credit for "saving the town," even though I have knowledge that, in fact, someone else was responsible for saving Bouring. Once again, Mighty Mike stumbles into his reward.

But you know what?

That's okay.

With the zombies gone, Mighty Mike's powers have returned and he's once again patrolling the skies of Bouring and beyond. Rescuing dogs from sewer drains. Moving trees felled by storms. Stopping fender benders.

Good for him. Really. I mean it. The world needs its heroes.

What I care about is this: My parents are okay. My town is okay. Mairi is okay and maybe someday I'll even find a way to talk to her again.

One additional bit of good news — when I pried

open the melted video camera with an awl and chisel, I found that the tape itself had survived. So that's a good thing. There's really no reason for it now, but I will watch it.

But first . . . I have something else to do.

Something to say.

Hello, there, Walter. Walter Lundergaard. I know you're reading this at some point in the future. You disappeared from the time capsule burial before the police could get the area locked down, but Mairi had you on video. That video clip of you absorbing energy from your plasma "zombies" has been on every news channel in the country. It's gone viral on YouTube. Now the whole world is looking for you.

Just like they used to look for the Blue Freak.

But the Blue Freak is gone now.

There's just me.

And I want you to know something: You may have a lot of money and a lot of secrets hidden around the world, a lot of places to hide . . . but it doesn't matter.

I'm going to stop you.

I don't know how, but I will stop you.

CHAPTER
THIRTY–THREE

Kyle stood at the closed door to his parents' bedroom. This would be the most difficult thing he'd ever done.

After long moments of waiting, he finally rapped on the door.

"Come in!" his dad called out.

Kyle went into the bedroom. Mom sat at her makeup table, brushing her hair as she did every night. Dad lay in bed, half watching the news and half reading one of the paperback mystery novels he never seemed to be without. It was so strange — just a day ago, to Kyle, his father had been a scrawny little squirt. And now he was a man. It was as though he'd grown up overnight.

And Kyle thought that maybe his dad wasn't the only one who'd grown up.

"What's up, sport?" Dad asked a little warily, a little less brightly than usual.

I lost my powers because of my trip through time. I lost Erasmus. But I may have gained something more important.

Kyle fidgeted. And then finally just spilled it:

"I just wanted to thank you."

"Thank me?"

"For what you taught me."

Dad stared at him, then grinned and gave a little shoulder shrug. "You're welcome!"

Kyle hugged his father and left. As he closed the door behind him, he heard his mother say, "What did you teach him?"

"I teach him a lot of stuff," Dad said confidently.

Kyle chuckled under his breath.

After his parents had gone to sleep and after Lefty was satiated with an abundance of yogurt drops and chunks of dried pineapple, Kyle lay awake in bed, unable to drift off. Too much had happened to him. Too much to think about. And with no more superbrain to process all of that information, he was having to do it like normal people did — one bit at a time.

There was still, of course, the lingering question of who Walter Lundergaard really was. And what he was up to. Lundergaard had recognized him back in 1987. So, someday in his own future, Kyle would meet Walter Lundergaard. For Kyle, it would be the second time. For Lundergaard, the first.

Well, that'll be weird.

He rolled out of bed, ignoring Lefty, who suddenly stirred and became very active now that Kyle was up and about. Kyle turned on his computer. He had already transferred the contents of his videotape to his hard drive, but he hadn't watched it yet. Why not do it now?

First, there was static. Then, framed by dry, dying cornstalks, Kyle could make out a chunk of the Bouring Middle School football field.

As Kyle watched, he saw himself walk into frame.

A few moments later, there was a flash of light from off-screen, and Kyle watched himself hold up an arm against it . . . and then pass out.

I didn't get Mighty Mike in frame after all. Oh, well. It doesn't matter anymore.

Kyle reached out to turn off the video, but just then Mighty Mike walked into the scene, still glowing from the plasma storm.

Oh, cool!

A slow, wicked grin spread over Mike's face as he leaned in close. . . .

Kyle watched. Watched Mike slowly approach his own unconscious body. Had Mike *done* something while Kyle was out cold? Something Kyle didn't remember?

The camera had good placement; he could see everything as Mighty Mike crouched down near Kyle's prone form. Kyle held his breath. What had happened? What was he about to see?

Mike leaned in close. Closer. His lips at Kyle's ear. His lips moved.

He said something to me that night! He said something! What, though?

The microphone on the camera wasn't good enough to pick up what was said. It was brief, whatever it was. It took only a few seconds and then — as Mike walked away — the video ended.

Kyle rewound and watched again: Mike approached. Leaned in. Spoke. Walked away.

Again: Approach. Lean. Speak. Leave.

He zoomed in as much as he could.

He watched those seconds over and over again, staring at Mike's lips for what seemed to be hours.

Eventually, he picked out four syllables.

Three words.

Just three words before Mike walked away.

Three words that made the hair on Kyle's neck stand on end. Three words that made his skin crawl with absolute terror.

The first two words: "It worked."

It worked.

And then the last word:

"Master."

CHAPTER
THIRTY-FOUR

Now Kyle *really* couldn't sleep. He tossed and turned, which meant that Lefty couldn't sleep, either. The rabbit stomped his feet and tugged at the bars of his cage. Which had the effect of making it even *harder* for Kyle to sleep, so he finally got out of bed, hoisted Lefty out of his cage, and plopped his fat bunny butt on the bed.

" 'It worked, master.' What's *that* about, Lefty? I was the only one there. He had to be talking to me. He was calling *me* master. Why would Mighty Mike call me master? And then go ahead and be all secretive and alien? Why, Lefty?"

Lefty cocked his head to one side and regarded Kyle with one pink eye. Somehow, that calmed Kyle down. He stroked Lefty's soft fur and the rabbit settled in for a nice, long petting. Before he knew it, Kyle's eyes were drooping and his chin dipped to the bed.

He awoke hours later to Lefty head-butting his fore-head with an insistence that meant either "Put me back in my cage so I can use the litter box" or "Feed me, you dolt!" Kyle did both, just to be safe.

It was early in the morning, around the time when Kyle would normally have to wake up for school. But school — which had just started up after Ultitron's rampage — was temporarily on hiatus again as Bouring recovered from being turned into time-stealing zombies. Kyle chuckled: The motto "Bouring: It's not Boring!" was becoming truer and truer with each passing day.

With his parents at work and the house to himself, Kyle had nothing to do, so he ambled down to the basement. A part of him wanted to go visit his grandparents, but he knew it would be a shock to see them so old, after having just seen them so young. Plus, he wasn't sure he was ready to see Gramps. Not yet.

Down in the basement, he began to clean up the remains of his workshop. He'd left the place a mess before leaving for the past. Once, he could have used these leftovers to build . . . something. Anything. Together, he and Erasmus would have figured out . . .

He sighed and sat on the bottom step leading upstairs. Erasmus. Oh, Erasmus . . .

After a while, he was tired of feeling sorry for himself. He needed to *move*. Needed to *do* something. He gathered up all the stuff that was now just junk again and hauled it outside, leaving it by the curb. People were still — weeks later — cleaning up from Ultitron's rampage, so it wasn't strange to see piles of random junk left outside for pickup.

As the morning became the afternoon and then early evening, the basement slowly began to resemble its old self, the version of it from before Kyle's exposure to the plasma shower and the arrival of Mighty Mike on Earth. All that remained were his two trophies: the leaded jar of irradiated dirt from Mike's landing site and the wooden mask that young Jack Stanley had worn as the Mad Mask. Next to them, Kyle placed his third — and final — trophy: the iPod shell that had once housed Erasmus.

And so ends the career of the Azure Avenger, he thought. *Some dirt, a piece of wood, and a piece of useless electronic junk. Way to go, Kyle.*

He stared at the mask. Its empty eyeholes seemed to stare back at him.

Project Steely. Project Brassy. Something like that . . .

He shook his head. No. He was done. He had no powers. He had no superbrain. He had no snarky artificially intelligent sidekick. He was just Kyle Camden again. For a moment, he considered trying to track down the grown-up Jack Stanley, but he realized that would be fruitless. Jack had had plenty of time to go wherever he wanted since 1987. He could be anywhere in the world, under any identity.

But his younger self is still out there. Still nuts. Kyle

remembered Jack's warning — *"Be on the lookout for me. . . . I'm pretty sure I did some nasty stuff to you to get back at you for destroying Ultitron." So, I have that to look forward to. Which is nice.*

Still . . . whatever Jack had done to Kyle in the past and whatever he would do to Kyle in the future, Kyle knew that a day would come when the Mad Mask would reform, would become an ally.

A friend.

Yeah, and speaking of friends . . . maybe it's time you start acting like one to the only one you have left.

That sounded about right.

Later that night, after dinner, Kyle bundled up (bundling up was something he would have to get used to again, now that he could feel cold) and walked over to Mairi's house. The devilish little prankster in him had considered wearing the Mad Mask's mask. Because boy oh boy would that have given Mairi a shock when she opened the door!

But, no. Sure, it would be funny to see the look on Mairi's face, but it would also be cruel to do that to her. She'd been *kidnapped* by the Mad Mask. Saying "It was just a prank" couldn't make up for scaring someone. Especially a friend.

So all Mairi saw when she opened the front door was Kyle's freezing cold face, ringed by a fake-fur-lined hood to ward off the wind that blew down the street.

"Hey," she said.

"Hey," he said back. And then they were silent for a moment until Kyle said, "So. I've been a butthead lately."

Mairi glared at him. Then she said: "A *total* butthead, you mean."

"Yeah. A total butthead." He shifted uncomfortably from one foot to the other and then said, "I'm sorry." *And not just for being a butthead. But also for lying to you and erasing part of your memory and all of that stuff. But mostly for being a butthead because friends shouldn't be buttheads.* "I'm *really* sorry," he added.

Mairi seemed to think about this for a moment, then nodded. "Okay. That's cool. Want to come in?"

CHAPTER
THIRTY-FIVE

Mairi couldn't believe Kyle was back. He was the old Kyle again — funny, interesting, fun to be with — but also somehow a new Kyle, too. A better Kyle. As if he'd grown up a whole bunch just in the past few hours.

But that was impossible, of course.

Whatever he'd had had going on in his head, she figured, he must have worked it out.

They spent time playing video games and watching Sashimi desperately chase a laser pointer — "You'll never catch it!" Kyle chortled — and watched some TV and then, before it was time for Kyle to go home, they went out on the back deck with blankets and two ginormous mugs of hot cocoa and stared up at the stars.

"Remember when you showed me Pegasus? The night the dirt monster tried to kill me?"

"How could I forget?"

Mairi sipped some cocoa. "You know, I didn't used to get it. Why you didn't like Mighty Mike. And I guess that's because he rescued me that night from the dirt monster. But I've been thinking lately. . . ."

"About what?"

She shrugged. "I don't know. You know, someone came and rescued me from the Mad Mask, when he had me down in the sewers. It wasn't Mighty Mike. I think it was the Blue Freak, but my memory's all . . ." She shook her head, frustrated. "The doctors say that trauma and shock can mess with your memory. They say I might never remember everything about what happened down there. But I know Mike didn't save me. And today . . . today, he didn't know *what* to do to stop the zombies or Lundergaard. I had to figure it all out and he *still* got the credit! It's not fair!"

Kyle put his cocoa down and gazed at her. "What are you saying?"

"I guess I'm saying that maybe I understand why you don't like him. There's something just . . . off about him."

Kyle surprised her by shrugging. "Oh, I don't know. Maybe he's not so bad after all."

"Oh, so now I guess you guys are best buddies and all?"

"Not really. I guess I've just come around on him, is all."

"And I suppose you're going to try to convince me I'm wrong."

"I'm not going to try to convince you of any-thing," Kyle told her. "You'll figure it out on your own someday."

"Well, isn't this ironic," Mairi said. "Suddenly, *you're* the Mighty Mike fan and I'm —"

Her cocoa was halfway to her lips and it almost spilled and scalded her when Kyle grabbed her by the shoulders like a lunatic. "What did you just say?" he asked.

"I said — get off my shoulders — I said that you're the Mighty Mike fan —"

"No, before that. You said it was *ironic*, didn't you?"

"Well, duh." Kyle's eyes had that crazy light in them, a light Mairi knew all too well. It meant he'd figured something out. That he was planning something. "It's ironic, Kyle. Ironic is when something happens that's the opposite of what —"

"I know what it means," Kyle said, evidently too busy thinking of something else to say it sarcastically. "But it . . . Oh, man!"

And then he did the most shocking thing ever: He leaned over and planted a kiss — a quick smacker — right on Mairi's forehead. It was so fast she barely had time to register it before he pulled away.

"You know how people say, 'I could just kiss you'?" he babbled. "Well, that's how I just felt. So I did. Oh, man. I think I have it figured out."

Mairi touched her forehead with the tips of her fingers. She didn't have *anything* figured out right now.

"I need your help, Mairi," Kyle said. "I need to . . . I need to pull a prank."

Mairi rolled her eyes. *This* she understood. "More pranks, Kyle? Really? After everything that's happened to this town?"

"Just one more. My last prank, probably. Will you help me?"

Mairi sighed. "Of course I will. You butthead."

Kyle grinned.

The next day, at noon, Kyle Camden threw himself off the top of the Bouring Lighthouse, much to the horror and shock of the people below.

A day earlier, throwing himself off the lighthouse wouldn't have been a big deal because Kyle could fly. But now he couldn't fly anymore. These days, when he flung himself at the ground, he only had one option: Obey the law of gravity and go splat.

Still, it was a tall lighthouse and Kyle had some time to think on the way down. Mairi had been instrumental to this prank, of course. She'd gotten him into the lighthouse, which was necessary. He needed some height. He needed to be seen. No other building in town would do.

Mairi had insisted on going all the way to the top with him. The trapdoor into the Lantern Room was still fused shut, so Kyle had climbed out a window in the Watch Room and — with Mairi fretting the whole time — scaled the lighthouse up to the Lantern Room, then the rooftop.

"Be careful!" Mairi had cried more than once.

"Oh, don't be such a worrywart!" Kyle had told her. And then jumped.

Right on time, Mighty Mike swooped in from above the clouds and snatched Kyle out of the air long before he could go splat.

"Kyle!" Mike exclaimed. "What are you doing?! Why did you jump? And why is there a bungee cord attached to you?"

Kyle could have explained, but instead he gave Mike a moment to think it through.

It took more than a moment, but eventually Mike got it. "Ohhh . . ." He hesitated, hovering in midair, as if unsure what to do. For a second there, Kyle thought Mike might just let him go and then Kyle would go all bouncy-bouncy alongside the Bouring Lighthouse.

"I needed to see you," Kyle explained, "and you've been all over the world, looking for Lundergaard. But I knew that if half of Bouring suddenly shouted for help, you would come running."

"You were wrong," Mike said sternly. "I did not come running. I came flying."

Once upon a time, Mike's banged-up brain annoyed the heck out of Kyle. Now it didn't seem like such a big deal. "Consider me corrected," Kyle said. "Take us up to the roof, all right?"

Mike complied. They passed Mairi on the way. Kyle saluted her. She grinned and saluted back.

On the roof of the lighthouse, Kyle unattached his bungee cord and gazed at Mighty Mike.

"Is there something else I can help you with?" Mike asked politely. "I have other things to do. . . ."

"Why did you call me 'master'?" Kyle asked.

Mike cocked his head to one side, and for a moment, he looked exactly like Lefty. "What do you mean?" Totally guileless. Completely sincere.

"You really don't remember anything from that night, do you?" Kyle had suspected this was the case. He wondered if it was a safety feature or just a glitch. It could go either way. "Or even before that?"

Mike shook his head. "I have been very front-up about that. I have no memory before being here in Bouring."

"It's 'up-front,' not 'front-up,'" Kyle corrected. Gently.

"Thank you."

"Look, Mike, I don't expect you to get this. . . . I don't expect you understand it all at once, but . . . I think we should work together."

Mike blinked rapidly. "Together? But you are just a person. No offense."

"None taken. I'm just a human being, yeah, but I'm smart. And you're not." He paused. "No offense."

"None taken."

Kyle fished in his pocket and brought out one of the few functioning gadgets he still had — the Bluetooth communicator he had once used. He handed it over to Mike. "With this in your ear, you'll be able to hear me and talk to me. I can help you figure out the best ways to use your superpowers. Make you more efficient."

Mike stared at the Bluetooth earpiece. "That . . . would be most helpful. Thank you."

"We have a lot of work to do," Kyle told him. "So you'll have to listen to everything I say. Like I said, I don't expect you to understand — not right away, at least. I sent a weapon back through time. Or, rather, my future self *will* send a weapon back through time. To help me in the fight against Walter Lundergaard."

"Lundergaard . . ."

"He's a madman. He was willing to wipe out the entire town of Bouring. He tortured a . . . a friend of mine. Made him a slave."

"He is not a nice man," Mike said. "And I believe he should be stopped."

"Excellent. Glad we're on the same page. But remember: You can't call me Kyle when you're out in public," Kyle told him. "I have to be a secret."

"Yeah. You'll need a namecode."

"It's 'codename.'"

"Are you sure?"

"I'm always sure. Anyway, here's what I'm thinking: Why don't you call me 'Erasmus' . . . ?"

EPILOGUE

Many years in the future, Kyle Camden staggered backward in pain. His laboratory was in flames and he collided with a control panel. Nearby, the Giggler lay completely still. Dead, maybe. Or maybe just unconscious. Either way, Kyle didn't care right now — at least that insipid giggling had stopped.

Lundergaard stood in the prototype version of the new chronovessel, a large, clear bubble of thermoplastics and transparent titanium. He was punching buttons, grinning like a madman. The Mad Mask was with him, his wooden mask shattered and hanging in jagged pieces off his face. For a moment, Kyle's eyes locked with Jack Stanley's.

And then Jack looked away.

Coughing through the smoke, Kyle shouted, "Don't do it, Walter! Don't engage the sequence! It's a prototype! It won't work the way you expect it to!"

Lundergaard sneered. "It *works*. That's all I care about." To the Mad Mask, he said, "Kill him."

The Mad Mask hesitated. "But —"

"Do it!" Lundergaard screamed, and the Mad Mask raised an odd-looking gun.

Kyle tried to dodge as the trigger was pulled, but the edge of the energy burst caught him on the left side of his body. He bellowed in pain and collapsed to the floor. He couldn't believe this had happened. He'd been *betrayed*. He had known the betrayal was coming, but not from which direction. He never could have imagined that he would be betrayed by M —

But that didn't matter. Not anymore. The present was no good, but there was still a chance. In the past.

"I'll stop you," he croaked, pulling himself to his feet, bracing against the control panel. "I'm sending a weapon to the past. To stop you."

"Shoot him again," Lundergaard commanded, not even looking at Kyle, still fiddling with the controls on the chronovessel.

The Mad Mask stared at Kyle. He shook his head just the tiniest bit and dropped the gun. "It, uh, it's out of power. . . ." he said.

Kyle felt for the proper buttons on his control panel. He couldn't stop Lundergaard — not now — but he could . . .

He bashed a button with his fist. Lights illuminated

the control panel. A siren sounded. And as Lundergaard and the Mad Mask began to fade into the timestream, a computerized voice filled the lab:

"Project Irony is now online," it announced. "Project Irony is now online!"

The chronovessel vanished into the timestream, taking Lundergaard and the Mad Mask with it. And the computerized voice droned on:

"Zero-point energy at maximum! Plasma field intact and ready for transmission!"

Kyle pushed another button. The last button.

"Project Irony, final phase!" the voice announced. "Now inserting the Mighty Mike Matrix into the timestream . . . Arrival scheduled for pre-designated temporal coordinates . . ."

Kyle laughed through the pain that filled his body. The weapon wasn't perfect — its databank was incomplete and it would have computational glitches and difficulties. But that was fine.

He knew what would happen next . . . because it had already happened. On a warm October night some time in the past, the sky above his hometown of Bouring would light up with the residual plasma effect of the chronometric insertion of the Mighty Mike Matrix into the timestream. To a twelve-year-old Kyle Camden, it would look like a plasma curtain falling in sheets from outer space. To the rest of Bouring, it would look like . . .

Well, the rest of Bouring would gaze up in wonder, in fear, in awe. And turn to one another and say:

Where were you when the stars fell down?

ACKNOWLEDGMENTS

My thanks go out, as always, to the folks at Scholastic, but especially to Jody Corbett, David Levithan, and Sheila Marie Everett. Also, a long-overdue shout-out to Andrew Trabbold and Christopher Stengel, the gentlemen who bring you those gorgeous covers. Please applaud for them when you have a moment, will you?

I'd also like to thank Faith Hochhalter, who's read each of these books as I wrote them and offered that special insight that only a first reader can offer.

But the biggest thanks go — no surprise here, really — to the man I still call "my kid brother," Eric Lyga. Before I even sat down to write the first words of Kyle's first adventure, I spent an afternoon with Eric, just spitballing ideas. His thoughts, insights, and probing questions forced me to rethink the project and take it a bit further than the original "kid with superpowers plays pranks" I had intended. He's also the one who read the first book and said, "So, you mention that Kyle's journal is encrypted — will it ever end up being decrypted by someone?" Heh. Thanks, bro. And I promise to try to stop calling you "my kid brother." (But let's be honest — we both know that's not gonna happen.)

Last but never, ever least — thanks to you, the reader of this book. Writing books is fun; getting them published is great. But it's all pretty pointless if no one reads 'em. So thank you for being at the other end of the page for me.